THE GRANTVILLE INQUISITOR

Bradley H. Sinor
and Tracy S. Morris

Cover designed by Laura Givens

Printed in the United States of America

First Printing: January 2021
1632, Inc.

E-book ISBN-13 978-1-953034-43-4
Trade Paperback ISBN-13 978-1-953034-44-1

CONTENTS

VARIATIONS IN THE MEDIUM OF INK

By: Tracy S. Morris

One wouldn't think that chocolate and Bigfoot paired well together. But at Mirari Sesma's chocolate shop in Grantville of the United States of Europe, the two went hand-in-hand. Or teacup handle in slightly furry fingers, as the case may be.

Mirari thought about this with some smugness as she hurried between the tables of her shop, delivering pastries, carafes of hot beverages, and hot-off-the-press copies of the *Grantville Inquisitor* to her patrons. The paper hadn't been her brainchild. It started as a one-off issue that Paul Kindred, managing editor of the *Grantville Times,* had used to bury a story that was too politically hot for its own good.

Or his own good, Mirari thought.

But the one-off paper had sold well. And Mirari, who prided herself on her business sense, knew a good thing when she saw it.

With stories like "Pope and Elvis Caught in Secret Love Nest," no one would ever take the *Inquisitor* seriously as a source of news. It nevertheless was famously entertaining.

One thing that Mirari immediately noticed was that more patrons turned up on the days when she put out a fresh issue of the *Inquisitor.* And patrons who read the *Inquisitor* tended to linger over their drinks. Then buy a second. Then a third. And maybe just one more éclair for the road, thank you for asking. What began as a joke was now a viable business tool in her shop. Last week, Betsy Springer-Sesma had even suggested that they start selling subscriptions.

As if the thought of her red-haired cousin-by-marriage had summoned the girl, Betsy pushed the shop door open. The door swung against the wall with a loud bang, knocking the bell off its tether and hurling it to the floor. Around the room patrons jumped in surprise, spilling drinks and crumbling pain-au-chocolate on their plates.

Betsy surveyed the damage with barely a wince, then spotted Mirari. With an impish grin, she raced across the room full-tilt. "You will never believe what happened!"

"Is it aliens, or the Loch Ness Monster this time?" Mirari asked. In addition to working as a reporter for the *Grantville Times*, Betsy was also the most prolific contributor to the *Inquisitor.* Paul Kindred would send Mirari anything Betsy wrote that was *just a touch too fanciful* for the *Times* to use.

"What?" Betsy looked confused. "No! Old Man Kindred is going to send someone over here to interview me and Denis for a change!"

Mirari sat down her tray of pastries and put her hands on her hips. "Is this about the travel book that the two of you wrote, or the play that you consulted with Cyrano de Bergerac for?"

"It's for the book!" Betsy clapped her hands together, and jumped up and down girlishly. "We gave a copy to Old Man Kindred to read, and he liked it! He really liked it! He's going to give it a review in the paper. I feel like I just won a major award! And it's not even from Frah-Gee-Ley!"

Mirari smiled at Betsy. When she was over-excited, Betsy made obscure references to uptime cinema. "Congratulations! I know that you and Denis worked hard on that book."

"You have no idea! It feels like Denis and I can't leave town without something interesting happening to us."

Just then Denis and his friend the typesetter, Alexandria, walked through the door. Denis closed it behind him and re-hung the bell. "I see Betsy came through this way," he deadpanned.

Betsy blinked at him in confusion. "Denis, weren't you supposed to bring Yuri Kuryakin with you? I thought he was going to interview us about our book?"

"*Sta cercando inchiostro!*" Alex said in Italian while snapping her fingers rapidly. "*Como se dice inchiostro in Inglese*? Ah!" She held up her finger triumphantly. "Ink! He look for ink." She said at last in broken English.

Mirari and Betsy traded puzzled expressions. "Ink? But the paper supplies us with writing tools," Betsy said.

"It's not for him," Denis put in. "We were expecting a shipment of ink for the press from Magdeburg this morning, but it hasn't arrived yet."

"I thought the *Times* made its own ink?" Betsy scratched her head. "Wasn't that one of those things that Old Man Kindred was working on to go with his improved fountain pen?"

Alex made a face. Denis knew that part of why she'd been hired at the paper was her extensive knowledge of ink recipes. Her father had owned a print shop in Venice. And when his apprentice proved to be a useless layabout, Alex had taken over his duties, which included typesetting and making ink. Her interest in chemistry had proved invaluable on one of their escapades.

"*Progetto diverso,*" Alex sniffed. "Different project. Separate inks."

The process for making ink was partially secret; Alex had once told Denis that most printers were proprietary about their ink recipes. From what he had observed, the steps that Alex used to make writing ink involved fermenting oak leaves for several months and combining the result with green copperas, water, and tree sap. The ink was suitable for Mr. Kindred's pen contraption, but too runny for use with movable type.

For that, Alex made lampblack pigment by melting oils with coal and distilling the whole mess. Then she boiled linseed oil for several hours; once it cooled, she added the lampblack pigment and turpentine.

Whenever he'd tried to examine the process more closely, Alex had told him to mind his own business. But he suspected that the whole undertaking was a smelly, dangerous, and unpleasant task. Which was why she had been the one to convince Mr. Kindred to outsource it.

"If you count the *Inquisitor* and the other tracts and newsletters that hire the *Times's* print shop, then the volume of work that our press produces is too high for us to make our own ink anymore," Denis shrugged. "We could either be an ink-making operation, or a print-making operation. But not both. Mr. Kindred outsourced the ink production shortly after we started to print Mirari's *Inquisitor* for her."

"Is that why sometimes the ink is faded?" Mirari wrinkled her nose.

"Bah!" Alex spit on the ground. "Gunther Schreiber! *Adulteri*!"

"We've had some quality control issues," Denis winced apologetically. "According to Alex, we had to change ink suppliers when she found out that our first contractor – that would be the Gunther Schreiber who she was maligning -- was mixing water in the ink to stretch it out."

"Figures," Betsy rolled her eyes. "And when the supply didn't arrive today, Yuri jumped at the chance to go looking for it? Anything to get out of interviewing me!"

Denis blinked in confusion. "I don't actually think Yuri was that upset about the assignment."

"I'm not letting him off the hook!" Betsy drove a fist into her open palm. "If he won't come here, we'll just go find him!"

"Really, Betsy?" Denis rolled his eyes. "I think this rivalry of yours is kind of one-sided."

"Besides, he could get in trouble out there in the countryside!" Betsy continued as if she hadn't heard Denis. "Old Man Kindred would be really upset if anything ever happened to that little brown-noser."

"Careful, dear wife. Your jealousy is showing," Denis sighed.

"Jealous?" Betsy squawked. "What do I have to be jealous of? Just because Yuri's stories end up on the front page above the fold more often than mine?"

He held his hands up in surrender. "I said nothing!"

"We're the ones with the book – soon to be a bestseller, thank you very much! And you, Alex, and I are the ones who have caught more killers than him!"

Alex pulled the brim of her cap low over her eyes and hunched over, as if to say, "Leave me out of this."

"That's not too difficult, seeing as Yuri has never caught a killer," Denis said.

With a scoff, Betsy turned on her heel and stomped toward the exit. "Come on! We'd better find him. Before he gets lost somewhere on the road between here and Magdeburg."

Denis sighed. "Yes, dear."

* * *

The three of them rode out on horses that they had borrowed from Mirari, following the road past where West Virginia red clay met rich black Thuringian loess. As the sun gradually rose in the sky the day grew warmer. Betsy put on her large straw sun hat.

"Ladies and gentlemen of the class of 1999: wear sunscreen," she grumbled. "You know how many freckles I've gotten since coming back to this time? At least now the ozone layer is intact."

Denis looked at Alex in mystification. The two of them shrugged. Whatever the ozone layer was, he doubted it was that important.

Just then, Alex stood up in the stirrups of her saddle, shading her eyes against the strong sunlight. She pointed to the roadside in the distance. "There!"

A giant black stain messily coated the right side of the road. At the center of the inky splatter lay a jumble of shattered barrels. Bent hoops and splintered staves curved upward to the sky like the bones of a roasted goose.

Betsy let out a low whistle. "It looks like someone's Jenga game got out of hand!"

Denis nodded absently as he took in the details of the wreckage. A dripping trail of ink continued overland across the hard-packed ground away from the shattered barrels. "This has to be from our ink supply," he said. "Who else in Grantville would have ordered barrels of ink?"

"But for some reason, the wagon left the road and went cross-country." Betsy drummed her fingers against the pommel of her saddle. "When the wagon left the smooth road bed, the load must have shifted, and these barrels fell off."

Alex circled the black puddle slowly. When she reached the far side, she pointed to a set of inky footprints that Denis had missed. "Yuri." She nodded.

The three of them followed the ink trail across the grassy hillside. Within minutes they came upon a stand of tall pine trees. Yuri's ink-stained boot tracks followed the splatter down a partially overgrown wagon track. Denis signaled for Alex and Betsy to dismount from their horses.

"We'd better walk from here," he said.

Sunlight slanted in golden shafts through the canopy of needles overhead. In the distance, a wren trilled its song.

Betsy put a hand on Denis's arm and pointed at a nearby tree. "Look at that," she whispered.

A series of neat pruning cuts had been made along the branches. Each cut dripped with sap. It looked like the larger branches that might have been snapped by the passage of a wagon had been removed, leaving only the growth that would spring back easily and make the passage look disused.

"Houston, we have a problem!" Betsy singsonged.

"My thoughts exactly." Denis pushed back his hat and scratched his head. "Highwaymen?" He tilted his head as he considered the obvious ink trail. "Really sloppy highwaymen?"

"Not acting this close to Grantville," Betsy said. "That would take nerves of steel. Does the *Times* have any rivals? Stealing our ink would be a good way to stop the presses. Would those hacks at *The Daily News* stoop to this? What about political enemies?"

"We know how to make our own ink if we need to, remember?" Denis said. "It's inconvenient, but it wouldn't stop us from printing."

"It's too bad Captain Pohl isn't here," Betsy said. "I would feel better with a few of his dragoons backing us up.

"That wouldn't be the best idea, since his dragoons are French." Denis said. "I don't think they'd be exactly welcome in Grantville, seeing as how the USE. is at war with France."

"Perhaps we should load our flintlocks? Just in case?" Betsy asked in a hushed voice as they led the horses through the underbrush.

Denis grunted his agreement. As the two of them moved back to their saddlebags where Betsy had packed the cartridges, Alex threw the reins of her horse's bridle over Betsy's saddle and walked on ahead. They had just finished loading their pistols when the typesetter ran back to them.

"Come quickly!" She hissed, pressing a finger to her lips.

Betsy held out her hands for the reins of Denis's horse, indicating that she would tie the animals up and follow behind. Denis tossed her his mount's reins and tiptoed after Alex.

Rounding a bend in the pathway, they came upon an opening in the trees. The wagon stood in the center of the clearing, it's ink-splattered canvas pulled over the bed. The wagon's oxen lazily ate the grass growing at their hooves.

The back of the wagon was open. Frayed rope ends and a large tear in the canvas showed Denis just how some of the barrels had fallen out. The torn fabric was halfway stitched back together. A sewing awl hung by a heavy thread from the half-mended tear, as if someone had been attempting to repair it when they had suddenly been interrupted.

Alex held up her index finger and twirled it to indicate that they should circle the clearing. Denis nodded in agreement. The two of them crept slowly through the underbrush along the tree line. Fallen pine needles muffled their steps.

As they circled the wagon, they could see Yuri, slumped over what looked like an equally unconscious deliveryman. Denis held his breath and watched until he saw Yuri take a breath. Then he inhaled with relief. Whatever was going on here, at least it wasn't murder. Not yet, anyway.

"Well, now we know what happened to our ink delivery and our wayward comrade," Denis whispered. "The question is, how did they get there?"

The cocking of a pistol sounded very loud in the quiet of the forest. Denis turned toward the sound, to see a man in ink-stained workmen's clothing emerge from the bushes. He held a weapon leveled at them. Denis groaned. A line from one of Betsy's movies came to mind. "I just hadda' open my big mouth!"

Alex gasped, covering her mouth with her hand. "*Tu*!"

"You know him?" Denis asked.

"Gunther Schreiber!" Alex huffed. "We fire him!"

"Then Betsy was right!" Denis snapped his fingers and pointed at Gunther. "You *are* trying to sabotage the *Times*!"

The inkmaker scowled at them. He motioned for Denis to drop his own firearm. Denis flung it into the pine straw, lips twisting in anger.

"Mr. Kindred hired me to make ink!" Gunther said. "If he wanted me to make *his* ink, he should have given me *his* recipe!"

"You tell us already you have *una ricetta* . . . recipe!" Alex scoffed. "*Promesso risultati!*" The Venetian girl groaned in frustration as she searched for the proper words in English. "Results! You promise!"

"Results!" Gunther laughed somewhat hysterically. The end of his pistol wavered. "I invested a lot of money in equipment because I expected the *Times's* business! I'm owed! And if Kindred won't pay, I'll take his ink and sell it to someone who will!" He turned to Alex, a mad gleam in his eye. "And now, I have his recipes too!"

Gunther motioned for them to walk ahead of him to the wagon. Denis turned, eyes scanning the clearing for some means of escape or some way to warn Betsy of their predicament. But just as Gunther turned his back to the road, their three horses stampeded into the clearing.

Startled, the oxen reared and bucked, sending the wagon rolling backward. The barrels in their wagon clattered against one another. One rolled to the ground, but did not break.

Gunther spun with a look of concern on his face. The nose of his flintlock drooped downward.

Denis and Alex threw themselves simultaneously at Gunther. Denis pushed the man's gun arm down so that the flintlock was pointed at the ground. Out of the corner of his eye, he saw Alex shove her thumb into the firing mechanism between the cock and the frizzen.

Gunther pushed away from the two of them, abandoning his pistol, and running off into the forest.

They looked at each other, open mouthed and panting, as if they couldn't quite believe what had just happened to them. Alex chuckled, somewhat nervously.

"Is everyone alright?" Betsy called as she emerged from the pathway, her brows knit together in concern.

Alex handed Denis the abandoned flintlock with trembling hands. Denis noticed that her thumb was already turning greenish with bruising.

"Cows! I go!" She hurried over to calm the oxen and retrieve their horses.

"We're –" Denis's voice faltered. He coughed. "We're fine here! Your timing is sublime."

Betsy's fearful expression melted like snow in April. "Where would you be without me, Denis?" She beamed at him.

He embraced her. The smell of her hair had a calming effect on his nerves. The trembling in his hands gradually subsided. "Languishing. Somewhere alone in a ditch."

Betsy pushed at his shoulder good-naturedly.

A groan pulled their attention to where Alex was helping Yuri to his feet.

"Are you able to walk, Yuri?" Denis asked.

"*Luis sta bene* . . . Fine! He is fine," Alex waved at them in reassurance.

"That's a relief," Betsy said. "I think Old Man Kindred would be more upset if Yuri was permanently hurt than if he lost all this ink."

Denis gave her a sideways look. "You know, Betsy. Mr. Kindred might like you more if you didn't insist on calling him *Old Man Kindred* all the time."

Betsy pursed her lips, then shrugged.

"We should get going, before Gunther comes back," Denis said. "We can put the deliveryman into the wagon with the ink. Alex, you take Yuri and drive the wagon back. Betsy and I can follow with the horses."

Betsy sighed. "I suppose our interview will have to wait for another day, on account of Yuri getting his brains scrambled." She brightened suddenly. "That means that I get to write this up for the *Times*!"

Denis laughed. "It just gives you more time to embellish all the other stories you want to tell Yuri."

Betsy sniffed disdainfully. "I always stick with the cold, hard facts!"

Denis knew that there was only one way to answer that. "Yes, dear."

"SECOND ISSUE?"

By: Bradley H. Sinor

The back door of the *Grantville Times* printing plant flew open with a bang. An icy blast of January air came rushing in, whipping the flames of several candles placed around Paul Kindred's worktable, scattering the numerous sheets of paper that he had spread out on it.

He muttered a comment about idiots, in this case himself, who forgot to lock doors at night. The middle of January, especially in northern Germany in the year of our Lord 1633, was not the time you left a door standing wide open.

Before he could get out of his chair, Paul caught a glimpse out of the corner of his eye of someone coming through that door. Who he saw was enough to know that this was no chance gust of wind, even though Paul realized that he definitely hadn't locked the door.

"Yuri Andreovich, would you shut that damn door!"

When Yuri Andreovich Kuryakin heard Paul he turned with a start, looking around for the source of the voice. With his small frame and twitchy on-the-move manner, he gave the impression of being younger than his twenty-some years, not to mention of being frightened by his own shadow.

"Oh, there you are, Paul," the young Russian said, letting a small sigh escape. "I'm glad to find you working late."

"Never mind that, just shut the damn door; in case you haven't looked at the calendar, it's January!"

"I know it's January!" he replied. "Just wait until it gets really cold, like in Mother Russia!"

"Unless you have a cord of wood with you, shut the damn door!"

Yuri made a big show of checking the pockets of his down jacket and thick leather chaps, in the processes of which he managed to push the door closed.

"Nope, no extra wood here," he said with a grin.

It wasn't that he was stupid, far from it. That much Paul had realized within five minutes of meeting Yuri. He just tended to be so enthusiastic that when he got an idea it pushed everything else, including common sense, out the back door.

This was not the first time Yuri had shown up unexpectedly. It had become a regular habit since he had come striding into the *Times's* office and asked for a job as a reporter. He claimed to have worked for several "local papers" in other parts of Germany, Russia, and farther south in the Balkans.

Paul's father hadn't been that enthusiastic about hiring him, but Paul had convinced him to hire the young Russian anyway. As his father's chief of staff, and managing editor of the *Times*, he had some say in who was on the staff. There was something in Yuri's intensity, his willingness to follow a story no matter what, that reminded Paul of himself just a few years ago.

Though there were moments, like this one, when he would have cheerfully strangled Yuri or taken a two-by-four to him, depending on what was handiest.

"So, why the late night visit?" asked Paul, picking up the papers from his table, designs for a fountain pen that local craftsman could make, shoving them into a box, and guessing that he wouldn't get any more work done on them tonight. He was a newspaperman at heart, but it never hurt to have several money-making enterprises going.

Yuri began to pace back and forth, occasionally glancing toward the windows as if expecting someone to be looking back at him.

"I've got a story, a big one. Okay, this goes back a few weeks," he said, "to the Christmas party at the high school."

That party had been a brilliant stroke, if Paul did say so himself. It had helped improve the morale of all of Grantville; some of the uptimers had been having major problems coming to terms with their "new reality."

"Yeah, Nina and I were there."

"I saw you," grinned the young Russian. He stopped again, staring out the window. "But I also saw something else that apparently you missed entirely."

"Such as?"

Yuri turned to face Paul, the smile on his face a little too self-satisfied for the older man's liking. "How about General Pappenheim himself there in the school."

"Gottfried Heinrich Pappenheim? You've got to be joking!"

"I wish I was; when that man shows up, there is trouble. It was him, of that I'm sure; the birthmark on his face marks him. Besides, I stood a dozen feet away from him a couple of years ago and got a good look at the man," said Yuri.

"Wallenstein's chief general, here? Now that might just be a story."

"It gets better. I spotted him going into the, what do you call it, men's room. He came out dressed all in red. Julie McKay made him start giving out presents to everyone."

Santa? Pappenheim had been Santa? Try as he might, Paul couldn't recall the man's face; that red suit dominated everything.

"Remember when "Santa" disappeared down the hallway? I was in one of the classrooms and saw what happened. There was some altercation involving two men and a barrel of gunpowder. A few minutes later I saw Pappenheim talking to Julie MacKay and President Stearns. I couldn't hear worth a damn, but I saw everything. I would swear on my mother's grave that the two of them knew who he was."

This story sounded so fantastic that Paul wasn't sure if he should kick Yuri out or take him seriously. Not that Paul trusted the government. Oh, Mike Stearns and the rest, individually, were good men and no doubt were sure that they were working for the general good. They were still politicians, and that meant you had to keep your eye on them.

Yuri pulled out several sheets of paper and passed them to Paul. "I've got it all written up. It can go in the next edition!"

One thing you could say about Yuri, he did have easily read handwriting and knew how to put an article together. The story covered everything the young Russian had seen, plus a lot of speculation.

"No, Yuri Andreovich. We can't run this story, not as it stands now." he said. "You cannot accuse the government of a secret conspiracy without proof."

"I've spent the last week asking questions! All that's gotten me are a lot of blank stares and denials. Though I think Leffert suspects something; I've been followed everywhere I go." Lefferts was Captain Harry Lefferts; he was part of the army, but he also functioned as the head of Mike Stearns's special security unit that was directly under the President's authority.

"I didn't say we wouldn't publish it, but we will need proof before we could even consider going to press with this," said Paul.

Yuri stared at Paul for a long time. "Very well, I will get proof." His voice suggested that his idea of getting proof would look something akin to a bull in a china shop. Yuri pulled his jacket tight about him and headed out the door without a word. A moment later he opened it again and leaned part way in.

"My byline, above the fold. Da?"

"Of course. I wouldn't have it any other way."

* * *

Yuri would not wait long, that much Paul knew. While the reporter was long on talent, he was at times short on patience, and Paul had a gut feeling that this could very well be one of those times.

Pappenheim playing Santa at the Christmas party was just so bizarre that it could have happened. Now if Yuri had suggested that it had been Wallenstein that would have been too much. It wasn't that Stearns wasn't capable of making a deal with Pappenheim; Paul was fairly certain he would, if it were necessary. Like all the other uptimers, Stearns had been forced to adapt to political realities in the seventeenth century.

Paul needed information, fast.

That meant Mirari Sesma.

Mirari was Basque. She had turned up in Grantville three months after the Ring of Fire. Just exactly why she had left the Pyrenees was a bit unclear; a few dropped hints suggested something about a vendetta, but she had never been forthcoming with details.

Mirari had taken over one of the empty buildings in town and set up a small café that had turned out to be extremely popular. People came, they ate, they drank, they talked, and, most importantly, Mirari listened. Her dark hair and dark eyes gave her an exotic appearance, but her manner was such that people just trusted her. It wasn't long before Mirari seemed to know everything that was going on in town, and if she didn't know about it, she could usually find out.

Paul found her in the back of her shop, just after closing at midnight. She was pouring a dark liquid into a cup. Before he could say anything she offered it to him and poured herself another.

"Chocolate?" he asked, savoring the familiar taste.

"I just got a supply in. I'll be saving it for special occasions," answered Mirari. "How is Nina?"

"She's almost over the cold. That herb tea you left certainly helped." Mirari and Nina, Paul's wife, had met weeks before he had been introduced to her. By that time the two of them were like long lost sisters.

"Besides drinking up my chocolate, what brings you out and about this late at night?"

"You always did know how to cut to the point." Paul wrapped his hands around the cup, enjoying the warmth. "I've picked up a rumor that General Pappenheim has been seen in the area, the night of the Christmas party."

Mirari was hard pressed to keep from laughing. "You've got to be joking. He's not stupid enough to come anywhere near here, not without a very large army at his back. Have you seen the reward for his head?"

Paul was very familiar with the reward. The *Times* had bid on and gotten the job of printing wanted posters of both Pappenheim and Wallenstein.

"And you're serious about this?" asked Mirari.

"Just see what you can find out, as soon as possible."

"There is something going on," said Mirari. She had shown up at Paul's front door just after six the next evening. She seemed more than a bit unhappy. "Since noon I've had the feeling that I was being followed, though I saw no one. It's not a feeling that I like."

Nina had been as pleased to see her as Paul was. The two women hugged and began talking about half a dozen different subjects as the three of them sat down on the couch.

Among other things that Paul discovered in the next few minutes was that Nina and Mirari were working on setting up some new classes at the high school, and were even talking about going into business together. This was the first time that he had heard anything about that.

"Hey, even the *Times* doesn't get every story," laughed Nina.

"We can try," he told his wife.

Mirari picked up a small glass vase from the coffee table and began to turn it over and over in her hand. "I've not been able to find anyone who might have seen Pappenheim the night of the Christmas party. Of course, there are the usual sorts of rumors about what he is doing, but none of them put him anywhere near Grantville.

"One thing I did put together; it may be related to this, it may not, but some of Harry Lefferts' men have been hanging around at all hours of the day and night near Edith Wild's house," she said.

"You're stumbling over Harry Lefferts' men, and Yuri was sure that they were after him. I am beginning to wonder if Lefferts might be the story, not Pappenheim," muttered Paul, leaning back in his chair and staring up at the ceiling. "And what does Edith Wild have to do with it?"

Edith Wild was a nurse, and a force of nature in the minds of many Grantville residents. She was the woman in charge of public health for Grantville, a job that required that type of personality to get the job done. She definitely took her duties seriously, and would brook no interference in performing them.

"I hadn't heard anything about Harry seeing Edith, and I'm not sure if even he could stand up to her should the situation arise," Nina said as she came back from the kitchen with a plate of cookies. "But I suppose it's possible."

"I wouldn't lay odds on his surviving," chuckled Paul.

* * *

"Are you sure you know the way?"

Paul didn't bother answering the question, as he hadn't the last four times that Yuri had asked it. His companion did seem to have sense enough to keep his voice down to a whisper, though.

They had been walking for the better part of two hours, gradually working their way through the forest toward the far end of Grantville. Edith Wild's house was less than a half hour's walk from the *Times's* offices, but just walking over and knocking on her door was not going to get the answers that Paul and Yuri wanted. Paul still wasn't sure that he believed Yuri's' story, but he had the definite feeling that something might just be going on.

Paul had made a point of not going anywhere near Edith's house during the day, not that he normally did so. There wasn't that much to see anyway, beyond the home that Wild had occupied for more than half her life.

There were enough other matters on his plate, concerning the *Times* and several business projects that his family had in the works, to take up Paul's time as he waited at the office for Yuri. A note to Yuri had told him to show up at midnight. The Russian was there at 10 p.m., champing at the bit to get on with it. Paul had considered taking Mirari along, but she had made it clear that she was not interested. Besides, Yuri and she usually ended up arguing about some damn thing or another and they didn't need that tonight.

"I still think that we should have gone this morning to the President's office and confronted him, in front of everyone. That way he couldn't have squirmed out of it," said Yuri.

"That isn't the way the *Times* does things; we need proof, Yuri Andreovich. There may be something going on, there may not; it may just be a lot of things taken out of context. If you don't like it, you can take your story somewhere else," he said.

Yuri muttered something, but it was in Russian and Paul couldn't be sure of exactly what he said.

In the just over twenty-four hours since Yuri had come sneaking in the back of the *Times*, the weather had not changed beyond adding a fresh layer of snow. It was still bitterly cold; the two men's breaths hung in the air, and the ground was frozen, grass crackling under their feet with every step.

In spite of the weather, Paul did not feel safe in taking a direct route to Edith Wild's house. There was a chance that Yuri could be right, so the two men doubled back, crossing and re-crossing their own trail, watching for any signs that they were not alone in the darkness.

At one point, Yuri almost tripped over a pair of foxes who were prowling the bushes, looking for food and, no doubt, a warm place to spend the night. It was a sentiment that Paul had come to identify with in the last few hours.

"We're alone," said Yuri. "Let's get on with it."

As they neared the house there was a movement a dozen yards ahead of them.

Paul tried to focus on it. Before he could say anything or point out the guard to Yuri, half a dozen figures came at them from three different directions. Voices and fists flew, and chaos drew Paul in. There were no faces, just colors and shapes and sounds.

Yuri kept moving, dodging the attackers, until he reached the house. He boosted himself up toward a window using a snow-covered box, hanging on the sill for only a heartbeat or two.

Paul had little time to watch Yuri. He managed to land several good punches, his fists connecting with bare flesh and clothing. As he turned, Paul felt a sharp pain in the lower part of his back and then a matching one at the base of his neck that sent him crashing to the ground and into darkness.

* * *

Paul opened blurry eyes and found himself staring at the business end of a double barreled shotgun about eight inches from his face. A million miles away, at the other end of the weapon, Paul could just make out the face of a man he did not recognize.

"Can I interest you in a subscription to the *Times*? Make a great after-Christmas gift for yourself," he gulped. In the back of his mind he was envisioning what the shotgun would do to his face; of course, he also knew that he would not be alive to see it. He figured flippancy could be the only way to go right now; it wasn't as if he had a whole lot of options right then.

Mike Stearns stepped out of the shadows. He looked at Paul for a moment, shook his head, softly chuckled, and waved the shotgun wielding man back.

"On your feet," said Mike, extending his hand to help Paul get up. "What the hell are you doing prowling around in the woods tonight? And before you ask, I already am a *Times* subscriber."

"I would say that shows your good taste, but I happen to know you also subscribe to *The Daily News* and *The Street* as well," said Paul.

Another man came up to Mike. It took Paul a moment to recognize Harry Lefferts. "There were two of them," he told the President. "We lost the trail of the other one, down by the creek. I'm fairly certain that it was a pain-in-the-butt reporter named Kuryakin. My men have been watching him for the last couple of days."

"Bloody great," muttered Mike. "So, Paul, you never answered my question."

Paul struggled to the feet, wiped himself off, and pulled his notebook and a pencil out. "I'm doing my job, reporting. I've come to interview your visitor."

"Visitor? Visitor? I'm not sure what you're talking about," said Mike.

"Mike, let's cut the crap. You and those playmates of yours wouldn't be prowling around the woods at three in the morning any more than I would, unless something important was going on. You could deny it, but I'd know you were lying," he said. This wasn't the first time he had run a bluff to get a story, though in the pit of his stomach Paul felt it wasn't a bluff. "The *Times* is going to run a story, speculating on just who that visitor might be and why you're going to all this trouble to hide him. Now, you can help me make this story as accurate as possible or live with the consequences of not bringing me in on it."

Mike went immobile for a moment. The only sound, beyond those drifting in from the woods, was their breathing. It was almost two full minutes before he spoke.

"All right, come inside. There's someone that you need to meet."

* * *

The "visitor" was awake. It was not who Paul had expected.

Wallenstein was sitting up in bed, with several pillows behind him. He looked pale, even in the light from the single candle next to his bed. The man's lower jaw was wrapped in bandages. There was bulge under the blanket that Paul suspected might be a loaded pistol.

Harry Lefferts stood in one corner of the room, an unhappy expression on his face.

"You, sir, present me with a moral dilemma," Paul said after Mike had introduced him. "You know I came here to get a story for my newspaper. But if I write it I cause major problems not only for my government, which I don't mind doing, but possibly for all of Grantville."

Wallenstein picked up a pad and wrote quickly.

Morals are for churchmen; statesmen cannot afford them.

"Thank you, Signor Machiavelli." Wallenstein looked at Paul oddly, but wrote nothing.

"We got word that he had survived *Alte Veste* through General Pappenheim, who came to us with a most unusual offer of alliance."

"Ah yes, Pappenheim, or should we also be calling him Santa Claus."

Mike smiled. "Not bad, not bad at all. He offered an alliance to help stir up a revolt in Bohemia, plus a few other little political actions that could work to our advantage; in exchange he wanted our dentists to repair the damage that Julie's bullet did to Wallenstein's jaw and teeth." said Mike. "Then there is also the matter of Chmielnicki."

Paul didn't recognize the name, but then he had never been good with European history. He looked at Mike for an explanation.

"It's a massacre of ten thousand Polish Jews in 1648. Wallenstein says that if we help him he may be able to stop it."

Wallenstein handed a hastily scribbled note to Mike, who in turn offered it to Paul.

NO MAY. I WILL STOP IT. BUT ONLY IF YOU HELP ME.

"You want me to sit on the story," Paul said. "That much is obvious."

His first impulse was to say to hell with this, publish the story, and expose the whole deal. He wasn't fond of secret government plots, but he could see the logic implicit in what the President seemed to be doing. It still didn't feel right to him.

"If I were to agree with what you're doing, and I am not saying that I will, there is one other problem. Yuri may or may not have seen Wallenstein, but he knows that you were involved with Pappenheim. That can cause a lot of problems in and of itself."

"Then he has to be dealt with," said Lefferts, his voice quiet and without emotion.

"I hope you're not going to try to arrange an accident for him," said Paul,

"Paul, please. There are certain levels I won't stoop to," said Mike. "You know he's going to want to get that story published, and he can do it. It's just a matter of time." There were newspapers outside of Grantville, some good, some bad. "We both know there are more than a few places that would be willing to publish it."

"If I agree to go along with you on keeping this quiet, I want an exclusive on it when you do go public," said Paul.

"Provided we haven't been exposed and strung up over this whole thing, you've got a deal," Mike said. "Seriously, I wish I were handing you an easy story to deal with, like a secret squad of ninjas setting up operations in Grantville, but I can't."

"Ninjas, yeah, I've heard those rumors, as well as the ones about aliens. You're sounding like you think I run the *Weekly World News* rather than the *Grantville Times*. Not that a fine upstanding gentleman like yourself would know anything about the *Weekly World News*," said Paul.

"At least with *Playboy* you could claim that you were reading it for the articles," laughed Mike.

Paul nodded, only half listening to Mike. Later he could not say when the idea had hit him. It was just suddenly there.

"I know exactly what I'm going to do. I think you will like the idea."

"And that is?" said Mike

"I'm going to do what I always do. I'm going to write the story about Wallenstein being alive and see it published," grinned Paul.

"Now stop me if I've got this wrong, but isn't that exactly what we don't want to have happen."

"Trust me."

* * *

Paul slid into a booth in the far corner of the inn's great room. The place was virtually empty at just after three in the afternoon. That was just fine with him; he could use a little down time. The beer and sandwich that sat in front of him looked very good.

From a chair near the booth he had picked up a copy of the latest sensation to sweep Grantville, *The National Inquisitor*. The paper had made its appearance five days before, turning up in bundles at taverns, stores, and any place else that a crowd could gather. There was nothing in it to indicate who had published it; the only bylines on stories were obvious pseudonyms such as Sarah Bellum and Noah Ward.

With its glaring headlines and outrageous woodcuts, it was definitely distinguishable from the *Grantville Times*, *The Daily News*, and most certainly *The Street*; the 75 point headline

---

WALLENSTEIN ALIVE, LIVING IN SECRET WITH BIGFOOT

---

said it all. A second story announced

PAPPENHEIM BUYS CONDO IN GRANTVILLE.

Paul's experienced eye slid over the pages, checking the text, the layout, and the content. Not that he needed to; he was quite familiar with every column inch of it. He had written most of it. Mirari, and a few others they had enlisted, had penned what he hadn't authored. The entire matter had been accomplished in a dozen intense hours after his return from Edith Wild's house.

That this had been done without anyone apparently being the wiser still astonished Paul. In the back of his mind he had been convinced that someone would spot them and put two and two together, especially when they were distributing the papers. But that didn't happen.

The lead story told how Wallenstein had survived the battle of *Alte Veste* with help from that legendary humanoid creature known as Bigfoot. There were not going to be many people who would put any stock in stories published in other papers that the man was alive, or that Pappenheim was anywhere near Grantville, at least for the next few months.

"Checking out the competition, now, are we? Or is it just admiring your own work?" said Mirari as she came up and sat down across the table from him.

"I just hope a few other people are "admiring" it," said Paul.

"That is something you don't have to worry about," Mirari laughed and motioned for a beer. "I've been keeping my ears open, and it is fairly obvious that you've got yourself a runaway hit. The uptimers are laughing their heads off about it. I heard some of them saying it reminds them of something called *The National Enquirer*, whatever that is. Downtimers aren't quite sure what to make of the *Inquisitor*, but they like it. I even saw a couple of priests reading it and giggling."

That was a relief. Mike Stearns had expressed considerable doubts when Paul had suggested the idea. Hell, even Paul hadn't been that sure it would work.

Short of sending killers after Yuri, it was the only idea they could come up with in a hurry that had even a glimmer of a chance of succeeding. Revealing the truth was out of the question; Wallenstein still needed weeks of recuperation, and the political repercussions would have been devastating.

"I heard some talk that Yuri has been kicked out of three newspaper offices in other towns; he can't seem to give his story away," said Mirari.

"Good," he reached down and tapped the copy of the *Inquisitor*. "It was kind of fun, but I am glad it's over."

Mirari leaned her head back, letting her eyes roll toward the ceiling. "Lord, please help me. The man is as slow and unthinking as a churchman who hasn't been bribed!"

"Woman, what in the hell are you talking about?"

"Okay, let's put this in simple terms. The *Inquisitor* is a success; everyone wants to know when the second issue will be coming out."

Second issue? Second issue? That was something that had never even been discussed, that he had never even thought of. The whole concept seemed utterly ridiculous. There wasn't going to be a second issue!

"I know what you are going to say," said Mirari. "There was never supposed to be a second issue. But this thing is popular; people are eating it up and demanding more."

"Yeah, but what does that do to the *Times's* credibility with me editing the *Inquisitor*?"

"You don't have to," Mirari smiled in a way that warned Paul that the woman had some ideas of her own.

"I suppose you know someone who could become the editor," he already knew the answer.

"Of course: me. I'll have a second issue out in no time."

There was that phrase, second issue. Mirari would make a good editor; that much he had learned during their marathon session putting the *Inquisitor* together.

As he mulled it over he kept remembering a lot of the more outrageous rumors that had escaped into the world since the Ring of Fire; a hidden battalion of 21st century Marines who just happened to be passing through town when it was transported back in time was only one of many.

"A second issue," Paul muttered, "I suppose it might be fun if we did a second issue."

"STILL LIFE WITH WOLVES AND CANVASES"

By: Bradley H. Sinor and Tracy S. Morris

"Werewolf?"

Denis Sesma caught himself chuckling as he retied three small strips of leather on his horse's saddle. This was not the first time that his traveling companion, Elizabeth "Betsy" Springer, had asked that question. Actually it was more like fifth time in the last two or three days that the tall redhead had said the same thing.

The first time, Denis had grabbed for the pistol that hung from his saddle, only to hear his friend's laughter coming from just behind him.

This whole "werewolf" thing was one of those "movie quotes" that Betsy seemed inordinately fond of repeating. Denis wasn't all that sure just what "movies" were -- other than that they were something like theatre. But he had a hard time grasping just exactly how.

He'd tried ignoring Betsy when she started spouting these lines, but there was one thing Denis had learned in the last five months since he'd met Elizabeth "just call me Betsy" Springer in the offices of the *Grantville Times*: That was a nearly impossible task.

Betsy was a tall thin girl with her shoulder length red hair tied back in a pony tail, dressed in a red woolen work shirt and strange blue trousers that Denis had learned were called "jeans". Denis had been in Grantville for just over six months and was still not accustomed to seeing women wearing what were normally considered "men's" clothes. His cousin Mirari had told him it was the Americans way of doing things, and that he'd better get used to it.

Without even turning toward her, Denis replied "There wolf, there castle."

"You're learning," she said. At that moment, a wolf's howl rang out; it could have been anywhere from fifty feet to five miles away, the heavy forest and mountains here in southern France tended to play tricks with sound.

"Now *that* was timing." She looked in the direction the noise seemed to have come from. "I couldn't have planned it better myself."

"I'd be happy to take credit for it, but somehow I don't think that you would believe I was responsible," said Denis.

"I think we had better find someplace protected to camp, or an inn," he said. "I am not fond of the idea of waking up and finding myself in the middle of a wolf pack."

"I told you: wolves are more afraid of humans than we are of them," said Betsy.

"Yes, but you also said that there are going to be a lot of wolf attacks in the next hundred years or so."

"Werewolf attacks," Betsy corrected.

"Wolf attacks," Denis restated firmly. He cleared his throat and began to recite. "Over three thousand people were killed in France between 1580 and 1830 by wolves. And over a thousand of those were not rabid.' That's a statistic that they don't mention in your *Time-Life Books: Mysteries of the Unexplained*, I'll wager."

"You read that?" Betsy blinked. "But . . ."

"You Americans were allowed to hunt animals," Denis cut across her argument. "Your wolves learned to be afraid of humans. Here a wolf knows who is the predator and who is the prey. And when his natural prey runs out," he threw a sly glance up at her red hair, "Red Riding Hood looks quite tasty."

"Ha, ha. Very funny. I think I would prefer not to put "wolf prey" on my resume." Betsy muttered. She sounded less sure of herself than she had a moment earlier. "Remember that was not exactly a fortune in expense money that old man Kindred gave us, so we might want to consider camping."

A wolf howled again, the sound was closer this time. "If we can find an inn, it might be safer," he said. "I have the distinct feeling that we are being followed."

Betsy immediately turned in her saddle. Denis winced and shook his head as she made a grand show of studying the terrain behind them.

"I don't see anyone," she reported.

"Nor will you," Denis said. "Especially since you've just alerted whoever it was to the fact that we're aware of them. Trust me, with some hunters there is no way you would see them if they were following you."

"Did you see a signpost anywhere to give us some clue where we are?" She asked.

"No," Denis said. "Nothing since we passed the crossroads."

"As long as there wasn't anyone playing a fiddle there, we're fine," said Betsy. "This is where my dad's *Rand McNally* would be a big help."

"Rand McNally? Who is that? A Scottish guide of some kind?" Denis muttered.

"No, just maps. They were a pain anyway, sometimes it seemed like it took a year for my father to get one folded back properly," Betsy said. "And he'd never let me do it. It always had to be folded back just the way it came."

"Well, there is no reason not to respect the wishes of your father," Denis deadpanned. "Until then, draw an X on the map and label it 'Here be Dragons'."

"Werewolves," Betsy muttered.

"Those too."

"We could stop and ask for directions at the first farmhouse we come to," she suggested.

Denis looked sideways at her. "One look at you and they will think we're mad. And that will be before you even open your mouth."

"So? Just tell them the truth. We're looking for missing blacksmith apprentices."

"Then they'll know we're mad for certain. After all, who would come all this way to find people that they aren't related to and don't even know? Should I leave out the part where we are on the road because you're fleeing from your engagement to *Sven*?"

"I'm not engaged to him and his name was Albert, not Sven," Betsy said. "And it was all a big cross-cultural misunderstanding."

"The kind that can only happen after one too many pints of Thuringian Gardens's best . . ." Denis trailed off and shook his head. "I'm not the one that you should be explaining things to; more like Sven…excuse me, Albert. I don't see why you didn't just let him ask your father's permission for your hand. Surely things would have been straightened out then."

"You don't know my dad like I do," Betsy rolled her eyes. "I love him, but he's hopeless. Besides, Albert should have figured things out by this point."

"And if he hasn't?"

"I'll just tell him that I eloped with you." Betsy batted her eyes at him.

"God save me." Denis said.

Just then another wolf howled off to the west, the sound was much closer than before.

"You may be right about us getting off the road," Betsy nodded in concession.

Denis pointed toward a small thatched hut that was set back from the road. It was a sturdy looking place with earth and wood walls. The trees and brush masked its presence so that it was easy to miss if you weren't looking directly at it; though it looked like no one had lived there for many years.

"Great," muttered Betsy. "Just great. First werewolves, and now this."

* * *

The hut was old, the air inside of it heavy with dust, its former owners long since gone. There were only two rooms; one that had served as kitchen, living, and sleeping area for the residents, while the other had been for storage and possibly a pen for small animals.

This was not the first place that Denis had seen in this condition, he was fairly sure it wouldn't be the last. While war might have stayed away from this part of France for several years, the conflicts between Huguenot and Catholic were going strong. Any kind of unrest usually meant that bandits would come out to play, and there were times when you couldn't tell them apart from the latest local authorities.

"I wish this place were big enough to bring the horses in with us," said Betsy. "If there are wolves around here I don't want to leave them out as a temptation."

The two horses that they were riding were ancient beasts, only one or two steps removed from plow horses or someone's next meal; tempting morsel would not be a description he would have used for either animal.

"Don't worry; I tethered them on the other side of this wall. If anyone or anything shows up, they should make enough noise to alert us," he said.

"And we can't even have a fire; wonderful."

Denis would have liked a fire as much as Betsy. It might be almost May, but there was still a solid winter chill in the air. A fire would scare away wolves, but it could also be a beacon to whoever might be following them, if there was actually someone out there in the darkness.

Betsy pulled herself to her feet and went into the hut's other room, where they had stored the saddles and other tack.

"Denis, come here a minute," said Betsy in a strange tone of voice.

Picking up his pistol, Denis went through the door in a half dozen steps. Betsy was kneeling down near a stack of refuse next to the wall.

"What's the matter?" he asked.

"Look at these. I almost tripped over them in the dark."

A heavy blanket had been pushed to one side and there were a good dozen rolls of canvas bundled together and piled one on top of the other. Betsy sat back on her heels and held the topmost roll out for Denis's inspection.

His questing fingers brushed the surface, electing memories of the dried oil paint, the rough feel of canvas to the touch, and the hand of his old master on his shoulder as he worked on an underpainting.

"Paintings? Who in their right mind would store paintings out here in the woods?" he asked.

A strange voice cut into his musings: "A good question. Perhaps you can ask my captain. But for now, if the two of you want to live long enough see the sun come up again, I suggest that you not move."

* * *

"Papers! My Great-Aunt Lilibeth has papers! It just depends on whether or not I believe your papers are real. And even if they are real, whether or not they actually belong to the two of you."

Denis looked around the room that was serving as an office for Captain Marcus Pohl. It was certainly not as opulent as he would expect to see occupied by someone who commanded the dragoons that served the Bishop of Mende holding court in. But he was a military man, and these rooms definitely had the plain Spartan look that went with that profession.

The region that governed Gévaudan, known as Mende, was at the crossroads of several major pilgrimage routes. Since bandits loved to prey on pilgrims, Pohl and his dragoons found much to keep them occupied.

"I've explained who we are: my name is Denis Sesma, and my companion is Elizabeth Springer," said Denis. "We work as writers for the *Grantville Times*. Why have we been arrested?"

"You haven't been arrested, just brought in for a friendly little chat. When my men find strangers lurking in the forest, I start asking questions about why they are there and who they are." said Pohl. "And I keep asking them until I am satisfied with the answers I receive."

When they had been brought before the captain, he studiously ignored them for a half an hour as he continued to sharpen a formable looking sword. Once he was satisfied with his work the blade had been resheathed and now lay on the desk in front of him. Once he looked at Denis and

Betsy his scowl seemed to indicate that he knew that they were trouble, and wanted very little to do with them before beginning his questions.

"I…" Betsy stood up from her chair, a look of irritation on her face.

Denis automatically put a hand to Betsy's arm to stop the sarcastic reply that he knew she was about to make.

"Judging by your manner of dress, you are Americans."

"Actually I'm not American; I'm part Belgian and part Basque," Denis started to explain. This was the third time he had told the story since the three dragoons had found the two of them in the hut.

"A handful of blacksmith's apprentices who worked for an American company vanished in this region while transporting raw goods, and our editor thought that it might be a good story," said Denis.

"And you've come all this way for a newspaper story?" Pohl shook his head. "Why?"

"Because the last reports of them were in Gévaudan," Betsy cut across Denis's explanation. "And there have been and will be reports of a lot of wolf killings in this area."

Pohl raised an eyebrow at that. "Wolves have been killing in this area for years. There have been rumors of wolves and men who turned into wolves all over this part of France for decades; what's different now?"

"Nothing unless you happen to be a crazy red-haired conspiracy theorist," Denis muttered.

The dragoon captain nodded. With a wave of his whetstone, he pointed at the rolls of canvas on top of their bags. "Very well then, explain that. My men said that you had those with you."

"We found them in the shack we were sheltering in," Betsy said. "Think about it, Genius. Does our baggage have room for this stuff? Where were the bags that we carried it all in? Those nags we were riding had the extra space on their saddles for all of this?"

Denis shook his head. "Elizabet, it might not be the smartest idea to offend someone who could have us killed without having to worry about the paperwork."

Betsy went over to the canvas rolls, and untied the topmost one with fingers that shook in anger. Then she held it up for Pohl to see. "Caravaggio, if I'm not mistaken," she said.

Denis blinked at that. "What? Caravaggio? Let me see."

"It is," Betsy insisted. "It's called *Fortune Teller*. The subject is a Gypsy girl."

Denis nodded in confirmation. "I remember seeing it. It caused quite a stir in the art world. My old master had me study it." He gave Betsy an appraising look. "How do you know this?"

Betsy rolled her eyes. "I got an Associate's degree in Art before I switched to geology. My father wanted me to have a real career instead of knowing just enough to ask if you want fries with your burgers. Besides, I went through a phase where I thought that I couldn't possibly be related to the rest of my family. I was hoping I was a Gypsy left on my parent's doorstep. So I studied everything about Gypsies that I could get my hands on. That way when my real family came back for me, I would be ready."

Pohl looked at her, arching his eyebrows in surprise. "You wanted to be taken by Gypsies?"

"Captain, on this trust me, once you get to know her, that will make complete sense," Denis said. He reached for the next canvas in the roll, and surveyed the panting of seven men bowling. "I don't recognize this one."

"*Game of Skittles*, by Jacob Duck." Betsy said. "I think it is supposed to be painted sometime in the next year. These are all Baroque paintings."

"They look fine to me, nothing seems broken." Denis said.

"That's Baroque, not broken. Who's on first?" Betsy said. "That's what art teachers call art from this time period when they want to lump it all together."

It was Denis's turn to scoff. "I've seen books of your uptime artwork. Christo? Thomas Moore? If you ask me, modern art can stay in the future where it belongs. I don't understand how your Thomas Kinkade can be known as the painter of light when your people knew of Rembrandt."

"I think that's a marketing thing…" Betsy began to unroll a second bundle of canvases, there were a dozen bound tightly together. Her eyes went wide as she lifted the corners of first one and then another.

"The ones in this bundle are exactly the same as in the first one," she said, pursing her lips. "I'm going to make a bet that there are more of the same in the other batch. They are all Baroque. I think that whoever did these is good. Very good."

Denis groaned. "Copies! I was afraid of that. I know for a fact that the original Caravaggio is elsewhere."

"Since there is more than one, I don't think I am going to go out on a limb to say that we are looking at more than just copies that art students make," said Pohl.

Denis and Betsy both jumped, and looked at each other guiltily. In the excitement of their investigation, they had forgotten about the captain. Now they looked at the man. In the space of just a few words he had gone from being a menacing force, ready to lock them up, to someone sharing the same experience as them.

"You know about that system?" asked Denis. He remembered how he had sweated blood over copying any number of works by Rubens and the Carracci brothers. The only comment he would usually get from his late master was a growl and to have him point out where he had gone wrong.

"I'm not a total idiot who only knows that you put the pointy end of a sword into people," said Pohl. "My nephew is apprenticed to Jusepe de Ribera, and in exchange for giving him patronage, I get long detailed letters from him telling me all he has learned."

"Ribera? He was one of my old master's pupils."

"You studied with Francisco Ribalta? I heard of his passing," said Pohl.

"Yes. Unfortunately, I'm just not as talented as Ribera," said Denis. "After Master Ribalta's passing, I could find no other master to take me on. Thankfully, my cousin found me work as an illustrator for the *Grantville Times.*"

Pohl walked over to where Betsy was kneeling and bent down next to her. "M'lady, if I may?"

"Of course, Captain." Betsy cast a quick glance over to Denis who simply shrugged. It wasn't as if either one of them was in any position to stop the dragoon captain from doing what he wanted.

The captain pulled out one of the canvases.

"I know that one as well," said Betsy. "*Landscape With Apollo and Mercury*. I don't remember the artist or the name. But I know it. I also am fairly certain that it won't be painted for at least another ten or twenty years."

Pohl looked at her oddly. "I don't really understand what is going on, but I do know one thing. I have seen this painting before, and within the last few days."

"Where?" asked Betsy.

"At the home of his eminence the Bishop. He was showing off his latest acquisition."

Betsy held her compact mirror out at arm's length, trying to use the small polished glass surface to get an accurate picture of how she looked in the dress that Captain Pohl had provided.

Hours ago, the captain had escorted them to a building located near the dragoon barracks, and requested that Betsy disguise herself as a member of the bourgeoisie while he made arrangements for her to meet with the art dealer who had sold the Bishop the possibly forged painting.

Now she wore a gown that was edged in lace with a double layer collar. Betsy stuck her tongue out at her reflection as she dressed, but once or twice Denis did catch her smiling and preening a little, when she didn't think he was looking.

Her American jeans, along with the rest of her uptimer clothing, had vanished into their luggage.

"Personally I think you look good, like a lady," said Denis. "Though that ponytail of yours, well….."

"I feel like the time I dressed up as a pilgrim girl for Thanksgiving." She gasped. "I just realized that the real first Thanksgiving was only a decade ago! This dress is probably closer to what the pilgrims wore than the one I dressed up in as a kid!"

"You're wearing far too much lace to look like a puritan." Denis said. "Although if we fix your hair correctly, we may be able to convince someone that you are sideways royalty, or at least connected to some up-and-coming merchant house."

Betsy reached up behind her and pulled the rubber band off of her pony tail, shaking her head to let her hair spread out. Then she curled the topmost layer into a bun, and let the rest hang in long, unruly curls. She stared at the mirror for a long moment, twisting her head to the right and left before muttering. "It still needs something."

With that, she turned away from him and her hands disappeared under the layers of her dress. A moment or two later she held up a set of diamond earrings, something that Denis had never seen her wear and had not even known she had with her.

Pohl came walking into the room and inspected Betsy. She smiled, turned around for him and then curtsied. Denis raised one eyebrow. That was something that he had never seen Betsy do before, though it didn't surprise him that she knew how. Things had reached the point between the two of them that little she could do would surprise him.

"These are valuable?" Pohl asked, as his hand brushed the side of Betsy's face, lightly touching the earrings

"Yeah, they are," Betsy said.

Another of Betsy's favorite expressions sprang to Denis's mind. "Lucy? You gotta lotta *splainin* to do." Denis said. "Where did those come from? You don't make enough to buy diamonds. Besides, do you know how dangerous it is to be carrying things like that with you through the countryside?"

"Your friend is correct, m'lady," said Pohl. "Within a half mile of these barracks I could find a couple of dozen cutthroats who would willingly slit your throat, not to mention rape you, for these."

"That's why I had them hidden in my bra," Betsy rolled her eyes. "And they *are* mine. They belonged to my mawmaw; she lent them to me for a friend's wedding, before the Ring of Fire. Usually I keep them in the family safety deposit box, but I didn't want to take a chance that Albert might convince my father to give permission for him to marry me and want to use those as a dowry gift."

Denis rolled his eyes.

"You know," chuckled Pohl. "This time I'm not going to ask for an explanation; it would just make things too confusing."

"It is my pleasure to meet you, Mademoiselle. I am Justin Quinniaro."

The art dealer lived in an opulent manor house just outside of Mende. Captain Pohl had brought a stylish coach to transport her to the place. Where he had procured it, Betsy hadn't asked; she'd learned that, although as a journalist it was her job to ask questions, every now and then it was better to just sit back and say nothing.

Betsy disliked Quinniaro at first sight. She had seen his type before; tall and dark, in a mafia kind of way, and insufferably sure of himself, the kind that either ended up buried in a work cube somewhere or doing time in a federal country club prison.

"I'm pleased to meet you, Monsieur Quinniaro. Your French is good, but I detect a hint of an Italian accent," she said.

"You have a good ear, milady. My family is from Venice, though I have not been back for a few years."

The bare walls in the living room of Quinniaro's residence were awash in candlelight and shadows. Three paintings were placed at intervals on one wall. Betsy recognized one of them as another copy of *Landscape With Apollo and Mercury*. A masterful rendition, and identical to the three others she had seen in the rolled up canvases that were back in the dragoon barracks.

"If you will excuse me, Monsieur Quinniaro, there is a small matter that I must attend to," said Pohl. "I'm sure that it won't take me more than a few minutes to deal with. One of my men will be close by, should the need arise." Although he looked at Quinniaro as he said this, Betsy knew that his words were for her benefit.

Pohl was gone with that, not waiting for a word from Quinniaro. The Italian looked at Betsy with an air of respect.

"I would be fascinated to know how you got that stick in the mud to accept a bribe. I've been trying for months," he said.

"Let us just say that it didn't cost me a cent," said Betsy, smiling her most seductive smile. "But let's get down to business; he won't be gone that long. First: officially I am not here, I have never been here, and this conversation is most definitely not taking place. Is that understood?"

"Of course;, should the question ever come up, I have been hunting with several of my good friends, in the forest to the south. I understand there have been reports of wolves. Dangerous filthy beasts," said Quinniaro.

"My brother and I are acquiring items for our family's new estates in the colonies; a place that, quite frankly, I find appalling to even consider. However, our parents have compelling reasons for the relocation. Thus, I suppose we shall have to endure for a few years," said Betsy with a melodramatic sigh. She watched the man carefully. There were reactions to her words, small signs that her poker playing cousins would have been proud that she noticed; but for the most part Quinniaro kept his face unmoving.

"Good reasons? I would suspect those reasons might be political, but far be it from me to inquire into another's business," he said.

"Unless it might profit you," Betsy said. "And trust me, if you can supply what I need, you will make a profit. I require . . . shall we say, transportable investments. I'm not particularly interested in how you acquire them. It's not as if anyone would ask too many questions in the colonies. I was thinking perhaps artwork: Caravaggio, Duck, Carracci, or even older works, such as the kind made by the contemporaries of Titian and Dürer, if they can be had for a decent price."

Quinniaro sat for a long time before speaking, his eyes not moving off of Betsy. She was reminded of the first time she had worn a bikini out at the lake; the boys's reaction was nice at first, but after a bit began to feel creepy.

"You must understand, I am simply a business man. While it is true I do come across art work from time to time, I can make no promises that I would be able to find any such items for you at this moment," he said.

"Well, that's a pity," as from inside her sleeve she produced a small leather bag of coins. "I was going to leave this as earnest money to prove that I am prepared to pay for what I want without explanation. But since you can't provide what I need, I suppose I will have to look elsewhere."

"I didn't say I couldn't find what you were looking for," Quinniaro's eyes darted to the corner of the room as he spoke, an action that Betsy noted for later. "I believe that an associate who specializes in acquiring such things may be presently under my roof. If you will wait but a moment, Mademoiselle, I can consult him."

As soon as Quinniaro stepped from the room, Betsy looked over to the corner where he had glanced. An ornate trunk caught her attention. She jumped from her chair and hurried over to it. Although it was locked, that was no match for one of Betsy's hairpins. Inside was a hardbound book with the Grantville Public Library card catalog designation.

"Hello! You definitely didn't come from France." Betsy looked up at the door nervously. She figured that she didn't have much time. Hastily, she opened the book, and tore the title page from the inside. Then she replaced the tome before jamming the lid in place.

She had just taken her seat again when Quinniaro returned. "I believe that I may have access to some of what we discussed." The smile on his face exuded the sort of calm confidence that Betsy had always detested.

"Very well, I will be in the area for a few more days. Let Captain Pohl know when we have business to conduct," she said.

"So, do you believe us now?" said Denis.

"I trust no one, and I believe only what I see," answered Pohl as he knelt on the ground, eyeing a set of horse's hoof prints. He'd said the same thing when Betsy had handed him the page she had liberated from Quinniaro.

"It's the title page from a book on Baroque art. It shows work that has been painted by this point and some that will be produced over the next few decades. I would have brought the whole thing out with me, if I thought that I could have stuffed it down my bra. Overall I would say a book of this nature makes quite a handy bit of source material for forgers. So do you believe your own eyes now?"

Pohl shrugged. "I will concede that Monsieur Quinniaro's behavior is most suspicious. And now, Mademoiselle, I must ask that you and your intended take your places behind my men where it is safe. One of my scouts reports that Quinniaro went to a small cottage not far from here."

"Her . . . intended?" Denis jerked back.

Pohl winked at Denis. "I'm starting to understand how the lady thinks. Trust me on this, Monsieur Sesma. You may not realize it, but you are a doomed man."

Denis glanced over at Betsy and was surprised to see that her face was almost as red as her hair. With a laugh, the dragoon captain mounted his horse, and signaled for the dozen men who had been waiting quietly in the woods to follow him.

Betsy coughed. "Funny guy."

"Hilarious." Denis said

"Don't get any ideas," she said, as Denis caught a whiff of something that he thought might be perfume when she slid uncomfortably close to him as he helped her onto her horse. There hadn't been time to retrieve her "regular clothes", so she was forced to ride in what Denis thought of as a "normal" manner, i.e.: side saddle.

Once the others had passed by, Denis and Betsy fell in behind them as they had been instructed. It took half an hour for them to reach the small cottage-- although apparently Pohl's idea of a small cottage and Denis's were radically different. The outbuildings were rather dilapidated, but the main house was large and definitely looked livable. Denis could see light coming through several of the windows.

Denis and Betsy rode up beside Pohl, who was conferring with a small man dressed in brown that neither of them had seen before.

"My associate here says that Monsieur Quinniaro went inside, and he is certain that there are others with him," said Pohl.

"A problem?" asked Betsy.

"Possibly," said Pohl. "Only one way to find out. You two stay here! In case of a fight I don't want you injured. Especially you, Mademoiselle Springer."

"I can handle myself in a fight," snapped Betsy.

"Perhaps you can," he nodded. "But the dress is on loan, and I don't want to have to pay for a seamstress to repair it should it be damaged."

Quiet as shadows, the dragoons advanced on the entrances to the house. There was the sound of shattering wood and breaking glass, followed by silence. A few minutes later, a lanky young man of perhaps fifteen or sixteen years came out of the house and brought word that Captain Pohl thought it was safe for them to join him inside.

"That was quick," said Betsy

Denis just shook his head at her words. He was no soldier but he had learned that most fights, whether they were a major battle or a one-on-one run-in with a thief, were usually over quickly. Later, when you were painting the picture to honor the skirmish or retelling the story over the fifth or six mug of beer, the events were always inflated to the level of a high adventure.

Denis hadn't gone more than four or five steps through the front door before the smell of turpentine hit him. It was thick and pungent; causing him to cover his nose even as memories of his days spent in his master's workshop assailed him.

"I'm beginning to think that the Mademoiselle and you were correct," said Pohl as stepped through a door at the far end of the room.

There were several dozen easels spread about the room, each bearing a stretched canvas painted with a work in progress. In the dim light from candles it was hard to see just what the pictures were, but Denis could make a few guesses.

"So where are the artists?" asked Betsy.

Pohl gestured for Betsy and Denis to follow him back into the next room. Crouching on the floor were five men, their hands tied behind them, their faces showed the evidence of close-quarters fighting with the dragoons who stood nearby.

"I haven't had a chance to question them, but I think they will be willing to explain what is going on and who their "patron" might be," he said.

"So where is Quinarro?" asked Denis. "These men are obviously just the hired help. I'm willing to bet that they are apprentices whose masters didn't think they were up to snuff."

"Apprentice!" one of the men on the floor yelled in heavily accented German. "I am no apprentice. I am a master at what I do. I have done nothing wrong!"

Denis looked at several paintings stacked to one side. A compelling portrait that seemed to show the painter Diego Velazquez standing before a canvas while a princess, two ladies in waiting, chaperones, a dog and two dwarves entertained themselves next to him. Behind the painter hung a painting of a very much older-looking Philip IV and a woman who Denis didn't recognize as the queen of Spain.

He looked to Betsy in question.

"*Las Meninas*; that has to be for practice, as there is no way they could explain that one, much less sell it." Then she made a wave of dismissal. "I'll loan you my fine arts textbook to explain who most of those people are."

Denis rubbed his chin for a moment, then picked up a brush and made a series of strokes, forming a shape in the lower right-hand corner.

"It needed something," he said, looking at the man on the floor.

"Let's get back to the barracks," said Pohl.

"Then far be it from me to delay that," said Quinarro who came out of a nearby closet and grabbed Betsy around the shoulders with one arm. He yanked her up against him and stepped backwards. In his other hand he held a cocked pistol, the barrel only inches from her face.

"You must know that you cannot escape," said Pohl, taking a step toward the man.

"Oh, I think I will, my dear Captain Pohl. I've seen the way you and this idiot Spaniard look at this girl. I don't think that you want to see her brains spread all over this charming little retreat," said Quinarro.

"If you harm her I will track you down, no matter where you go," said Denis.

Quinarro, shook his head and chuckled, twisting to look over his shoulder. The inattention was all the invitation that Betsy needed. She threw herself backwards against him. The move was unexpected enough to throw them both off balance and cause him to loosen his grip around her. She pulled away, twisted, and rammed her knee into her captor's crotch.

"Aaaahhh!" he screamed, the pistol dropping out his hand. Betsy slammed her elbow up and into the man's throat. The pain drove Quinarro to his knees in front of her.

"This dress is on loan," she said. "If you've caused me to tear it, Captain Pohl will be most unhappy."

* * *

Denis dropped a couple of pieces of wood into the campfire. The flames flared brightly orange, dancing high into the air for a moment before settling back into a comfortable yellow glow.

"You realize that Captain Pohl would have been quite happy to have us stay. Or at least you," said Denis slyly.

Betsy's head shot up from the other side of the campfire. "Don't you start in on that again! I had enough of that kind of thing from Albert back home."

"All right, all right," laughed Denis. He turned to the saddle bag next to him and dug around inside of it until he found two wrapped packages. He passed one of them to Betsy, then turned his attention to the remaining one.

Inside the cloth was a thick piece of bread and a reasonably fresh-looking apple, at least that's what it looked like. Denis had been hungry too many times in his life to be that picky about his food. Besides, this and some of their other supplies had come from the Bishop's kitchen, so it should pass muster. That, plus the wine that had been a parting gift from Captain Pohl, would serve to make a passable meal.

"I wish that the Bishop hadn't insisted on keeping my earrings," Betsy said as she shifted her shoulders. "I couldn't stuff all the coins he gave me in payment down my bra."

Denis stared at her incredulously. "Where did you put the rest of them?"

"Don't ask."

"Yes, dear." Denis handed her a share of the rations.

"Do you think that Quinarro is going to hang?" Betsy asked after several bites.

"For forgery? I seriously doubt it," said Denis. "You can find bad copies of almost any painting on the streets of Amsterdam. Quinarro should be more afraid that his customers, who thought they were buying originals, will find out what he did."

"Did you see the look on the Bishop's face when he saw so many copies of the same painting that Quinarro had sold him?" Becky snorted. "I thought he was going to explode. Somehow I doubt that our Italian friend will be seeing anyplace outside of a dungeon for a long time."

The Bishop had also sworn both of them to secrecy regarding his involvement, saying it was a matter of the church's honor; i.e.: he didn't want anyone to know that he had been fooled by a copy.

Denis leaned back against the fallen tree trunk and stared up at the sky. A gibbous moon looked down on them, and the stars were spread out like a blanket. Right now, things felt rather good and sharing this quiet time with Betsy was nice as well.

"Of course," he said finally, "We still haven't found any trace of those missing blacksmith's apprentices. That is the story that Kindred sent us out here to get. Besides keeping you apart from Albert."

Betsy glared at Denis. For a moment he expected her to throw something at him, but she didn't; instead a smile slowly broke across her face.

"The less said about Albert, the better. As for our wayward apprentices, one of the dragoons said that a few weeks ago he saw a couple of guys who matched their description sitting in a tavern and drinking through a windfall. I'll bet that if we ask around, we'll find that they probably sold their master's raw goods and drank away their profits. Not much of a story there. But I do have an idea that might just satisfy old man Kindred."

"Would you care to enlighten your traveling companion," asked Denis. "Or do I have to guess?"

"Simple. I'll just write up a story about the forgery for the *Inquisitor*. We'll spin it differently, so that the Bishop won't get his cassock in a bunch. In our version a group of werewolves was operating the forgery ring, killing off anyone who discovered their secret. You supply some very nice woodcuts and that will keep Kindred happy with us."

Denis began to laugh, rocking back and forth. "You have an evil mind woman."

"Thank you," Betsy said with a grin. "I do my best."

Just then a wolf's howl echoed through the forest from the south.

"Werewolf?" asked Denis.

"There wolf," replied Betsy.

"A STUDY IN REDHEADS"

By: Bradley H. Sinor and Tracy S. Morris

"Paul, we need to talk!"

Paul Kindred, managing editor of the *Grantville Times*, stifled a groan when he heard that voice. Betsy Springer came toward him at a dead run, her red ponytail bouncing like an excited rooster's tail, and would have collided with him had he not stepped aside at the last minute.

"Hello, Betsy," he sighed. Paul had been hoping for a quiet day. The political hijinks that fed both the front page and the dull ache just behind his eyes had been running at high tide lately, getting hotter as summer approached.

But Betsy Springer only called him 'Paul when she had another wild story idea to pitch to him. When she thought he couldn't hear her, he was 'old man Kindred.'

"Hello, Paul! Look, this is important: Rosebud and Watergate all wrapped up in one! We need to talk, but not in the street."

Paul couldn't count the number of times he had heard that phrase. Like the common cold germ, it would get under his skin, make his pulse race, and leave him in a cold sweat, and before long he would have a major headache.

He gave Betsy a pleading look, hoping she would at least wait until he got into his office before she pitched another hare-brained conspiracy theory story idea. But as Betsy hopped from one foot to the other in excitement, he knew that there was little chance for peace.

"Indeed," Paul consoled himself with the thought that if this story turned out to be too wild for the *Grantville Times*, at least Betsy wasn't opposed to letting him "re-direct" it into the pages of the *Inquisitor.*

Paul also knew it would only be a matter of time before Betsy would start in on the movie quotes that were her trademark. It seemed like she could remember every detail of every movie she had ever seen.

One of these days he really needed to convince his father, the publisher of the *Times*, to send Betsy on a "Nellie Bly" style tour of the USE and surrounding areas, just to get her out of his hair. If sending her around the world were practical, he might have considered that.

As they neared the paper's offices, Paul could see Denis Sesma's gangly frame leaning against the front door. Denis was one of the artists he kept on staff to do woodcuts, one of the few who turned his work in on time, if not early. He should have expected that Denis would not be far when Betsy was around. They were a couple, though neither would admit it.

"Good morning, Mr. Kindred," said Denis, doffing his cap the moment he spotted his employer.

"Hi, Denis. Come on inside," Paul unlocked the door and gestured for the two of them to follow him. Betsy whispered something to Denis, who nodded and sprinted away. A few moments later he returned, followed by a skinny boy dressed in a typesetter's apron and a square paper hat.

"If you want to stop the presses, you need to hijack more backshop people than that, Betsy," Paul said. "So, what's the story?"

In response, Betsy snaked her arm around the kid and pulled him forward. The boy seemed reluctant, like he would have preferred to hide behind Denis.

"This is Alessandrio…Alessandrio?" Betsy looked to the boy with a quizzical expression. "Alexandrio." She said firmly. The boy made a noise of protest, but Betsy waved it away with a dismissive gesture. "I like that better. It's more American. Paul this is *Alexandria*, actually." Betsy began again. "She's from Venice"

Hearing Betsy's words, Paul looked at the young typesetter again and realized this wasn't a scrawny young boy, but a girl.

She wore her red-blonde hair in a close-cropped masculine style, but her overly large blue eyes made her seem more like one of those Precious Moments figurines of a street urchin rather than an actual person.

"Betsy," Paul said with the caution of a man stepping through a minefield, "Do you have Alessandrio's permission to discuss personal business like this?"

Before Betsy could respond, Alessandrio waved away his concern. "Before. We talk."

"You see!" Betsy said with a sunny smile at Alessandrio. "Everything is copacetic between me and Alex."

The young typesetter sighed in tired resignation. "Bene. Alex."

Paul sympathized. This was why most of his staff now called him *old man Kindred* behind his back. Betsy had this way of wearing you down: much like a hurricane wears down the rock face of a cliff.

"Alex here found something important," Denis said. The younger girl nodded and began to speak quietly in a string of broken English mixed with German, Venetian and Italian. Paul thought he heard the words "reading" and "murder," as well as the name of a town not that far from Grantville: "Hildburghausen."

"Okay, you've got my attention," Paul said. "Let's go in the office."

If it were possible for Alex's eyes to get bigger, they did at the prospect of going into Paul's office. Most of the time when an employee went in there it was to be fired.

"Come on, he won't bite," said Betsy, and then turned to Paul. "You better not!"

"Yes, ma'am." He led them into his office and slid into the high-backed chair that had been a gift from his father when he took over as managing editor. "Now, what the hell are you three talking about?"

"I read." Alex blurted out.

"Alex's father was a printer in Venice. His chief apprentice, Vito, turned out to be a lazy lout; unfortunately, he couldn't get rid of him, because of the boy's family political connections, so Alex had to help in the shop to take up the slack," said Betsy.

"Small fingers," Alex held her ink-smeared hands out so that they could see that she had the nimble fingers that were perfect for setting type. "Typesetting for Papa, that's how I learned to read English and German, besides Italian."

"Unfortunately, her father was killed in an accident a year or so ago, and the family business was seized by creditors," said Denis.

Paul could almost finish the story himself. Even though she was trained as a printer and typesetter, there was no way any other printer would take on a girl, no matter how good she might be.

"Alexandria had two choices," said Betsy, waving away the girls protest about the Americanizing of her name. "Become a prostitute, or hope she could find a convent that would accept her; neither idea was to her liking, so she made a third choice. She sort of reminds me of myself in that way."

"I heard about USE and how women have rights to work here," she said slowly, picking her English words carefully. "Only way I could travel was disguised as boy. Took me four months, walking mostly. I had gotten used to having my hair like this, wearing pants and even answering to the name Alexandro, so when you hire me I didn't bother tell you I was girl."

"I only found it out by accident." Denis rubbed the back of his neck, cheeks staining red. "We were taking a wagon of supplies and the wheel broke. It threw Alex off and knocked him, er… her out. When I tried to see if he…. she, was all right I opened his shirt and ……"

"I get the picture," Paul said. "But how does this lead to murder?" Paul could feel his right eye start to tic. Betsy often had that effect on him.

"I read!" Alexandria cut in. "Always I read, books, pamphlets, even the type that I set. In library I find books about -- what you call them?" She snapped her fingers as she searched for the correct words. Then her eyes lit up and she pointed at Paul. "Serial killers!" She said triumphantly.

"Wait!" Paul sat up straight. "Back up! Serial killers?"

"Yes, I see it in the type! I'm sorry my English not as good as I would like. I read it in the stories I set. I even read the other newspapers we get in here."

Betsy nodded and gave Paul an apologetic smile. "I guess she was reading about criminal profiling at the library; how she got on that I still haven't figured out. But she's been setting stories about a series of strange deaths in Hildburghausen, and began to notice things that look like deliberate arsenic poisoning to her."

As Betsy said this, Denis pulled out tear sheets of the stories and pointed to the pertinent passages. "The victims seem healthy. They eat enough to get fat – there's a clue right there. How many people do you see who are actually overweight anymore? – And the poison stays locked up in the body fat. When the poison stops, they lose their appetite and as they get skinny the poison works its way back into their body and kills them. By the time they die, the poisoner has gotten away."

"And she knows about poisons, how?" Paul asked, a number of possibilities running through his head.

"Her uncle was an alchemist," Denis said. "But he was murdered by a client so that he couldn't give testimony before the tribunal."

Alex sniffed. "Typesetting is better. Nobody . . ." She snapped her fingers as she searched for the correct word. "Incazzato . . . mad! Nobody mad at you, at least not that much."

"I saw this in a movie once," Betsy said. "I think it was about the Borgias and how they used poison."

Alex pointed to the article on top of the stack that Paul held. "Sickness in Hildburghausen. And here." She pulled a third article out of the stack. "Again, and again."

Paul looked from the articles to the two reporters and the typesetter. "You think it was murder?"

"Yes," proclaimed Betsy. "The three of us spent a good while at the library. The symptomology matches."

"Some of them could have been accidental," Paul pointed out, though as he glanced over the articles there was something in the back of his mind that said there might actually be a story. "How do you intend to prove your theory?"

"We read up on a couple of tests, and scrounged what equipment we could. Alex thinks she can perform what's called a Marsh test if we can find tissue samples and bring them here to her."

"What tissue samples?" Paul asked pointedly.

Betsy gave him a blank look. "Swabs from dishes, or maybe leftover meals?"

Paul rubbed the bridge of his nose as he realized that the young redhead hadn't thought this through. "To prove anything, you need tissue samples from the actual victims. You do realize that the authorities, not to mention the families, would not be pleased to have you digging up their relatives?"

"That is just gross," said Betsy, "And I wouldn't even think about it unless it were absolutely necessary."

"You may be on to something here." Paul said slowly, "But I think that you three are going to have to be very careful, very circumspect in what you do and what you say. Do you hear me, Betsy?"

"Right!" Betsy grinned. "We won't let you down, Ol–er–Paul!"

"Scusi," said Alex. "You say 'you three'?"

"Yep, you're going with them," he said.

"B-b-but I'm supposed to work," she stuttered. "Mr. Kelly will fire me if I not there!" Kinkelly ran the newspaper's back shop and ruled it with an iron hand, though Paul knew that the man actually had a very soft heart.

"Don't worry about Kelly, his bark is worse than his bite. You're on full salary for as long as it takes to get this matter settled. No matter what happens, you will definitely have a job to come back to, on that you have my promise."

"Oh," she said in a little girl's voice, and looked uncertainly at Betsy and Denis.

* * *

"You may have to be both a boy and a girl," said Betsy.

Alex looked up at Betsy with a start. "Scusi?"

They had arrived in Hilburghausen that morning and gotten rooms at a small inn on the south side of town. It was the sort of place where strangers were the norm, so no one looked at them twice when Betsy, Denis, and their *younger sister* checked in.

"It's just a matter of letting people see one thing while something else is going on," said Betsy. "It's a kind of magic."

Alex jerked back at the mention of magic, crossing herself and muttering something in Italian as she looked back and forth between Denis and Betsy.

Denis laughed and tore the corner off a piece of paper from the edge of a copy of the *Inquisitor* that lay on the table. He rolled it up in a ball, showed it to her, and then holding it between two fingers, he passed his hand in front of it and the ball was gone. Alex's eyes grew even wider than they normally were. Denis smiled, then reached across the table, touched her ear with one hand, and seemingly produced the paper ball from her ear.

"How?" she stuttered.

Denis didn't say anything, he repeated the move, making the ball disappear, but then held his hand up and turned it around to where Alexandria could see the piece of paper hidden between two of his fingers.

"I let you see one thing, when something else was going on. That's what Betsy's talking about. It's just a little misdirection; you're expecting one thing while I'm doing another. Like they do it in the movies." Denis looked over at Betsy, smiled and ran his finger down the side of his nose; hoping that was the gesture she had talked about in that movie, *The Sting.*

Alex laughed and picked up the paper ball rolling it over and over in her hands.

"The fact is that everyone saw us check in with a young girl, so I doubt anyone else will be paying attention if a young boy is seen wandering around town, listening and maybe asking the occasional question," said Betsy.

"I see," Alex said with a mischievous smile as she waved the crumpled paper around. "I sneak around, quiet as mouse, and listen in dark alleys and back corners." She folded her hand over the paper ball, hiding it from sight.

"Exactly," Betsy said. "Do you think you could sneak into one of the victim's homes and get a look at the dishes?"

"It's probably been too long to even try," Denis said. "The first case was three months ago, and the second was a month later. Whatever possessions were left would have been distributed to their heirs."

"You don't suppose that's the connection, do you?" Betsy tapped her upper lip with her forefinger. "The people in the second case. The Fuchs, yes?" she looked to Alex for confirmation. "Maybe they bought something that had been in the first home."

"The home of Herr Zedler," Denis said. "That may be the case, but we won't be able to find the connection that way."

"I'm just afraid that the trail, as they say in detective movies, has gone cold."

"They always made this look so easy on the detective shows," Betsy muttered. "Old man Kindred may be right. We may have to dig up the bodies, no matter what he said or how gross it might be. We could find out for certain that way."

"Even if this is the USE, our German hosts take a dim view on grave desecration," Denis shuddered. "I have no desire to face a hangman for the sake of a story."

"Oh all right," Betsy said reluctantly. "I'll tell the stable hands that I don't need to borrow a shovel after all."

* * *

"I hope Alex had better luck than we did," Betsy said moodily as she dug into her bratwurst and potato buns. There were hardly any other people in the common room of the tavern. It was still relatively early; even the tavern girl had disappeared into the kitchen after dropping their plates in front of them. "Do you believe that those guys actually thought that breathing onions would stop the spread of illness? The thing is, in a couple of hundred years this area will be one of the first places to regulate food. They already regulate beer."

"Not everyone believes the Committee of Correspondence when they talk about germs," Denis said as he poked his maultaschen suspiciously with a spoon. "Knowing what may be going on makes me reluctant to eat anything in this town."

"Don't be silly," Betsy said around a forkful of food. "Dad always told me that if I go anywhere, I should try and eat like a local. That way I learn more about the culture." She bit her lip and looked down. Betsy's father had died suddenly of the plague while serving as a minor bureaucrat somewhere outside of Grantville. Betsy had taken death by disease particularly hard, having come from a time and place where plague was rare.

"We always did stuff like that on family vacations. Sometimes I wasn't sure just exactly what cultural experience I was supposed to get, but I suppose it didn't matter as long as it was an experience and it was cultural, and it was with my dad."

Denis nodded; he reached over and patted her hand. Betsy didn't often let herself slip into melancholy, but thoughts of her dad always caused her eyes to water. "What would he want us to do?"

"Go get the bad guys, pilgrim," she said.

"Pilgrim?" Denis shook his head. He was used to most of her movie references, but not all of them.

"Time to watch some John Wayne movies, then." She squeezed his hand.

Just then, Alex slid into the seat across from them. Her wide, dark eyes looked serious. "Others sick." She folded her hands and rested her chin on them. "So far, no one dead. But many ill." She looked at Betsy's plate. "I speak to Herr Zedler's neighbors and Herr Fuchs neighbors also. Servants too."

Denis nodded in approval. "It's always the servants who know more about what is going on in a house than the family that lives there."

Herr Zedler buy a cow for meat . . . tre . . . three days before he died," Alex said. "Everyone know Frau Fuch for her beef sausages. The cook here," she pointed at the floor, "at this inn is her cousin."

Betsy's eyes bulged. She looked down at her plate, her stomach rolling. "I . . ." She set the sausage down. "Suddenly I don't feel so good."

* * *

Denis held Betsy's hair back as she threw the contents of her stomach up into the chamber pot.

"I think I just threw up my toenails." She wiped at her mouth, and then flopped onto her side on the floor. "Wurst food I ever ate. Pun intended."

Denis patted her shoulder in sympathy. "You're fortunate," he said to her. "You're only suffering from your own overactive imagination. But you must be feeling better if you're making bad puns like that. "

Betsy lifted her head from the floor and looked at him weakly. "Are you telling me that there wasn't any arsenic in my dinner?"

"Alex checked your sausage." he smoothed her hair back. "It was poison free. Now that you're okay, she'll start testing samples of meat from the families who are ill. I think we may have found the connection there."

"She's getting the samples how?" asked Betsy.

"She said 'Don't ask', so I didn't. There probably are things that it is better for us not to know."

"So, I guess this means the butcher did it. Although that doesn't quite have the ring of saying the butler did it." Betsy grimaced as she sat up, a little pale, but the color rapidly coming back into her face. She gave Denis a sheepish smile. "Now I feel silly."

Denis extended his hand to help her to her feet. "You say that like it's a new feeling? There is someone I know here in town that I think we should talk to."

Betsy looked surprised at that. "Who?"

"His name is Calvin Norcross," Denis said. "We were apprenticed to Master Ribalta at the same time. If anyone knows things that are going on in this town, it will be him."

"You ought to take up investigative journalism yourself," Betsy said. "Everywhere we go you seem to have connections from the old days."

"I can't write with your flair," Denis said, noncommittally. "Besides, don't you always say a picture is worth a thousand words?"

* * *

"I figured that you would either be dead or in the army by now," laughed Calvin Norcross.

The air in the studio was heavy with the smell of turpentine and paint. Half-finished paintings and sketches filled every nook and cranny. Norcross stood just an inch shorter than Betsy and was thin enough that it looked like a good stiff wind would blow him away. The studio was bigger than what Denis had expected, but still little more than a closet. The accumulated work showed him that Calvin was doing well, and that fanned a tiny bit of envy in Denis. Calvin had obviously found another painter to take him on after Master Ribalta died.

"I figured you would have been beaten to death by some jealous husband or boyfriend," returned Denis, taking his old friends outstretched hand.

"It helps to always know where the exit is and to be able to get your pants on while you are running," laughed Calvin. His laugh cut off abruptly as Betsy stepped through the doorway around Denis. "And who is this stunning beauty?"

"This is Betsy Springer." Denis took her hand protectively. "She's a reporter for the *Grantville Times*."

Calvin looked at Denis and Betsy's clasped hands, and then smiled at his old friend. "And what does the *Times* want in Hildburghausen? Obviously, something that is very important to send someone as lovely and talented as you. If you have the time, I hope you would consider modeling for me; with that beautiful face and red hair I would call it *A Study in Red*."

"Well, now, aren't you just the one? Perhaps I might consider posing for you once our business here is completed," said Betsy. Denis heard a familiar tone in her voice and knew that she didn't buy into Calvin's flattery. "We're here investigating some mysterious deaths. There's a chance they may have been from deliberate arsenic poisoning."

Calvin looked from Denis to Betsy and back. Then let out a low whistle. "That's a very serious matter," he said. "If someone has been doing so, they would very quickly be hanged."

"We hoped that you might be able to tell us if you had heard anything suspicious? As I recall, when we were studying with Master Ribalta you were always aware of what was going on around town," Denis said.

"It never hurts to listen to what people are saying, Denis. I suppose you could say that it is only common courtesy. As for suspicious, I'm not sure what you're looking for. I did lose a commission awhile back. Herr Fleischer wanted me to do a portrait of his daughter, but then canceled it at the last minute."

"That would cost a lot of money, yes?" Betsy looked to Denis, who nodded in confirmation.

Calvin walked across the studio and pointed to a half-finished canvas where a figure had been sketched out. "I haven't had a chance to reuse the canvas; there's always a chance he'll change his mind. Although the man actually had the audacity to ask for his deposit back."

"Shameful," said Denis.

"Sounds to me like Herr Fleischer ran into money problems," said Betsy. "We need to follow the money, just like Woodward and Bernstein in *All the President's Men*."

"Woodward and Bernstein?" Calvin whispered to Denis.

"Don't ask so loudly," warned Denis. "If you set her off, she'll wax rhapsodic about it for hours!"

"Strange." Calvin said, staring at his old friend.

"Tell me about it," shrugged Denis.

Their room looked like something out of a mad scientist's lab when Denis and Betsy returned to the tavern. Alex stood over a burner with an odd array of glass flasks, copper tubing and bent beakers. A copy of the

Grantville library's *Fun With Chemistry!* book was propped open before her like a cookbook. A number of tissue samples arrayed in bowls across the table reminded Betsy of the time in Charleston that she'd tried sushi on a dare.

Alex looked up from the burner, eyes enlarged behind a pair of goggles, and waved them over to her. "If I no make mistake, then it's arsenic in all samples."

Denis and Betsy looked at one another in trepidation.

"Ordinarily, I would say that we should go to the authorities, but . . ." Denis rolled his hand in the direction of the table. "What evidence do we show them? I barely understand this, and I have my doubts that the burghers in this town will."

"We could try," said Betsy. "Combined with what we know from your friend, Calvin, we can at least set the authorities on Herr Fleischer. I'm sure they can figure out how his money problems," she held out a hand to her side, "and his poisoning people with bad meat," she held out her other hand to her other side, "all fit together." She drew both hands together, interlacing her fingers like a puzzle.

"I'm not sure just how much I trust Calvin," Denis said. "He was always out for himself, but something felt off about him when we visited; I just can't put my finger on it."

"Do you have another idea?" Betsy asked.

"We've got to force Fleischer into a corner, but under circumstances that we control, not him. There is no one quite as dangerous as a man in that position. Besides, we still don't know why he's killing these people."

"Maybe we should just ask him? Sometimes you have to just march right up to Jabba the Hutt's palace and knock on the front door," said Betsy.

* * *

"Hello?" Betsy called out as she looked around the stables behind Herr Fleischer's home and shop. "Herr Fleischer?"

"He doesn't appear to be here," Denis said as he stepped around Betsy and into the stable.

"And he looks like he left in a hurry," Betsy replied as she pointed to the floor. Tack and slightly tarnished coins lay scattered across the ground. "I wonder if his daughter knows that he's gone on the lam?"

"The droppings here are still warm," Denis said as he held his hands over a pile of steaming animal leavings in the stall. "Maybe we can catch him if we hurry." He grasped Betsy's hand and the two of them ran out of the stables and toward the river, in the opposite direction from whence they came.

"What did your sources at the Committee of Correspondence have to say about Herr Fleischer?" Betsy asked.

"They said to be careful," Denis replied. "Dieter Fleischer used to be a Feldwebel in the army. He curses like a soldier and kicks like an angry mule."

Betsy stopped abruptly, just over a mile beyond the city limits, pointing toward a shape lying just off the path ahead of them. "I don't think we have to worry about that anymore."

Denis followed her outstretched hand to see a man lying there in a rapidly spreading pool of blood. Half his head had been blown away. Judging by the mule grazing at the roadside with saddlebags filled to bursting, not to mention the physical description, the dead man was Dieter Fleischer.

"Definitely gross," said Betsy. Even so, she knelt close to the body and began examining it. "He's still warm. We may have just missed his killer."

"So much for getting a confession out of him," said Denis.

Denis touched the side of Fleischer's head and rubbed a drop of blood between his fingers. The smell of gunpowder hung in the air, but there was something else, something familiar that Denis couldn't place. He began to pace back and forth along the bank, looking down at the ground, wishing he could do something like that fellow in the movies and books that Betsy talked about, Sherlock Holmes. The idea that he was starting to think in terms of movie characters scared Denis just a little.

"I'm thinking that we don't have a lot of options now. This was murder and we should report it to the authorities," said Denis as he passed close to some low bushes and trees. He had taken a few steps beyond them when he thought he heard the rustling of an animal within. Denis was about to investigate when Calvin Norcross charged out toward him, swinging a stout, jagged branch. The blow from his attacker's cudgel was enough to put Denis on the ground.

"What the hell?" Betsy stepped backward in shock. Before she could charge to Denis's rescue, Calvin dropped his club and produced a flintlock pistol.

"Old friend, I would not advise you, or your rather well-endowed companion, to move; I won't hesitate to shoot either of you," he said.

Betsy scoffed. "It figures; even in the 17th century men only notice one thing."

"Why, Calvin?" asked Denis as he raised himself up to a sitting position.

"Money," said the little painter. "That idiot cheated me out of my earnings! He was trying to get away with a fortune. I simply intercepted him as he left town. If you hadn't interrupted me, everyone would have assumed that bandits took his ill-gotten gains." He looked regretful, as if trying to convince himself that he had no other choice in what was about to happen. "Now I'm going to have to eliminate you, old friend, and your rather attractive traveling companion, to avoid a hangman's noose myself. I would much prefer to have had her posing for me."

"I think not." Alex came from behind a nearby tree, her two small hands around the grip of a rather large and outrageous looking pistol.

Denis gaped at the device. It looked futuristic and frightening: wrapped with pieces of bent copper tubing and bits of glass on it. If he hadn't seen the component parts in Alex's lab, he would have believed it to be yet another frightening and wondrous uptime device instead of just a clever prop.

Alex pulled a lever as if underscoring that she meant business. "You will drop your pistol, or I use this and it will make what happened to Herr Fleischer seem like a nice thing. Do it now! You will drop your weapon and get down on your knees."

Calvin looked at her and then the weapon. He seemed to be weighing his options.

"I wouldn't," Betsy said. "That's a .44 Magnum, the most powerful handgun in the world. It would blow your head clean off. So, you've got to ask yourself one question: Do you feel lucky? Well, do ya, punk?"

Calvin swallowed, and dropped his own weapon. Then he slowly dropped to his knees.

Denis scrambled over and picked up the gun while Betsy pulled rope off the mule's saddle and tied Calvin's hands behind his back.

"He would have gotten away with it if it hadn't been for us meddling kids. But this still doesn't explain the tainted meat." Betsy threw her hands in the air. "If I can't explain that, then I don't have much of a story. I'll have to invent something for the *Inquisitor* and I would prefer to avoid another lecture from old man Kindred about my 'wild flights of fancy."

"There is an old horse trader's trick," Denis said. "You give a little bit of arsenic to a nag to fatten it up. The poison makes the coat glossy and soon the nag looks like a respectable mount. It's possible that Herr Fleischer purchased some very poor cattle at a very good price. Herr Zedler purchased a cow and took it to Herr Fleischer. Herr Fleischer may have substituted his own poor-quality meat for Herr Zedler's good meat, without realizing that it was tainted."

"And Frau Fuchs purchased sausages from Herr Fleischer. Who pays attention to the quality of meat in sausages?" Betsy concluded with a grin. "This is going to make an incredible story. But what do we do with him?" she waved a hand at Calvin.

"I think we had better take this man to the authorities," Denis said slowly. "With the three of us as witnesses I think that should be enough."

"How did you know he was in the bushes?" asked Betsy as they walked.

"I caught a whiff of turpentine. It's hard as hell to get out of your clothes and most painters get to the point they don't even notice it," he said. "I almost didn't."

He pointed up the path to indicate that Calvin should lead the way. Alex backed up his motion by gesturing with her improvised weapon.

As the four of them walked down the street in a bizarre parade, Betsy leaned over to speak to Alex. "I meant to ask you earlier, were did you get the idea for the ray gun?"

In response, Alex reached inside her jacket and pulled out a rolled-up comic book that she passed to Betsy. On the cover, Ming the Merciless threatened Flash Gordon with a ray gun that looked remarkably similar to Alex's creation.

"I read," she said.

"PORTRAIT OF BEES IN SPRING"

By: Bradley H. Sinor and Tracy S. Morris

"Now this won't hurt a bit."

Betsy Springer rolled her eyes, remembering the first time she had heard that phrase: her family doctor had been about to give her a booster shot. Despite what the nurse said, that one had hurt.

"Like I really believe that, Nurse Rached! Do you also have a bridge in Brooklyn that you can make me a great deal on?" Betsy muttered the last part under her breath.

The dark-haired nurse gave her patient a baffled look before continuing to wrap a long strip of bandage around the young reporter's ankle. Actually, Betsy thought that the woman tied the bandage too tight on purpose, but she was determined not to give the nurse the satisfaction of hearing her cry out. Instead, she tightened her grip on Denis Sesma's hand, driving her nails into his palm. The fact that he stoically refused to react was typical of the half-Basque artist who had become her closest friend in the months since he had come to work for the *Grantville Times.*

"My name is Miller, not Rached," said the woman said with a sigh. She spoke reasonably good English, but every now and again Betsy could catch just a hint of Swedish in her voice when she became irritated – like now. "I've told you that several times. Why am I not surprised that you uptime young people don't pay attention to what your elders say?"

Denis suppressed a chuckle, this was not the first time he had heard that statement around Betsy.

"You are really a very fortunate young woman," Nurse Miller said as she gently placed Betsy's leg on a stool. "This could have been a lot worse. It's what the doctor calls a grade one sprain. It will take several weeks to heal, but you should have some mobility with the use of crutches. If you don't move carefully though, you could easily hurt yourself again and make it much, much worse." She shook her finger in warning at Betsy.

Normally Betsy would have had a good comeback on the tip of her tongue, but right now all she could do was grit her teeth and try to endure the throbbing in her leg.

"How long have you two been married?" asked Nurse Miller, in what Denis guessed was an attempt to distract Betsy.

"We're not married!" both Denis and Betsy spoke at once.

The nurse said nothing, though her expression suggested she was thinking "Yet."

"Are you finished now?" Denis asked nervously.

"You can go, but make certain that Miss Springer stays off her injury and does what she is told," said the nurse.

"Like I have any control over that," muttered Denis.

"I will fetch you some crutches. You're lucky that the doctor has a side business manufacturing them; otherwise, you would have to wait for a carpenter to make some for you," said Nurse Miller. "How did you say you hurt yourself in the first place?"

"I wish that I was doing something really cool, like fighting off a bunch of mercenaries on our way here. But I stepped wrong getting out of a coach. The trip here to Hamburg is one of the most boring ones that I've ever taken in my life." Betsy looked down, embarrassed at her own clumsiness. "At least it isn't as bad as an injury a friend of mine in high school had. He fractured his ankle hitting it on the side of a concrete curb."

"I believe you. It sounds like you were having--what do you Americans call it? 'A really bad day.'" Nurse Miller ducked her head to hide her smile.

Betsy frowned down at her sprained ankle. "For the record, this not the way I wanted to get close to the story."

The nurse continued as if she hadn't heard Betsy. "Now that I'm done I'll send Dr. Kunze in to see you."

Once the nurse was gone, Denis let go of Betsy's hand and went over to the door. He waited for a good thirty seconds before he spoke, all the while listening to the sounds outside the office that doubled as an examining room.

"I think we're alone, at least for awhile. I don't know why, but I just have the strangest feeling that something is going on here that they're not telling us," said Denis.

Betsy looked up from her ankle with a startled expression. "Aren't you and old man Kindred the ones who are always accusing me of being paranoid and seeing conspiracies where there aren't any?"

"Mr. Kindred just wants you to have proof of them before writing the things up,"

said Denis.

He retreated from the door to a nearby chair where he had left his drawing pad and a piece of charcoal. "Besides, I told you it was just a gut feeling. I hope I'm wrong. Mr. Kindred said this trip was supposed to keep us out of trouble."

"Yeah right," said Betsy as she pushed herself to the edge of the chair and gingerly lowered her right leg. She inhaled, as if preparing herself for an excruciating task, then grasped both arms of the chair and pushed up. The result was a sharp sensation of pain that forced her back into the chair.

"You weren't listening to the nurse," Denis laughed. "You're supposed to stay off that foot and keep your leg elevated."

"Yeah, elevated…. check," groaned Betsy.

Denis turned his drawing around so that she could see it. "This is the image I plan to submit with your story. What do you think?"

"You're just trying to distract me," Betsy said.

"Of course I am," he replied.

"You can be just as much of a baby when you're injured." Betsy stuck her lip out in a pout and crossed her arms. After a moment of silence, she put her ankle back on the stool. "I guess it's the thought that counts."

Denis's sketch showed a man, his chest bandaged, lying on a table. A second man, obviously a doctor, judging by the stethoscope that hung around his neck, was pouring something from a jar onto the bandage.

"Not bad, but how will we be able to tell that its honey he's using?" Betsy wondered.

"Your story will tell them that," Denis said.

"But what about people who can't read?"

"If they can't read, why would they have a newspaper?" Denis asked.

"Because they like the pictures?" Betsy shrugged. "Or maybe their Aunt Gertie is reading it to them."

"If you think it will help, I could draw a label with a bee on the jar," Denis said.

"Then people who can read will see the image and wonder why that doctor is putting honey on that man's bandages," Betsy said.

"Which will make them want to read your story about how the navy doctors who don't have antibiotics are using honey to keep infection out of serious wounds," Denis retorted.

"Just like the Egyptians did in the time of King Tut." Betsy smiled in satisfaction.

"King Tut?" Denis tilted his head to the side in a thoughtful pose. "Was he in the movie about the archeologist with a bullwhip?"

"He's from history, not movies." Betsy waved her hands in the air as she spoke. "He hasn't been discovered yet. But when he will be – or was in the future -- those archeologist types that found him figured out that the Ancient Egyptians were using honey to fight off infection in wounds long before antibiotics. "What do you think of this for a headline--" She spread her hands in front of her face as if to picture the headline on a newspaper: "Teaching a New Dog Old Tricks."

A new voice chimed in. "Not bad."

Betsy and Denis turned to see a rather large man standing in the doorway. The pair of crutches he held in one large hand suggested that this was the one they had come to see, Dr. Johannes Kunze.

"I'm sorry that I am late for our interview, young lady," said Dr. Kunze, apologetically. "But we've had a bit of… trouble with Thomas Radetzki, the bee keeper who supplies our honey."

Denis and Betsy exchanged a look.

"What kind of trouble? Denis asked.

"He was supposed to bring us a fresh shipment of honey this morning, from his latest harvest. I saw him only two days ago and he confirmed his plans to me," the doctor said. "But he has not kept his schedule, which is most unusual. The man is normally quite punctual."

Dr. Kunze lifted a shoulder in a helpless shrug. "Since he is a civilian, I can't justify sending a seaman to go check on him, not for just being late.

But I remembered that you said you wanted to speak to him for your story. I thought that perhaps you could go to his apiary and check on him."

"Normally I would be happy to help, Doc. But . . ." Betsy pointed at her leg.

The doctor smiled in that *I was expecting that comment* way that had always irritated Betsy. "I hate to send you so soon after your injury, but there is no one else available right now. If you go it will help put my mind at rest. I just have a bad feeling about the whole matter. We can loan you one of our wagons so that you can stay off of your injured leg. If everything is fine, you can fetch back the honey with you. And when you return we can finish your interview. I would go with you, but we are short-handed."

"You must be busy," said Betsy. "You haven't even had your pants repaired."

"My pants?" said the doctor, glancing down at his trousers where a ragged piece had been ripped out. "Yes, they got caught in a wagon wheel earlier today. Nurse Miller has offered to repair them when we have time. So will you do me this favor and look in on our missing beekeeper?"

"All right," Betsy chuckled, and then muttered under her breath. "The things I do for a story."

"Would you mind if I asked a question?" Denis asked as the doctor handed Betsy her crutches.

She braced them against the floor and tried to use them to stand. Her first attempt was not a glowing success, since she rammed her bandaged foot against a side table and dropped back into the chair. She stifled a muffled groan through closed lips. "I feel like one of the Stooges here."

Denis winced in sympathy, and moved to help her. Betsy's glare caused him to back out of her way with his hands raised in mock surrender.

After a few deep breaths Betsy levered herself up to a precariously balanced standing position. While keeping her weight on one foot, she tucked a padded crutch under each arm, and then began to hobble forward.

She moved only a few feet before she tottered as if about to fall. This time, when Denis stepped forward, she allowed his steadying hand on her shoulder.

"Ready?" Denis asked.

Betsy gave him a reassuring nod before tottering forward a step. Her smile brightened as she took another step and then another, aiming herself toward the door. The doctor nodded approvingly and stepped aside to let her pass.

"Now, about that question?" the doctor asked Denis

"Would I be right in assuming that there is more worrying you than just a late shipment of honey?" Denis asked.

"We are at war," The doctor shrugged. "This is a military hospital and that honey will save soldiers' lives. With the number of spies traipsing around the USE, it would be one more way to strike back at the Navy."

"I'm sure the beekeeper just lost track of time," Betsy said over her shoulder as she stumped down the hall. "We'll go out there, collect the interview and the honey, and be back here before you know it."

* * *

Outside, the stable hands brought out a one-horse buckboard wagon. Denis lifted Betsy into the seat carefully. Then he tucked his drawing tools alongside her before vaulting into the driver's place.

The road between the hospital and Radetzki's apiary was fairly well maintained, but Betsy winced in pain with every stone or rut that the wagon bounced over.

Denis slowed the horses to a sedate walk.

"You don't have to go this slow; it will take us twice as long," Betsy touched his shoulder. "I'm fine."

"It should only take a few hours by wagon," Denis said. "Since it is still early in the day, we can afford to take a little extra time."

"I would rather get our work here done with and get back to Grantville." She frowned down at her bandaged ankle. "This is so inconvenient."

"The nurse said that if you stayed off of it for a few weeks, you should be as good as new."

"I'm no good at sitting still," Betsy crossed her arms and looked out across the field that bordered the road. Denis pinched his lips together to keep from laughing.

* * *

As the hours passed, the city gradually gave way to rolling countryside. In an obvious attempt to distract herself from the throbbing in her ankle, Betsy described, in extreme detail, the plot of several different movies. It hadn't taken Denis long, after he had met Betsy, to master the art of looking like he was listening, while letting his mind wander.

"Then Marv says: All the great ones leave their marks. We're the wet bandits. . . Are you listening, Denis?"

"Yes, dear," Denis said.

When the wagon crested a hill, Denis wished he had time to sketch the picturesque scene in front of them. It would make an interesting paintng, very different from the things he had been doing for the newspaper. He missed doing art like that, but a regular paycheck was a really nice thing to have. Fresh yellow straw thatched the roof of the beekeeper's cottage. Around the yard a riot of roses, chamomile, and lavender bloomed.

"Hey, look!" Betsy broke off and pointed to a field bordered in shrubs that were covered in pink flowers. Denis craned his neck, seeing dozens of insects darting back and forth between the flowers. "Bees!"

Denis pulled the wagon to a stop and squinted at the cottage. "No smoke coming from the chimney. He may not be home."

"One way to check," Betsy said.

"You wait here. I'll go look."

"No way!" Betsy shook her head. "You aren't leaving me out of things. I don't care if I end up having to crawl after you."

Denis sighed. So much for any hope of her being reasonable because of her injury, not that there actually had been much hope of that to begin with. If Betsy had been agreeable, he probably would have been worried about what she was plotting.

As the two of them crossed the yard to the front door of the cottage, they could hear excited barking from inside the building.

Betsy looked at Denis with a sly smile. "Sounds like someone has a little yappy dog."

"If the beekeeper is home, one would think that he would come out to see what his pet is barking at."

Betsy shrugged and reached out her hand to knock. The door creaked inward under the pressure of her rapping. The little dog that they had heard then squeezed through the opening and began to run in circles around the two of them, barking as it did.

"Hello? Anyone home?" Betsy called out as she hopped through the doorway, holding her crutches awkwardly. "Your door is open and --Uh oh!" She froze, with one hand on the doorframe to keep her balance.

Denis stepped behind her and looked over her shoulder, and then he swallowed hard. A man that he presumed was Thomas Radetzki sat at the table in the tiny kitchen, facedown on a tray of sausage and cheese. A bread roll and cloth napkin lay upside down next to one of his open hands. A knife, sticky with what Denis guessed was honey, lay next to the other. It looked as if the beekeeper had died right in the middle of sweetening his Brötchen.

The two of them looked at one another, and then Betsy clomped her way into the kitchen with Denis at her heels. She moved to the table and held her hand over his mug.

"His tea is cold," she said. "He's been dead for a while."

"We had better fetch Dr. Kunze. He may be able to tell us why this happened," Denis said.

Betsy pulled a second chair away from the table and plopped in it, allowing her crutches to clatter to the ground. The dog ran up to her, barking and nuzzling at her uninjured leg at the same time.

"Oh, you poor dear," she said as she picked the animal up, put it in her lap and began to scratch it behind its ears. "You're an orphan now."

At that moment, a figure stepped through the door behind them. Betsy twisted and saw a man in a dark jacket standing there staring at them. The stranger scanned the room slowly, then turned suspicious eyes on Denis and Betsy.

"May I ask who you are?" One of the newcomer's eyebrows winged upward.

"Dr. Kunze sent us. I think we should be asking who you are?" Betsy countered.

"Abelard Gottschalk, Seaman Apprentice with the USE Navy."

Betsy wrinkled her forehead. "I thought Dr. Kunze said that he couldn't send a seaman. Are you part of the hospital staff?"

"I am not assigned to the hospital. I'm with the Naval Criminal Investigative Service and here to see Herr Radetzki on USE business."

"NCIS? You're like a Navy detective," Betsy grinned. "Just like Sherlock Holmes on water, only real! I bet that would make a great addition to the story that we're working on. When this is all over with, can I interview you?"

Abelard looked to be no more than a year or two older than Denis, but he moved in the manner of someone who had complete confidence in his authority. He ignored Betsy's request. Instead he walked over to the body and stared down at it for a time, as if cataloging everything in front of him; then bent down to bring his eyes to the level of the table.

"Dr. Kunze sent us to check on him." Denis said to fill the awkward silence. "He was supposed to be delivering a shipment of honey today. Was he expecting you to visit?"

"That information is classified, I'm afraid." The weight of his gaze made Denis feel nervous

Gottschalk reached over and carefully lifted the dead man's hand, the limp fingers drooping down in reaction. "I would estimate that he has been deceased less than three hours."

"Because rigor mortis hasn't set in?" Betsy asked.

"Correct. Plus the jars of honey for today's shipment are sealed," said the seaman, pointing over to the workbench that occupied the other end of the room.

There were nearly a dozen jars of wax-sealed honey sitting there next to a brazier, tripod, and lumps of beeswax that were no doubt used to seal the jars for transport. On the floor was a box filled with identical wax-sealed jars. While there were several projects under way in the USE for manufacturing and marketing Kilner-style screw lids, they were still a long way from being widely available, so this was still the best way to protect the contents of a jar.

"I bet he got up early, which was probably his usual routine." Betsy surmised. "You can set your watch by some farmers. I don't know how often he robbed his hives, but he had obviously done it in the last day or so. Then he came in here, sealed the jars, sat down to eat, and then bam!"

She paused in scratching behind the dog's ears to wave at the dead man. "Luca Brasi ends up sleeping with the fishes."

Abelard stared at her for a moment. "I do not know this Luca Brasi that you speak of. He sounds Italian. The man before you is definitely Thomas Radetzki, not Luca Brasi." A growl of frustration escaped the seaman's throat. "I don't have what I need to process this crime scene."

"Why do I get the feeling that this isn't your first murder investigation?" Betsy

asked.

"Because it isn't," said Abelard.

The seaman's expression hardened in a way that made Denis feel even more worried. Law enforcement types always seemed to have that effect on him. Perhaps it was because of all the detective movies that Betsy had told him about. There were a few matters in his past that he had not mentioned to her that could still come back to haunt him.

"I am afraid that I will be the one asking questions, since you and your friend are either suspects or witnesses." said Abelard. "I have long suspected Herr Radetzki of selling Naval secrets to spies. But I could not figure out who was supplying him with the information. He could not have gotten it on his own. Not with the limited time that he spent on navy property. I intended to confront him with what I knew and see if I could get him to admit the identity of his contact. However, I suspect his associate became aware of my investigation and decided to silence Radetzki before he could talk to me."

Betsy's eyes widened in surprise. Her grip on the little dog loosened. It jumped from her lap and skittered under her chair, from where it growled at Abelard.

The seaman's hand crept to the folds of his own clothing in an unmistakable hint that he was armed. He pointed from Denis to a chair next to Betsy in a silent demand that the artist take a seat. Abelard then began to move around the room, studying items with a magnifying glass that he produced from his pocket.

"You don't suspect us of killing this man," said Denis. "Do you?"

"Should I?" said Abelard.

"I've never been a murder suspect before," Betsy whispered to Denis. He wasn't sure if her tone implied surprise, fear, or that she was pleased with it; knowing Betsy, the latter might have been the most likely scenario.

"We just got here maybe a minute or two before you," Denis said to the detective with confidence that he didn't really feel. "We couldn't have possibly had the time to murder this man."

"Well," mused Betsy. "I suppose we could have had time if we had driven the wagon at a normal rate of speed instead of really slowly. Our friend here might assume that we were working for the French. Heck, Cardinal Richelieu himself could have hired us when we went to France on that wolf story."

"Betsy, you're not helping us; besides, a lot of people go to France and don't come back working for the French government," Denis said.

They looked up when Abelard cleared his throat. "I've seen all I can here. When we return to the hospital I will bring a doctor back to check for poisoning, along with a full field kit to allow for a closer examination of the scene."

"Good idea! We can wait for you here," said Betsy, figuring she could do her own investigation while the man was gone.

"No," the young man snapped. "You will not. You both will be coming back with me to the hospital, where you will be held for further questioning. If you were simply unlucky enough to stumble on the body, it will be a matter of your own safety. After all, the killer could still be lurking around here."

"Despite what I said, we couldn't have killed the beekeeper." Betsy set her chin in a defiant expression. "In case you didn't notice, I have a sprained ankle, which is not the easiest thing to move around on. I doubt a cold-blooded French assassin would be hobbling around on borrowed crutches. That whole scenario doesn't fit. And 'if it doesn't fit, you must acquit.'" She balled one hand into a fist and slammed it into the open palm of her other hand.

"You may be correct, but nevertheless, you are coming back with me, if only to provide statements about what you have seen here," he said. Denis couldn't help but think this was the young man's way of admitting that Betsy was right without saying it. "We will leave everything as it is, until I can return to examine the scene."

"Fine," Betsy said with a huff. "But I'm taking the dog with me! Poor thing was locked up in the room for hours, with a dead body!"

As if the dog knew that it was being spoken of, the animal sprang from beneath her chair. Betsy made a grab for it, but the dog danced backward, barked at her and then raced in circles around the room. Abelard and Denis both made attempts to grab the animal, but it evaded them, pausing only to nip at the detective's heels before dashing out the door.

"Denis, don't let him get away!" Betsy started to rise and then fell back into her seat. "He's a witness, too!"

"If we don't catch him, I will never hear the end of it!" said Denis, angling his head in the direction that the dog had run.

Abelard looked at the two of them helplessly. Denis sensed a shift in the man's demeanor. Before, the detective had seemed cold toward them and ready to explode at Betsy's eccentricities. Now that they didn't appear to be suspects, he looked like he was suppressing a chuckle.

Finally, the detective shook his head. "We'll both go. I don't think that the young lady will be making any swift getaways in her condition or getting into any kind of trouble."

"He don't know me vewey well, do he?" Betsy muttered in her best Bugs Bunny voice as the two men disappeared out the door. She waited a full minute, then forced herself up onto her feet and hobbled across the room to open a window. The heat of the day had begun and the odor from old food and decaying flesh was intensifying.

Having a long time to search a place was a luxury that wasn't available to Betsy; Abelard and Denis could come back at any time--not to mention the crutches were cumbersome. But she still wanted to have a closer look at things. Betsy was certain she could find something that Abelard might have missed. Seeing the look on his face when she found the evidence he missed would be worth it.

Her breath came in hard gasps as she struggled to stay on her feet and not knock anything over. In her haste, she slammed her injured ankle into the leg of a side table where Radetzki had left several bowls and a blue porcelain pitcher.

"That's all I would need. Abelard would be convinced I'm the killer and was trying to destroy evidence. He'd haul me off the hoosegow without a second thought," she said.

Everything looked like what Betsy would expect to see in a bachelor farmer's home, but something bothered her. The beekeeper had a few utilitarian possessions, but his home was lacking in feminine flair. So why was it so clean? Weren't all bachelors a little bit messy --especially bachelor farmers who had more important things to do than to be sweeping up the dust on the floor? It seemed to her like the killer had cleaned up after himself. The one thing that seemed out of place in the room was a torn piece of ragged green cloth lying on the floor, obviously one of the dogs' toys.

Betsy had made her way around half of the room when she stopped and carefully rotated herself so she could look back at the table where the late owner of the apiary sat as silent and still as he had when she and Denis had come in. There was something about the table that didn't seem right, but Betsy couldn't put her finger on it for the longest time, until she moved closer and stared down at the bowls in front of her.

She gasped as the realization hit her.

"It's so freaking obvious that I should have seen it from the start," she laughed, staring at what she had thought was a napkin.

* * *

"I didn't think a dog that small could run that fast," said Denis as he skidded to a halt. The animal obviously knew to keep well away from the hives.

"You should have seen the little dog that my mother kept," said Abelard. "That mutt could outrun a horse, not to mention climb straight up a vertical fence."

Denis scanned the grassy knoll looking for any sign of the dog, though the little beast probably had the full run of the countryside and knew every nook and cranny along with every tree and bush.

"Do you see it?" asked Abelard. "If we don't find it quickly, I don't care if your wife does get mad; we're going back."

"She's not my wife. Why do people keep trying to marry the two of us off?" snapped Denis.

Before Abelard could answer, the two men heard the dog's barking coming from the base of a small tree ahead of them. On one of the tree's branches above it, a blue jay chattered irritably at the dog.

"There, now. Maybe your wife will be happy and I can do my job," said the detective as he cautiously approached the animal. The little mutt turned, growled at him and took off running.

Denis paused to look at the flower-covered bushes that spread out in the field. They had wandered a long way away from the apiary property, but the bees were obviously collecting honey here.

"That's it!" Abelard bellowed as he put his hand on Denis shoulder. "We go back now."

"Do you know what those are?" Denis said, gesturing at the bushes.

"Flowers?"

"Rhododendron! I think I know what killed Thomas Radetzki. And If I'm right, it proves that Betsy and I are innocent."

* * *

As Denis and Abelard stepped from beneath the cover of the shrub-filled meadow, the little dog darted out of the underbrush a few feet away from them and weaved between their feet. Abelard threw his hands up in disgust and muttered something about accursed dogs.

"Betsy!" Denis called out as the two men came through the cottage door. "I think I know what killed the beekeeper. It was--"

"Poison!" Betsy said as she looked up from where she sat on the floor of the room. She had pulled a crate from beneath Radetzki's worktable. The contents were spread across the floor in a seemingly chaotic pattern.

"You already know?" asked Denis, feeling his enthusiasm evaporating with each passing second.

Betsy paid no attention to his reaction. Instead she reached over and grabbed a jar to show him. "This bottle is marked with the skull and crossbones. Someone tried to hide it among the jars of honey. And look at the cloth under the beekeeper's hand. I thought it was a napkin, but it's a handkerchief. There are several more in his laundry. Radetzki was sick. The honeyed tea was to make him feel better."

"If he was sick, the poison would have killed him quickly," Abelard said.

"How did you figure out that the honey was poisoned?" Betsy asked Denis.

"I saw some Rhododendrons outside," Denis said. "Remember how your research for the article said that feral honey made from rhododedrons can be poisonous?"

"He was working, so his illness wouldn't have made him weak enough for feral honey to kill him, but good thinking." Betsy said.

"You haven't opened the bottle, have you?" Abelard knelt on the floor next to the crate, glaring up at her several times.

"I'm not stupid! I've seen enough mystery movies to know not to disturb evidence," Betsy snorted at him, trying to seem like she was insulted by his assumption.

"That never stopped you before," muttered Denis.

"Never mind that," she hissed. "Whoever poisoned him was someone who was acquainted with him well enough to know where he kept his personal honey."

"That's not the sort of information that you would share with every Jonathan, Dick and Harry," Denis said.

"Tom, Denis. The expression is Tom, Dick and Harry. And I think I know who it is!" Betsy said triumphantly.

* * *

Despite her throbbing leg, Betsy attempted to look as relaxed and comfortable as possible when Denis pulled the cart onto the hospital grounds. The ride in had taken half the time that the trip out had, but had seemed longer as she was anxious to get back.

Betsy was sitting on the back of the wagon, dragging her crutches in the dirt when Dr. Kunze emerged from the building and staring at his two emissaries and their companion. The doctor stared at Seaman Abelard for a moment before turning his attention back to Denis and Betsy.

"You're...back?"

"Don't sound so surprised; it didn't take all that long to get there and back." Betsy said. "We ran into Seaman Abelard there. He was happy to accompany us back. Denis wanted to baby me because of my ankle, so it might have taken a lot longer. But I wouldn't so much as let him drive the cart slowly. We made good time."

Dr. Kunze's eyes grew comically wide. "And Herr Radetzki? He was . . . well?"

"Indeed he is," Denis replied. "He said to apologize for worrying you. He was feeling ill this morning, but he took a purgative and has since recovered. He looks forward to seeing you soon so that you two can discuss some business. He even gave us a tour of his apiary. You should have seen Betsy scream when a bee landed on her."

Betsy made a grunting sound at Denis' words and then took a blanket off of several boxes full of honey. "There we go, Doctor. Herr Radetzki promised he would bring the rest soon, but this should be enough to handle any patients you may need to care for."

The doctor took a few steps over and stared at the boxes. He gingerly lifted one of the jars out and squinted at the hand-written label on it.

He chuckled uncomfortably and tugged at his collar. "That is most excellent. I'm glad that my worries were for nothing. We can do that interview this afternoon, Miss Springer. I'm sure you and your companion are tired and would like a few hours to rest and freshen up."

"Of course, Doctor," said Betsy "That's an excellent idea; my ankle is hurting a bit."

"You will excuse me, then. I have several patients that I must see to. I'll send someone to unload the wagon." Dr. Kunze whirled on one heel and hurried away.

Once the doctor was out of sight, Betsy looked over to Abelard who had quietly dismounted and was headed after the man.

"He went thataway, pardner!" she said.

Denis just smiled and said nothing; a few months ago he would have been perplexed, but now he just assumed her remarks were film related and saving himself a long-winded explanation.

"Come on." He jumped from the wagon. "I have a feeling that things are going to be getting very interesting, very quickly."

"I think you're right on the money," she said and tucked her crutches under one arm as she let him lift her from her seat.

Inside the hospital, the members of the staff were standing around with bewildered looks on their faces. Betsy was about to ask where Abelard and the doctor were when the sound of furniture crashing came from Kunze's office. Denis took off at a run with Betsy, doing the best she could on her crutches, a few steps behind.

Denis stood just inside the doctor's office door when she arrived. Inside the office, papers littered the floor. The doctor lay among them like a child who had spread out in a pile of autumn leaves. Abelard stood over him, holding a sword with the point pressed up against the man's throat.

"Don't move," the seaman said. "It will not bother me one bit to put you down like a rabid dog." He threw a quick glance over his shoulder at Denis. "Herr Sesma, would you be good enough to fetch some rope so we can tie this fellow up?"

It took Denis only a minute to find a set of the hospital's restraints. Then he and Abelard hauled the restrained prisoner up and put him in the wooden chair that Betsy had used to rest her leg on when they had arrived.

"You were correct, Miss Springer," Abelard said, reluctantly. "Dr. Kunze was the one responsible for poisoning Radetzki."

"I knew it!" Betsy pointed to the tear in Dr. Kunze's pants. "You told us you haven't seen Radetzki for several days. But I'm guessing you knew that NCIS was onto Radetzki, so you decided to eliminate him and get the heck out of dodge. You added the poison to the honey that he had set aside for his own use, and that was all she wrote for your partner in crime. I'll bet that the beekeeper's dog attacked you then and tore your pants, because I saw a bit of the torn fabric at his house. I thought it was a doggy toy."

"And these will prove that you are the one selling Navy secrets," Abelard said as he gathered the papers up quickly so that Denis and Betsy couldn't see the contents. "I suspect that somewhere around here is a bag of French silver, payment for his little 'sideline'. I would be willing to bet that there are also traveling papers somewhere in this office that would have given him passage to safety in enemy territory; good doctors are hard to find, I'm sure they would have welcomed his arrival."

"Our being here probably gave him the perfect culprit for the murder." Betsy lifted her hands from her crutches to point an accusing finger at Dr. Kunze. "Denis and I took twice as long getting to the apiary because of my ankle. If we had hurried, we would have had the means to commit murder."

"There is more than enough evidence here to convict Dr. Kunze of treason," Abelard said. "I'll send someone back to the apiary to process the scene."

"What about the dog?" Betsy said suddenly. "Who is going to take care of the poor thing?"

"Miss, if you are volunteering, you can have the job!" Abelard sounded exasperated.

Denis looked to Betsy in horror. A smile of triumph crossed her face. "Since he helped us solve the murder, we should name him "Asta," after Nick and Norah Charles's dog."

A chuckle from Abelard drew Denis's attention. "Whatever the missus wants, eh?"

Betsy didn't seem to hear him. "That was a nice bit of sword work; you're a regular D'Artagnan."

Abelard turned a suspicious eye on her. "Just what do *you* know about D'Artagnan, Miss Springer?"

"THE PLAYS THE THING"

By: Bradley H. Sinor and Tracy S. Morris

Mirari Sesma looked up with a start when the front door of her chocolate shop slammed open so hard that she feared it would come off the hinges.

Elizabeth "Betsy" Springer's familiar, lanky redheaded form made a beeline across the room, weaving in and out of patrons to get to Mirari's personal table in the far corner. Two recently hired waitresses dodged out of the way as she passed, barely keeping a hold on the plates they were carrying. A few of the customers looked up, the expressions on several of their faces showed that they recognized the newcomer.

"Hello, Betsy," Mirari said.

The young girl leaned across the table and looked down at the Basque woman.

"If I see him again, I'll kill him! And I will do it slowly! Very, very slowly!" She raised one hand, finger pointed skyward for emphasis. "I'll cut his heart out with a fork. No! I'll use a spoon!"

Mirari took a sip of her chocolate, set the glass down and smiled at her guest. "Why a spoon?"

"Because it's dull! It'll hurt more!"

"Why don't you sit down and tell me what my dear cousin Denis has done?" Mirari waved to an empty chair in invitation.

Betsy dropped into the chair on the opposite side of the table and glanced back toward the front door as if expecting the devil himself to be standing there. Mirari thought she could hear her friend counting backwards, first in English then in Latin, which surprised her, since she hadn't been aware that the young redhead knew any Latin.

In the few months since they had met, the reporter had become one of her favorite people in Grantville. Betsy was a little quirky, definitely not like the young women that Mirari had grown up around. That was something she liked about these American women; they were not inclined to follow the path expected of a seventeenth century woman, which suited Mirari quite well.

"It's not Denis! He's one of my best friends," said Betsy finally. "It's that supreme idiot Albert!"

"Albert?" Mirari blinked in confusion. "I'm not really sure who you are talking about. Personally, I know four Alberts, so you need to be a wee bit more specific."

Betsy leaned back in her chair and covered her face with one hand. "There can be only one! Albert Haleman! His family lives southeast of here. For some damn reason that I don't understand he's decided that he and I are soulmates and that we should get married and have eight or twelve or twenty kids," she said.

"Big families can be a good thing." Mirari said cautiously. She had five brothers and three sisters -- at least those were the ones that her father would admit to. Things did get a bit crowded at the dinner table, but there was always someone to talk with and to take your side in an argument.

Betsy sat up straight again to throw Mirari an incredulous look. "I don't mind having kids! I actually like the idea," she clarified. "Someday. A long time from now. After I'm secure in my reporting career. And not with . . ." Her face twisted like she'd just tried lutefisk. "Albert."

Mirari smiled in amusement. "So how did Albert get the idea that you two should marry?"

"I owed Albert's cousin, Hans, a favor for an interview. He said 'Let me set you up on a blind date with my cousin Albert." She puffed out her chest and cheeks while lowering her voice in an imitation of what had to be Hans. "Then we'll be even,' he said. 'He's curious about Americans. It would only be once,' he said. Unfortunately, he neglected to tell Albert that this was a one-time only event. Now the idiot thinks we're made for each other, and that I just have to realize it. He won't take no for an answer!"

Mirari couldn't help but smile. The Basque woman could think of at least a half dozen ways to get rid of an unwanted suitor. One or two would even leave his ego intact.

"You could always tell him that you were madly in love with that young navy man from Hamburg. The one with NCIS," she suggested.

"Abelard Gottschalk? He was kind of cute." Betsy looked thoughtful. Then she shook her head. "It wouldn't work."

Just then one of the waitresses walked up to the table. "Mirari? He's here." At those words Betsy went pale.

"Thank you," Mirari said. "Bring him right over." She turned to Betsy. "I think I've got just the thing to take your mind off of Albert."

* * *

The waitress led over a young man of perhaps thirteen years who was dressed in browns and grays. Like a good reporter, Betsy studied him while he approached. The first thing she noticed was his large, hawk-like nose. She actually thought it gave him a unique look. As he crossed the room, patrons moved aside to avoid brushing the sword that hung from his belt. As he neared, his startling dark eyes zeroed in on Betsy. She flushed at being caught studying him so openly.

"Madam Sesma," the young man turned to Mirari. "It's a pleasure to see you again."

"As it is to see you," Mirari said and then turned to her friend. "Betsy, I would like you to meet Cyrano de Bergerac."

"Cyrano? Oh! They wrote plays about you!" All thoughts of Albert flew from her mind. Betsy stood to offer de Bergerac her hand. Rather than shake in the American style, he turned it over and kissed her knuckles. If he had been a few years older, Betsy would have been flattered. As it was, she thought it was cute. She could easily see where the older Cyrano would get his reputation for being a great romantic.

"I'm told they exaggerated the size of my nose, somewhat," he said ruefully.

"You know what they say about a man's nose," Betsy replied. Then her eyes grew wide as she realized what she had said.

Cyrano lifted a single eyebrow in question. He was obviously trying to appear worldly and cool, but a furious red blush darkened the back of his neck and cheeks. "That would be where my other reputation comes from."

"Mondemoiseau de Bergerac is taking a grand tour of Europe. He and his companion have traveled out of their way so that he can speak with you, Betsy."

"Really? Where is your companion?" By the way that Mirari said the word, Betsy assumed that by "companion," Mirari actually meant "guardian."

Cyrano's eyes twinkled. "Regrettably, my cousin was detained in Badenburg on pressing business. I decided not to wait on him."

Betsy took an instant liking to Cyrano. Her favorite girlhood adventures were the ones she'd undertaken while the babysitter was "detained on pressing business" elsewhere. "So, what can I do for you?" she asked.

"Mondemoiseau de Bergerac is interested in your knowledge of uptime cinema," Mirari looked from Betsy to Cyrano in bemusement, as if she wasn't quite certain that introducing the two had been a good idea. "He is a budding playwright and he wants to write a play based on an uptime movie in order to gain some notoriety."

"Which one?" Betsy asked. She ran through a mental list of movies that could easily be converted into stage production. One that was adapted from a stage production, such as *The Odd Couple* or *The Front Page*, would be perfect, she thought.

"Have you ever heard of *Our Miss Brooks*?"

Betsy tilted her chair back and suppressed a laugh. "As a matter of fact, I have! But it wasn't a movie. It was a radio sitcom when my Papaw was my age. They made a TV show of it when my dad was a little boy. We used to watch reruns together when I was a girl; Eve Arden played Miss Brooks. Of course, that was years before she was Principal McGee in *Grease*."

"Greece?" de Bergerac tilted his head in confusion. "What does the Balkan Peninsula have to do with it?"

"Don't ask," said Mirari with a tone of warning in her voice that he apparently understood.

"You have seen the drama, which is the important thing!" The young playwright said in triumph. "I want to write a play based on this story. While other uptimers I've talked to remember the name, none of them admit to having seen it. Which makes it all the more intriguing to me; a story so forbidden that even now people will not speak of it!"

"*Our Miss Brooks*? Forbidden?" Betsy snorted in an effort to hold in her laughter. "I wouldn't call it scandalous. Just obscure."

"Mirari said that if anyone in Grantville remembered classic uptime cinema, it would be you." He continued as if he hadn't heard her.

"TV isn't exactly cinema, but it just so happens that I think I can help you anyway!" Betsy said.

Just then the bell over the door rang again. Betsy's head whipped around. She paled as a young man walked into the room, his eyes scanning the patrons intently. "Oh, no! Albert!" She dove under the table and then looked up at Mirari. "I was never here!"

* * *

"Tell me that it isn't really true," Denis Sesma said when Betsy walked into the room at the back of the *Grantville Times* offices where he and the other staff artists did most of their work. The air in the room was heavy with the scent of freshly cut wood, and long thin shavings were scattered all across the floor.

"Ok, it isn't true. What are we talking about?" Betsy stared down at the woodcut he had been working on. It showed a number of men and women sitting around a large table filled with piles of books and papers.

She picked the carving up and turned it upside down to stare at it. Then she righted it and looked again. "What is this? One of the Committee of Correspondence gatherings?" She asked, while obviously trying to make sense of the reverse image cut into a print block.

"No, it's a parliamentary subcommittee meeting," said Denis. "And don't try to change the subject."

Betsy didn't look up at her companion. "Then why do these guys look as if they like each other? That doesn't sound like most politicians that I know."

"Trust me, the disagreements came quickly. But Mr. Kindred wanted to show that the two sides could work together. It's in the spirit of . . . now what did he call it?" Denis broke off to search for the word while snapping his fingers in the air. "Bipartyingship."

The corners of Betsy's mouth twitched. Denis knew then that he'd made a mistake with the word.

"Bipartisanship is what I think you mean," she said slowly.

Denis waved away her comment. "That doesn't matter, you're dodging my question. So, tell me that you didn't do it!"

Betsy drew a deep breath and smiled at him serenely. "I really don't know what you're talking about."

"Betsy, I've seen you change the subject on someone too many times to just let you get away with it. Tell me about what happened yesterday."

Betsy picked up the woodcut and studied it again. She spent nearly a full minute ignoring him. Denis knew that she was doing it on purpose to goad him for being nosy.

"What did you hear?" she said finally,

"That you and Albert were seen out together, in fact that you were quite the pair of lovebirds. Is this becoming serious?" He asked.

She scoffed. "No! It is not becoming serious! Not in any conceivable way, shape, or form. If Albert has been telling tales like that, I will teach him the meaning of the words 'unending pain!'" Betsy sputtered.

"There are some people who would say that pain is a definition of marriage." Denis mused. Seeing Betsy's scowl, he held up his hands in a defensive pose. "But I'm not one of those people. I also heard something about a table that you were hiding under."

Betsy's eyes grew as big as coins and her face flushed red with embarrassment. "Oh Lord! Please tell me that you heard that story from your cousin and not one of the town gossips!"

Seeing her distraught expression, Denis took pity on her. "You can rest easy. I did hear that from Mirari. Did you meet with that playwright that she wanted to introduce you to?

"Cyrano de Bergerac, in the flesh!" Betsy grinned and bounced on her toes. In her excitement, she appeared to have instantly forgotten Albert. "And he looks nothing like Steve Martin!"

Denis knew better than to ask who Steve Martin was. Not asking the *who* question too often was one of the first things he had learned after meeting Betsy Springer. "What did he want? Mirari wouldn't tell me."

"He wants me to write down everything I know about some obscure sitcom from the fifties. He thinks it's an uptime classic that would be perfect to adapt it into a play." Her eyes got a faraway look in them. "I think he may even give me writing credit!"

"If you're going to work on this play with him, then that should keep you out of trouble. And out of Albert's notice as well." Denis said. "Will you be hanging around the office for a while?"

She glanced around the room warily. Denis couldn't be sure if she was looking for emergency exits, or to see if Albert was lurking in the shadows.

"Why not? Albert knows where I live. I don't want him hanging around there, getting too friendly with my mother." Betsy looked a little sad. "Ever since dad died, she's been hinting that I should find a good man, settle down, and start giving her grandkids. She doesn't need any encouragement from *him*."

Betsy slipped from Denis's mind as he worked on the woodcut. At least until Mirari ran into the workroom.

"Denis, have you seen Betsy?" Mirari looked shaken.

Denis's wave took in the room. "She was working on her notes for Mondemoiseau de Bergerac's play and hiding from Albert until about a half hour ago. But she decided to get some air."

"Oh, dear," Mirari said. "We need to find her, and soon! Mondemoiseau de Bergerac has challenged Albert to a duel!"

"What? Why?"

"Albert must have seen Betsy with us at dinner last night after all, and assumed that I was trying to set her up on a date. So he insulted Mondemoiseau de Bergerac's nose."

Denis blanched. "Good Lord! I thought she was exaggerating, but I guess Albert is as much an idiot as Betsy said he was!"

Mirari nodded at that. "And Mondemoiseau de Bergerac's cousin has yet to appear. If he were here, he could probably put a stop to all of this foolishness. But now . . ." She trailed off and shook her head. "If we don't get Betsy to intervene, I'm afraid that Mondemoiseau de Bergerac will kill Albert!"

"Not that she would think killing Albert would be that bad of an idea," said Denis. "You *know* how many times she has threatened to do it herself."

"I've threatened to kill men all my life, but I've never done it," said Mirari.

Denis arched an eyebrow at his cousin. There were family stories about her that said otherwise. Although he was sure that if she had killed someone, it was not without justification.

"Besides the paperwork that we would have to fill out, it would be a pain, yes?" He smiled. "You did happen to mention to Mondemoiseau de Bergerac that dueling is illegal in the USE?"

Mirari rolled her eyes. "I did. But he doesn't care. And I've seen Cyrano fight. He's already good enough to cut Albert to shreds without breaking a sweat," she said.

"In that case," he put down his drawing tools, "I think Betsy couldn't have gone more than a block or two."

"I'm glad you see it my way," she said.

"We would be doing Mondemoiseau de Bergerac a kindness. If Betsy gets a hold of him after he's killed Albert . . ." Denis broke off his speculation. "I think she wants to reserve that privilege for herself."

* * *

Betsy's mind was so filled with the play that she almost walked into danger.

"Look out!"

She snapped out of her reverie to see a large horse rear above her. She scrambled out of the way even as the horse's rider pulled tightly on the reins to keep the animal from bolting.

"What kind of nutcase--" she broke off muttering as she heard a small engine splutter across the street. She looked up at rider as he struggled to control his animal. Obviously, the horse -- and therefore the rider -- was from out of town, since the local mounts were used to engine noise

Betsy eyed the rider with predatory interest. A stranger like him would be a good subject for her series of features profiling newcomers to Grantville.

Once he had his horse back under control, he dropped to the ground and faced Betsy.

"Pray forgive me!" he said, whipping off his plumed hat and bowing to her. "I am most shamed that I almost caused such a lovely young woman as yourself harm. I am Charles de Largo."

Betsy swallowed the inclination to hold her hand to her heart and giggle. She would not behave like some kind of swooning damsel. "I'm Betsy Springer with the *Grantville Times*. You can make it up to me by agreeing to an interview."

She felt a little like Lois Lane just meeting Superman for the first time and having the gumption to ask for an interview after being rescued. De Largo's accent was slightly familiar. But she had never been as good as Denis with accents. He could identify where someone came from by their voice, right down to a side of town. That was sheer spooky as far as she was concerned.

Charles de Largo started at the name of the paper, and then stared at her for a moment. Betsy gave him her impression of her mother's *you're going to do this* stare before he could decline. Then she launched into her first question. "What brings you to town?"

"Actually, Mecklenburg was where I had intended to go," he said with his own nervous laugh.

"Oh? Are you a soldier?"

"I have more than a bit of experience in the army, yes. I thought I might be able to find employment there," he said. "Unfortunately, I got mixed up on directions about thirty miles outside of town and here I am." He spread his hands to indicate Grantville.

"You should have turned left at Albuquerque," she said with a smile at her small joke. She wasn't sure if she believed him or not; enlisting in the army was the excuse a lot of men used for coming to town.

A look of confusion ran over de Largo's face. "Your pardon, mademoiselle; is this Albuquerque you speak of a town or a local landmark, perhaps?"

Betsy felt her checks run crimson as she sighed. Sometimes she missed having fellow movie geeks to talk to. Her humor was completely lost on everyone in this century. But she had to admit that de Largo was quite good looking, perhaps even someone she might like to get to know better. Despite this, her reporter's instincts were pinging like broken radar. Something seemed off with him.

"Betsy!"

At the sound of her name the young reporter turned to see Denis rushing toward her.

Denis slid to a stop and doubled over to catch his breath. "Betsy," he said between gasps for air. "We need to talk!"

Betsy smiled at de Largo. "I'll be right back. Don't go anywhere." She turned to Denis and pulled him aside. "Can it wait? I'm about to interview this fellow for the paper."

Denis looked over her shoulder at de Largo. He narrowed his eyes suspiciously. Then he shook his head in dismissal before turning his attention back to Betsy. "Only if you want to miss your chance to see Albert being killed."

"What?" Betsy stiffened.

"Mirari said that Albert must have seen your business meeting last night. This morning he insulted Mondemoiseau de Bergerac over your honor and your playwright benefactor challenged him to a duel."

Out of the corner of her eye, Betsy noticed de Largo perk up at the name de Bergerac. But she couldn't spare more than a second to wonder why. She had more pressing matters to attend to.

"Well, at least he didn't say anything about Mondemoiseau de Bergerac's nose. That would take things from bad to impossible!"

Denis coughed and looked away.

"He didn't," Betsy slapped her hand to her forehead. "Great! Now what am I going to do? Mondemoiseau de Bergerac is famous for killing men who insult his nose! He'll obliterate Albert to satisfy his own honor, no matter what I say!"

"Excuse me, Mademoiselle," de Largo said. "I couldn't help but overhear. You said Mondemoiseau de Bergerac, yes? Would that be Cyrano de Bergerac?"

"That's right," Denis said.

"Then perhaps I can be of some assistance," de Largo suggested. "Mondemoiseau de Bergerac is a fellow Frenchman. He will naturally want to observe the rules of engagement; so if he has not yet appointed a second for this duel, perhaps I can offer him my assistance."

"What did Albert do to offend you?" she asked.

"Nothing, but if I were to act as Mondemoiseau de Bergerac's second, then perhaps I can help you save the life of your boyfriend. We may be able to control the outcome while still satisfying Mondemoiseau de Bergerac's bruised sense of honor. Would your boyfriend Albert know enough to name his own second?"

"He's not my boyfriend! And, no, he wouldn't," Betsy snorted. "He barely has the brain cells to tie his shoes. But your idea might work, if *I* can convince him to name me as his second. This is like a scheme right out of the Three Musketeers."

De Largo raised an eyebrow at her words. "Truthfully, I have never heard of a woman standing as second in a duel."

"You've never run into Betsy before, obviously," said Denis. "I think I should point out the fact that dueling is highly illegal. Everyone involved --or at least the survivors --could wind up in jail! I've been there; it's a place I prefer not to see the inside of again. Even if it's only the Grantville lockup."

Betsy scoffed. "It's only illegal if it actually happens; talking about it isn't illegal! Neither is scaring the hell out of Albert in the process," she said.

Denis sighed. He had a really bad feeling about this whole thing. He hoped it didn't come crashing down around them.

Betsy put a finger on her nose and pointed to de Largo. "No time to waste. I'll find . . . Albert." she broke off to make a face. "You and Denis find Mondemoiseau de Bergerac. Once we get them to name us their seconds, let's all meet back at Mirari's shop to go over the rules of engagement."

"Just be careful around Albert," Denis said. "This is likely to give him the wrong idea about you."

"I'll burn that bridge when I get there," Betsy muttered as she set off in the direction of Albert's family home.

* * *

Denis, Mirari, de Bergerac, and de Largo already had seats around Mirari's personal table by the time that Betsy led Albert into the chocolate shop. The four of them had large pots of chocolate and steaming mugs set out before them. Denis thought that Albert looked, to borrow an uptime phrase, *as low as a snake's belly*. No doubt Betsy had told him exactly what she thought of his behavior. As the two of them sat at the table, Mondemoiseau de Bergerac scowled at Albert. Albert ducked his head and pretended to find fascination in the wood grain of the table.

"Since I'm more familiar with the rules of engagement, Albert agreed that I will act as his second in this duel," Betsy said. When Albert failed to acknowledge her, Betsy turned and slapped his shoulder.

"Da," Albert mumbled. "My second."

"Cyrano has agreed that I will act as his second," de Largo confirmed, winking at Betsy in the process. "I suggest that we decide on the details at once. It is after all a matter of honor."

Mirari joined in without waiting for Cyrano to agree. "And Denis and I will observe to make sure that everything goes well."

"I will give no quarter, sir," said Cyrano looking directly at Albert. "Understand that I will slowly flay every inch of skin from you, then I will run my sword through first your knees, then your elbows; if I am feeling merciful, I will let you keep your manhood before I finish you, or I might not."

"If you're going to kill him anyway, why would he care about preserving his. . ." Betsy trailed off speculatively. Then she shook her head in dismissal. "Never mind."

To say that Albert's face went from pale to fish belly white was an apt description. Betsy appeared to relish this reaction in her unwanted suitor. Denis winced in sympathy for Albert.

"Let's begin," Betsy said. "There are decisions to be made."

Cyrano looked at her in consternation. He appeared more than a bit uncertain on how to react to a woman standing as second in a duel, especially one in which he had seemingly had a working relationship only hours before.

"We can, of course, avoid this duel all together if Herr Haleman will simply apologize to Mondemoiseau de Bergerac for insulting his person," said Mirari with a pointed look at Albert.

Albert sank deeper into his chair, refusing to look up at the others seated around the table.

"Stubborn ass," Betsy mumbled.

"We need to choose a field of honor. The authorities do tend to frown over dueling, so we'll probably have to take this little dust-up out into the countryside where we stand less of a chance of being caught." Mirari said after bestowing her own frown of disapproval on Albert. "I know several farmers who would be willing to loan us an empty pasture for the purposes of this duel. No fields, though. It won't do to trample their crops."

"Maybe a barn at night," Betsy suggested. "That would be plenty private."

"Not roomy enough," de Largo put in.

"But it would be dramatic!" Betsy leaned over the table. "If someone knocks over an oil lamp, it could burn the barn right down." The others stared at her. Finally, Betsy crossed her arms. "Poo. You're no fun."

"The best time for a duel is morning," de Largo continued as if Betsy hadn't spoken. "We can get it over with, and the survivor can buy the rest of us breakfast."

Betsy nodded at that. "What weapons? If I understand the rules correctly the challenged party is allowed the choice of weapons. At least that's how it always is in the movies."

"I am most proficient in the sword," de Bergerac said.

"But Albert is inept at it," Betsy replied. Albert glared at her with an expression of betrayal on his face. "Well, you are!" she added.

"Pistols," Denis suggested. "They're a great equalizer. And both men should have only one shot. If both miss, then everyone must forget this whole mess." Albert nodded at that, looking slightly more hopeful. De Largo lifted a single eyebrow as he looked at Betsy, a signal that Denis took to mean that they should pay attention to what he said next. "And I should remind each duelist that if either fails to participate in the duel for whatever reason, the seconds must take over."

"Agreed!" Betsy said quickly.

"Wait! What?" Albert looked up in consternation. "I don't want Betsy to take my place!"

"You should have thought of that before you insulted Mondemoiseau de Bergerac," Betsy said in sing-song. "The two of you will stand back to back. Then we'll count off and at ten paces, you'll turn and fire!"

"Five paces," de Bergerac said. "His insult to me was intolerable!"

"I've changed my mind!" Albert beat on the table to get their attention. When everyone broke off to look at him, he repeated. "I've changed my mind. I don't want Betsy involved in this barbarism! Will Mondemoiseau de Bergerac's accept my formal apology?"

Cyrano de Bergerac stood and leaned over the table looking at Albert. "If you will allow me to strike you once across the back with my cane, I will consider my honor satisfied."

Albert glanced once at Betsy and then nodded. "Let's step outside to finish this, then."

The two men stood. Betsy made to follow, but Denis grasped her arm to stop her. "Leave Albert some pride. I'll go along to make sure everything goes as planned"

Betsy watched as the three of them exited Mirari's shop through the back way. Then she nodded. "I think I've let Albert's affections get out of hand. Maybe this will make him understand that I am not in love with him."

"It would be kinder to let him down hard." Mirari said. "He doesn't seem to understand being let down easy. Or perhaps he just chooses not to see that you have no interest in him. And being strung along is proving hazardous to his health."

Betsy nodded. She looked up when the door opened. It wasn't Cyrano or de Largo, just Denis. For a panicked moment she was afraid that Cyrano had gone ahead and killed Albert.

"He's all right," Denis said. "I sent him off with some friends of mine who happened to be passing. I told them to take him somewhere and let him soothe his hurt pride in some ale."

"Men," smiled Mirari. "They think alcohol is a universal cure for everything."

"If he comes back I suppose that I could tell him that I won't marry such an impetuous man as he has proven himself to be."

"That might do it," Denis said. "One impetuous person in a marriage is enough."

"What's that supposed to mean?" Betsy folded her arms and scowled at her friend.

"You could just tell him that you're engaged to Denis," Mirari put in.

"That's all I need," Denis said. "Pistols at ten paces with Albert."

"This sounds like something that Cyrano would put in one of his plays," Betsy said and then paused. "Speaking of him, where is Cyrano?"

"A good question, Mademoiselle." A new voice chimed in.

The three occupants of the table turned as a new person approached the table. His dress was similar to that of Cyrano's. Once he had their attention, the man bowed. "I am the boy's tutor. Abel de Cyrano, lord of Mauvières and Bergerac placed the boy in my care. But he managed to escape my watchful eye in Badenburg. I've managed to follow him here."

"You just missed him," Denis said. He left with Monsieur de Largo. De Largo said he had something that he needed to talk to Cyrano about and, in fact, had been looking for him for several weeks. I had the impression that they were going to be heading out of town rather quickly."

The stranger's eyes grew wide at hearing the name, "de Largo." He clapped his hand to his sword. "Please excuse me." With that, he turned and ran from the room.

"What was that about?" Betsy asked.

Mirari shook her head and smiled. "You *do* know that Charles de Largo is not his real name?" she asked.

"Well, then, who is he?" asked Denis, glancing back toward the door as if expecting either of the two men to make a dramatic entrance.

"Charles D'Artagnan." she said.

"D'Artagnan," said Betsy. "You mean as in 'D'Artagnan and the Three Musketeers?"

Mirari reached across the table, picked up a pitcher of hot chocolate, and refilled her mug. "I've known a few Musketeers. I suppose Charles knows some, but I don't know."

Betsy just shook her head; she had images of Michael York and Chris O'Donnell running through her head.

"Oh, by the way," said Denis, fishing in his pocket. "Cyrano asked me to give you a note."

"I wonder if it's a love poem," Mirari speculated. "He seemed quite taken with you, Betsy."

Betsy ignored her friend as she scanned the brief note.

My dear Betsy,

Regretfully, I must cut my visit to Grantville and our association short. A situation in France has developed that I must deal with. Unfortunately, this means that I must put aside my work on Our Miss Brooks. I realize now that I do not yet have the skill to write in the way that the story demands. However, I have heard of another up-time story that I think I may adapt. It is about a lunatic red-haired woman who repeatedly falls into trouble. I believe I have enough material to adapt this into a series of comedies. I shall call it I Love Betsy.

Betsy crumpled the note in her hand and growled.

"Bad news?" Mirari asked.

"When I see that boy again," Betsy said between clenched teeth, "he's got a lot of *splanin* to do."

"IT'S ABOUT TIME: AN ODE"

By: Bradley H. Sinor and Tracy S. Morris

Elizabeth "Betsy" Springer came awake with a gasp. She could barely breathe! The last thing she remembered was the coachman's yell and the way the world had tilted as the carriage slipped off of the road. Then . . . nothing.

I must have died; I know it!, she thought. A picture of the headline for the next edition of the *Grantville Times* flashed through her head.

Daredevil Reporter Killed at 22. King Decrees an Extended Period of Deep Mourning. Editor Calls Springer an Irreplaceable National Treasure.

"Meow?"

The sound cut into her fantasies of her own rose-strewn coffin proceeding through the streets of Magdeburgin a grand state funeral. She opened her eyes and saw a dark grey, fur-covered face staring at her from only a few inches away. That was when Betsy sneezed, not once but twice. She always sneezed twice.

"Evil creature of darkness in the shape of a feline," she muttered. She must have gone to hell. Why else would there be a cat?

The sneeze didn't send the cat running away; instead it rode the sudden upheaval like a master surfer. Apparently, this cat thought that her chest was a fine place to sit and did not intend to give up its nice warm bed.

"Let me guess," she muttered, her throat feeling rough and raw as she spoke. "For your next trick you disappear, except for your smile."

The cat in question didn't deign to answer her. Instead it calmly turned around and began to groom itself.

"I wondered when you were going to wake up." A familiar voice spoke from the darkness beyond the bed.

Betsy looked past the furry annoyance. The speaker sat in a shadowed corner of the room, but it sounded like Denis. She raised herself up on her elbow enough to dislodge the cat and send it running.

"Was that all it took to get rid of you?" she asked the feline. Just speaking made her throat hurt, although less so now that she had banished the furry nuisance. Then she turned to her unseen minder. "Is that you, Denis?"

"Who were you expecting? Tom Cruise?" Denis turned in his seat and lit a candle from the small fireplace. He held the candle near his face so that Betsy could see him.

"You making a movie comment? I really must be dreaming."

"I guess you're just a bad influence on me."

Betsy chuckled as she examined the room. Even with the light from the small fireplace and the candle that Denis had in his hand, she could see very little. She knew she was in a large bed with a heavy quilt spread across her, but much more than that was beyond her.

"What happened?" She asked in a raspy voice as she noticed a glass of water on her side table. When she rolled to reach it, pain shot through her ribs. Betsy lay back with a groan. Denis stood to help her, but she waved him off.

"I'll be fine."

In the dim firelight she saw his wry smile of disbelief. Instead of returning to his seat, Denis moved to the foot of the bed in case she changed her mind.

Just for that, I've got to get that glass on my own now. thought Betsy as she wriggled across the mattress, feeling weak as a baby with every move. Eventually she managed to get her hands around the glass, take a couple of swallows, and return it to the nightstand without spilling the contents all over the bed.

She flopped back in an exhausted pose and smiled at him in triumph.

Denis shook his head at her antics. "The road washed out in the raistorm and the coach ended up on its side in a gulley."

Betsy winced as she suddenly remembered the events of the previous night: the lighting, the heavy rain, horses bolting, people screaming, and then the world turning upside down. "Was anyone hurt?"

"Hurt, yes, but thankfully, no one died. You got the worst of it; I only pulled a muscle in my leg and got a few scratches," he said. "Of course, if my cousins Carlos and Antonio hadn't found us almost immediately, who can say what kind of condition we would have been in?" He shrugged. "We could have both caught pneumonia."

"Cousins?" She muttered in confusion. Then she recalled the reason that they had been on that coach to begin with. "Oh, yeah."

* * *

"Denis, I need your help!"

Mirari waved a letter at them from her seat in the corner of the chocolate shop when Denis and Betsy both walked in.

"Is it your ankle?" Denis frowned at Mirari's foot where it sat on a stool. "You're worse than Betsy was that time she sprained her ankle. She was supposed to stay off it, and instead she pulled us into investigating the murder of a beekeeper."

Betsy shoved Denis's shoulder affectionately. "How can you expect me to stay off my feet and out of the action when there are wrongs to right? Speaking of which . . ." She turned to Mirari. "What's the matter?"

"This letter is from home, from Great-Aunt Serina." Mirari passed it to Denis. He took the letter with a frown and started to read. As he did so, Mirari explained the contents to Betsy. "Our Grandmama is turning eighty, and there is to be a family celebration. We have to be there, if at all possible"

"And the implied part of that is 'it better be possible'," said Betsy. She knew how her own aunts had been when it came to family gatherings.

"Exactly! You know this family like you were born into it," said Mirari.

"Mirari, *you* can't possibly go," Denis said with an apologetic frown. "Not with your leg in the shape it is. Next time someone tries to rob your shop, run get the authorities. Don't try to hold off the thieves with nothing but a pistol and a sword."

"I was better armed than they were." Mirari shook her finger at Denis. "I would not have them rob me blind!"

"Better than robbing you lame," Denis countered, knowing he would not win the argument with his cousin.

"I had them on the run." Mirari argued. "If I hadn't tripped over a chair, I would have been fine. But that's not important now. Grandmama is! And from the hints that Great-Aunt Serina dropped in this invitation, I fear that her mind is slipping away."

"Is there anything I can do?" Betsy wasn't sure it was even her place to offer. But she hated to see either of them so down. Righting social wrongs and stopping murderers and bandits were more her forte, not nursing a sick, possibly crazy, granny.

Mirari looked at Betsy. Immediately, her face brightened. "*You* can go with Denis in my place! I've written to the family about you often enough; in fact, they've been asking when they were going to get a chance to meet you. This is a perfect time!"

Denis looked a little worried. "I don't think--"

"Nonsense!" Mirari cut him off with a wave.

At that point, Denis's cousin took over travel arrangements; and before she knew it, Betsy was giving her bags over to a coachman in preparation for a trip to the ancestral Sesma family home.

While Denis and the coachman labored to pack the carriage, Mirari hobbled up on her crutches with a new letter clutched in one hand. She nodded for Betsy to follow her and when they were a little way off, she held the letter up for Betsy to see.

"This came in the mail this morning. It's a letter from my cousin, Carlos."

Betsy took the letter, but couldn't read it. She turned it sideways, and then upside down. Neither action helped. Although she had picked up spoken French in the time since the Ring of Fire, reading it was still difficult. Not to mention that she thought the author had terrible handwriting.

"And?" she asked Mirari.

"It tells me everything that the last letter didn't." Mirari said. "And it's worse than I thought. Grandmama has given her patronage to a young . . . poet." She frowned at that. "The family worries that he might be taking advantage of her in her dotage. They want Denis to come home immediately. He always was one of her favorite grandchildren. Hopefully he can convince her to cut the purse strings on this layabout. But I'm sure there is something more to this whole matter,"

"Why do I feel like I'm going straight into an Agatha Christie movie?" Betsy muttered.

"Agatha Christie? Oh, yes, I've read her books from the library," Mirari said. "I'm sure this journey will be nothing like that. I doubt seriously that you'll be tripping over any bodies."

"For a change," Betsy muttered.

* * *

"Why is it that *I'm* the one who always seems to get knocked around whenever you and I go out of town?" Betsy muttered.

At that, Denis got up from his seat on the bed and hobbled up to her. As he drew closer, she could see the injuries that he mentioned earlier.

"I didn't exactly come though this whole thing none the worse for wear," he said. "From what my cousin Soro says, you got a mild concussion and a whole lot of bruises, but it could have been worse."

Betsy sneezed; followed by a second one several seconds later and then a bout of coughing that made her ribs throb again.

"At least I wasn't injured tripping over a body this time." Betsy said. "Was anyone else hurt?"

"No –" Denis started to say.

"Denis, will you stop tormenting that poor girl! She needs her rest!" A new voice sounded from the doorway, interrupting him in mid-sentence.

At the sound of that voice Denis jerked back and turned, his face as pale as one of the sheets on Betsy's bed. "Grandmama," he gasped.

Betsy craned her neck to see who could have provoked that kind of reaction. The voice came from a woman standing in the doorway. She had a ramrod straight posture and long, neatly coifed hair held in place by an intricate comb. Even though Betsy couldn't see her face clearly, she could sense disapproval in the woman's bearing.

Betsy's eyebrows climbed her forehead. *This* was Denis's Grandmama? From Mirari's words Betsy had been expecting a tiny, hunched woman doddering about on a cane, barely aware of what was going on around her. But this woman had the commanding presence of Judi Dench's *M* in *The World is Not Enough*. Betsy would have expected to see her on the floor of the USE senate or in the middle of a presidential cabinet meeting.

"I wasn't bothering Betsy. She just woke and I was…."

Denis' grandmother snorted in disbelief as she stepped into the room and pointed at the doorway that she'd just vacated. "Don't fib to me young man. Go downstairs and make some tea for her! Make it chamomile, and use the mint honey in the kitchen. We have to beat that hacking cough before it sets in her chest," she said. "And take this infernal cat with you!"

Denis glanced at Betsy and then at his grandmother. The most Betsy could do then was to shrug, at which point he snatched up the cat and headed out of the room.

Denis's grandmother watched him disappear, and then turned back towards Betsy. "He's a good boy. He just needs a firm hand from time to time."

"Yes, ma'am." Betsy replied. Her own upbringing kept her from saying anything to an elder that would be considered "sass." Not to mention the fact that if she got into trouble and needed to make a fast exit, she was in no shape to do so.

The woman came over and pressed her hand against Betsy's forehead. She had the same sharp green eyes as Mirari, obviously a family trait. With swift moves she checked Betsy's pulse and then began to rearrange the covers over her.

"You seem to be doing all right," she said. "You should be rather stiff for the next couple of days; that much is to be expected. We still need to keep a close eye on you for any effects from hitting your head as hard as you did."

Betsy's head swam at the list of her injuries. "A concussion, yeah," she muttered.

"Indeed." The older woman said with a pronounced nod. Then she froze as if in sudden remembrance. "Oh! We have not been formally introduced, since you were only semi-conscious when they brought you in. I'm Juliana Anihoa Maria Constance Sesma, Denis's grandmother.

"I'm honored to meet you, ma'am," Betsy put her hand out for a good old-fashioned American handshake. She wondered what Grandmama would make of that. But if it was good enough for Gustavus Adolphus the Second, it was good enough for Juliana Anihoa Maria Constance Sesma. "I'm Elisabeth Springer; you can call me Betsy."

"My dear, Elizabeth, I know all about you. You're my grandson Denis's intended and will soon be his bride," said Denis's Grandmother Juliana.

Betsy's brain shut down as she pulled her hand back. Her mouth moved under its own power. "What?"

At the same moment, Denis walked back into the room with a fully loaded tray. He froze in place. The tray slipped from his hands and clattered to the floor. The teapot shattered, splashing steaming tea across his trousers.

"What?" He repeated.

Juliana Anihoa Maria Constance Sesma, looked from one of them to the other in confusion. Her eyes narrowed in a way that reminded Betsy of a hawk diving for prey. "Denis! Surely you are engaged! Mirari writes to me of the two of you traipsing about the countryside for that newspaper. You must be engaged to do so without an escort for the young lady! Unless you've taken up with a fallen woman?" She lifted an eyebrow at that.

"Fallen woman!" Betsy spluttered as she struggled to push herself into a sitting position. Her ribs gave another painful throb, so she settled for rising to her elbows. "Now just a second here! I'm one of the most highly-paid reporters in the USE!"

"Only because the Kindred family pays by inch of copy," Denis muttered.

"Not the point here!" Betsy shook her finger at him the way that she'd seen Mirari do. "I'm a woman of independent means! I don't need a husband to escort me!"

Grandmama turned to Denis, her face as dark as a thundercloud. "You will not bring scandal to the Sesma family name, Denis." She crossed her arms under her chest. "Before this visit is over, you will do the honorable thing!" With that, she strode from the room. She paused at the door and pointed to the shattered tea things. "And pick that up!"

Silence descended in the wake of her leaving. Betsy plopped back on her pillow and blew her bangs out of her face. Then she sneezed. Twice. "Well, that went well."

* * *

"Okay," Betsy said. "Start talking, and now. Just what did you and Mirari tell your *dear* Grandmama?"

Denis sighed and stared out toward the lake. There was a stiff breeze coming across the water, but he was absolutely certain that the chill running through him had nothing to do with the wind.

It had been a day and half since Betsy had woke up; this was the first time that his grandmother had allowed her to do more than huddle in front of the fire, drink tea, and eat soup. "Denis, you will have the rest of your lives together. I just want to make certain that they are long lives, so we have to make sure Elizabeth stays healthy." She had told him, in a tone that said she would not brook any arguments on the matter.

At lunch Betsy had insisted that she felt fine and wanted to go for a walk with Denis. The staring contest between her and Denis's grandmother had lasted for a full minute before the older woman had nodded.

"It's kind of scary how alike you two are," Denis had said as they walked outside. Betsy scoffed at that. Her ponytail seemed to bob and weave like a prizefighter looking for an opening as she turned her nose in the air.

"It wasn't me that started the rumor," said Denis. He motioned her to follow him to a fallen log near the edge of the water. "This sort of thing was why I didn't want to come back."

"So who started it? Louella Parsons?" she demanded.

If there was one thing that Denis had learned, it was that there were times it was best to ignore Betsy's Hollywood references, some of which he understood, but with many he was still at a total loss. This was one of those moments.

"Ever since Master Ribalta died, the family has, shall we say, been worried about my future. That settled down a bit when I got the job on the newspaper. But when I decided not to apprentice with a different artist, Grandmama Juliana and the rest decided that what I needed was a—"

"...a wife to keep you on the straight and narrow," she groaned.

That pretty much summed up the situation. "I was ready to tell my relatives what to do with their "suggestions." That was when Mirari stepped in. She didn't want me to cut myself off from the family."

Betsy reached over and patted his hand. "It's never good to be feuding with your kin, no matter how irritated they make you." She said with a melancholy air. "You never know when they'll be gone."

Denis knew Betsy was thinking of her father, and how quickly he had contracted the plague and died while stationed away from Grantville.

"Anyway," Betsy shook off her sadness. "Where did they get this idea that we're engaged?"

"Indirectly from Mirari." Denis grimaced. "She's been writing to our various relatives, including Grandmama Juliana, ever since she came to Grantville. She never came out and said that we were.... interested in each other."

"But she let your grandmother think what she wanted." Betsy smacked her forehead with one hand. "This is really sounding like one of those Doris Day and Rock Hudson romantic comedies. That was why you seemed worried when Mirari wanted me to come with you."

Denis picked up a round flat rock and sent it skimming out over the water. The stone bounced three times and then sank out of sight.

"I will have to inform Grandmama that we are not getting married and that this was a massive misunderstanding. That should bring me full circle: Right back to being estranged from the family." mused Denis. "Of course, with a few of them that might actually be a blessing in disguise."

"I don't want to come between you and your family." Betsy leaped to her feet and began to pace back and forth, her face lost in deep thought. "There has to be a way out of this mess that still leaves your relationship with your family intact. Maybe we could have a nice, long engagement? We could just never get around to marrying?"

"I don't think we could stall a wedding that long." Denis shook his head. "But if we go along with them, we'll be in front of a holy man before we leave."

"Maybe we could stage an argument where I break up with you; I could find you in the arms of another woman, that sort of thing; you know very, dramatic"

"Then how do we explain to them that we plan to continue our working relationship? Besides, it would take a miracle of epic proportions for me to quickly find someone I'm not related to around here who might be interested in me. I'm just not that gifted with the fairer sex."

Betsy face ran red to match her hair. "Denis Sesma! Any girl should count themselves lucky to have you interested in them!" She leaned over and kissed him on the cheek. "You are a prime catch, remember that!"

"I hope I'm not interrupting anything." Betsy and Denis both looked up and saw a familiar figure approaching them from the woods.

"Captain Pohl?" they wondered simultaneously.

"This is a surprise!" Betsy added. They'd met the captain on a trip to France for a story just before hostilities between their two countries erupted. As the USE was now at war with a French-led coalition, Betsy hadn't expected to see Captain Pohl again.

"For me as well." Captain Marcus Pohl said. "I thought the two of you were back in Grantville."

"Ordinarily, yes. But Denis is from this area. We came for a visit and to stop . . . Ohmygosh!" Betsy's eyes grew round. "That poet that your grandmother was patronizing! Between the carriage accident and your family deciding that *it's a nice day for a white wedding*, we completely forgot about him!"

"Why would you wear white to a wedding?" Captain Pohl scratched his head.

"It's an American custom," Denis said. To Betsy he said: "It's patronage, not patronizing. There is a difference. One is money, the other is an insult."

"Whatever!" Betsy waved him away as she turned to Captain Pohl. "This whole marriage thing is a complicated and somewhat bizarre misunderstanding." She quickly explained to Captain Pohl how they came to visit Denis's family, the carriage accident, and the ensuing mix-up.

"You being right in the middle of something complicated and bizarre does not surprise me in the slightest," said Pohl as he plucked at his goatee. "However, I may be able to help you."

"How?" Denis asked.

"How much do you know about this poet?" the soldier asked.

"Actually, a good deal. I've been able to interrogate my cousins while Grandmama was distracted with nursing Betsy back to health." Denis said.

"Nursing? Ha! More like torturing." Betsy muttered.

"Aren't they the same thing, sometimes? He goes by the name Jean LaRue de Rhizoy," Denis said. "No one in the family really knows much about him. He simply showed up on Grandmama's doorstep one day with a letter of introduction from an old family friend -- whom, by the way, no one has seen for several years. He spouted off a few poems and Gandmama Juliana seemed to fall head over heels for him. Since then, no one has seen a page of this epic poem he is supposed to be composing in her honor. Although he has been overheard spouting off a number of bawdy songs in the local tavern. From what my cousins tell me, he is gaining a reputation in town as a minor rake."

"But you can't get rid of him while he is under the protection of your grandmother," Pohl said. "Unless you decide to kill him. I could arrange for him to simply vanish, if you want." The dragoon captain held up his hands in the manner of a stage magician.

"No," Denis and Betsy said simultaneously.

"Good. I would have been worried if you had agreed to that plan," Pohl said. "Especially since I think I know of this man."

"What has he done to earn your interest, anyway?" asked Denis. "And it just occurred to me to wonder where your dragoons are encamped?"

"Most of them aren't even here; they are doing guard duty for a few merchant companies several towns over. Dull, but it pays well," Captain Pohl shrugged. "We may be lending our swords to the war effort in the near future."

"I hope not," Betsy said jokingly. "I would hate for the USE to hand you and your men a whuppin' the way we've been whuppin' up on the rest of France." Pohl tried to pass himself off as a simple soldier, but after their first encounter Betsy had the distinct feeling that there was a lot more to the man than he liked to portray.

"I shall keep that in mind," Captain Pohl said in a dry tone.

"Did Mr. de Rhizoy con you out of something?" she asked, her reporters' instincts roaring to the fore.

"Not me. Several years ago this man, if he is who I think it is, swindled a good friend of my family in such a manner that he was ruined. All because my friend wanted to be a patron of the arts.

"Since taking interest in the matter, I have found at least three different occasions where the same thing has happened: this scum passes himself off as a poet, occasionally an artist, and garners patronage from wealthy families. He hangs around as long as he can. And when he is expected to present his promised master work, he vanishes in the night."

"This sounds like your Grandmama's poeeeet buddy," Betsy said, deliberately mispronouncing the word. "Why don't you just speak with Grandma Juliana? She can force Jean to show you his portfolio. If we're lucky, she'll forget all about making Denis and me get married."

"I wouldn't count on it, but if she doesn't, I may have an answer to that problem as well. Rest assured, Miss Springer, you won't need to worry about having to wear white." Captain Pohl said, as he arched his eyebrow just slightly.

"I'd never wear white," Betsy said. "My colors would be blush and bashful." She affected a stronger southern accent, and hoped she sounded like Julia Roberts in *Steel Magnolias.*

"Is blush a color?" Captain Pohl asked Denis

Denis shrugged, rolled his eyes, and said nothing.

* * *

"Denis! I can't believe you would stoop this low!" Grandmama Juliana glared at the three of them. "I knew that you wanted to avoid getting married, but how could you sully a man's reputation like this? And you Elizabeth, I expected you to keep Denis from running off on a tangent of nonsense such as this."

Betsy and Denis looked at each other in surprise. "She don't know me vewy well, do she?" Betsy muttered in an imitation of Bugs Bunny.

"Grandmama, Captain Pohl is well-respected gentleman." Denis said while waving for Betsy to be quiet. "Shouldn't you take his word about…this man?"

"The captain is a friend of yours, so he would probably say anything to aid you in distracting me from the real issue." Grandmama Juliana said. "I meant what I said before. The two of you will not tarnish the family name! And I'll thank you not to upset Jean by mentioning this to him!"

With that, Denis's grandmother gathered herself to her full height and stormed from the room like one of the USE Battleships.

"Well, that went well." Betsy said. "Any ideas now?"

"I suppose the two of you will just have to get married," said Denis's and Betsy's companion.

Betsy looked at the captain in askance. "Captain Pohl, forgive me for saying this, but are you out of your ever lovin' mind?"

The captain smiled at her in amusement. "Not at all, my dear Betsy. My backup plan should take care of both of our problems."

That comment was enough to pique Betsy's interest.

"I only brought a few of my men with me, six to be exact. One of them, a Russian fellow named Illya, studied for the pastorhood. Let us say that things did not work out in that area; he found his true calling with a sword. But he knows enough to be convincing, and no one knows him around here.

"Betsy, since you are an uptimer, you can say that want your marriage as close as it can be to a traditional ceremony in your own faith; Illya will provide that. And then Denis's family will leave the two of you alone, thinking that the two of you are actually married.

"Meanwhile, you suggest to Madam Sesma that it would be a wonderful thing if you were to have a special poem composed in honor of your wedding".

"And when de Rhizoy fails to produce one, we trap him in his own lies!" Betsy said. "Hoisted on his own Picard!"

Both Denis and Captain Pohl winced at Betsy's mispronunciation.

"And if you want to stall the wedding further, you could insist on a dress made of those strange colors you were talking about. That should take a little time." Captain Pohl continued as if he hadn't heard Betsy.

"Maybe not; from what Denis has said about his Great-Aunt Serina, I could see her coming up with the material," Betsy said. "But I think I should insist on a bleedin' armadillo red velvet cake!"

"This is *insane*!" Denis said, and threw his hands in the air. "It'll never work,"

Pohl laughed and pointed at Betsy. "She's involved; of course it's insane. Besides, it isn't as if you have an alternative plan, short of sneaking off in the middle of the night. Are you two sure you haven't been married for several years and just not noticed?"

"No." snapped Denis

"Of course, it's insane," laughed Betsy. "That is exactly why it *will* work!

You realize that de Rhizoy will know that we are onto him, probably within an hour."

Denis shook his head. "A lot less than that. It wouldn't surprise me that one of my cousins was listening at the door. If by chance someone was, then I am sure they would tell him in hopes of driving him off.'

Pohl nodded but said nothing.

* * *

Denis watched in bemused horror as his Great-Aunt Serina wrapped Betsy in yards and yards of pink fabric in preparation for making her wedding clothes. He had no idea where they'd found the material, but it seemed to swallow Betsy whole. The redheaded reporter stood on a stool with her arms straight out, as if afraid that Great-Aunt Serina would stick her with a pin at any moment.

"Are you sure you want to wear pink, dear?" Great-Aunt Serina looked up at her in concern. "With your coloring, this shade does nothing for you. And I don't understand why you insisted that we make your dress out of a pair of drapes."

"Just like Scarlett O'Hara in *Gone With the Wind*," Betsy said. The twinkle in her eye told Denis that she was enjoying the play-acting. "It's curtains for me, see!" She sounded just like a gangster in one of her old movies.

This is quickly becoming what the up-timers call a train wreck. He thought. When it seemed like Great-Aunt Serina was done with her fitting, he cleared his throat. Both women glanced up at him in surprise, as if they hadn't been aware that he was there.

"I could definitely use a drink right now," he said.

"Sounds great to me!" Betsy wriggled out of the pieces of her new dress. "If that's alright with Great-Aunt Serina here." She waved to the venerable old woman.

"You children behave yourselves," Great-Aunt Serina said with a smile. "I'll have nothing happening that would disgrace this family on my watch."

As they headed out the door Denis couldn't keep from laughing.

"Are you going to share the joke with the rest of the class?" Betsy asked.

"Considering the tales I heard about Great-Aunt Serina when I was growing up, she's the last one who needs to be talking about disgracing the family."

"That would explain one or two of her jokes," Betsy said. "I'll be glad when this wedding nonsense is behind us. I felt so badly today when your Grandmama paid that jeweler to make us a couple of rings."

"You are the one who wanted to indulge Grandmama in this for the sake of getting rid of that swindling poet," Denis said. "I would be happy to just tell her the truth and accept the consequences."

"I know," Betsy nodded. "But it works out better this way. I won't be the cause of you being disowned by your family."

Denis's steps slowed as they neared one of the local taverns. "Oh, do I remember this place! I used to sneak bread and cheese from the kitchen when I was a boy. The matron who ran it was a bit sweet on me."

"So why didn't you ask *her* to marry you?" Betsy teased.

"Maybe because she's three times my age." Denis said. "When I say she was sweet on me, I mean that I reminded her of her own son."

"You miss being here." Betsy observed.

"Occasionally," Denis replied. "Why?"

"I was just thinking that we needed to make sure that you can come back when we take our leave."

Just then, Captain Pohl emerged from the alley between the tavern and the shop next door. His hawk-like gaze zeroed in on Denis and Betsy. "Ah! There you are! How go the wedding plans?"

Both Denis and Betsy jumped at the captain's sudden appearance.

"You are entirely too good at sneaking." Denis said at the same time that Betsy said: "I'm having way too much fun with this! I missed my calling! I should have been a wedding planner."

Captain Pohl and Denis traded horrified looks at the thought.

"Why are you lurking in a dark alley, anyway?" Denis changed the subject.

"Keeping our friend de Rhizoy on his toes," Captain Pohl directed a pointed look up the street.

A block or so away the door to another tavern came open and two men came stumbling out. One was a heavyset fellow with a beard half way down his chest, the other a tall thin man in his twenties. The two of them were singing a song in what seemed a combination of Italian, French and some eastern dialect that Denis didn't recognize.

Betsy lifted an eyebrow at their antics. "Are they auditioning for the Gong Show? And who are they anyway?"

"The heavyset man is my associate, Sargent Dimitri. He is one of the best soldiers I have ever known," said Pohl. "As for the other fellow, that is none other than Jean LaRue de Rhizoy, poet and trickster."

"Good! Now we know who we're aiming for with our metaphoric sucker punch." Betsy muttered as she cracked her knuckles.

"He seems to be having a good time, which is exactly what I instructed Dimitri to show him," said Pohl. As he pulled his hat further down on his head to hide his face. "Let's make things interesting."

"Oh, good! I like it when things are interesting!" Betsy's grin was positively feral.

"That's God's own truth." Denis rolled his eyes, checked to make sure he knew the nearest exit routes, then linked arms with her and Pohl and the three of them sauntered up the street as if they hadn't a care in the world. As they passed Dimitri and de Rhizoy, Betsy stumbled into the two of them with feigned ill grace.

Pohl took an exaggerated look at his Sargent, allowing his face to be seen for the first time as he did so. "Dimitri, is that you?"

Dimitri's eyes narrowed in a shrewd expression that he promptly hid behind a guileless look. "Captain Pohl? I didn't expect to see you here!"

At the mention of the captain's name de Rhizoy's head shot up. He directed an uneasy look at Captain Pohl.

"I hadn't planned on visiting the taverns today, but then I ran into my dear friend Denis Sesma and his lady, Betsy Springer. Betsy is an uptimer. They're in town so that they can marry in the presence of Denis's family. When she promised to tell me tales of the future that she is from, I couldn't resist."

At the mention of Denis's family name, Jean LaRue de Rhizoy looked even more uncomfortable. He turned as if to slip away, when Dimitri grasped his shoulder.

"What a coincidence!" Dimitri slapped de Rhizoy in a friendly gesture that caused the poet to stumble. "My new friend Jean here is a poet in the employ of the Sesma family."

"He is?" Betsy clapped her hands in excitement, her voice sounding as if she didn't have two brain cells in her head and her eyes sparkled in a way that told Denis that she was enjoying every minute of their act. "Please Mr. LaRue, would you recite one of your poems for us?"

De Rhizoy shifted from one foot to another and looked away. "I'm afraid I couldn't do my work justice on such short notice. I would need a little time to prepare."

"How very unfortunate," Captain Pohl said. "I would very much like to hear your work."

"I know!" Betsy said, holding her index finger up the way Charlie Chaplain would if struck by sudden inspiration. "Captain Pohl, why don't you come to the wedding? That way when Mr. LaRue recites the poem that he's writing for the occasion, you can be there!"

De Rhizoy's head whipped around as if he'd been struck. He stared at Betsy, eyes widening and mouth opening and closing as if he were a caught fish. Denis felt torn between pity and laughter.

"I beg your . . . that is . . ." The poet stammered and trailed off.

"That is what you do for Grandmama Sesma, isn't it?" Betsy asked the poet innocently. "Write commemorative poems? I can't think of anything that will be more memorable than this wedding."

Denis had to turn away to fight down his laughter. Between Betsy's wide-eyed innocent expression, Pohl's vaguely threatening presence, and the grey-purple hue that de Rhizoy's face seemed to be turning, Denis felt like he was enjoying his visit home for the first time.

"I . . . Yes." De Rhizoy trailed off. "In fact, I was just about to retire to my quarters to continue my work." He sketched a short bow to them all. Then he backed away. Once he'd walked four storefronts distance, he broke into a run.

Pohl watched de Rhizoy's retreat like a hawk. "Follow him," He instructed the sergeant. "And make sure that he does not feel the urge to suddenly find inspiration in another town."

* * *

"Three weeks," muttered Denis as he poured himself a cup of wine. He wished there were something stronger available. But the small room that had been put at the disposal of "the groom" had not much else beyond the wine, some bread, and cheese. His cousin Carlos, who was acting as his best man, had to smuggle that little bit of nourishment in to him. There would, of course, be a rather large wedding feast waiting after the ceremony.

"What about three weeks?" asked Captain Pohl as he walked into the room with an empty goblet. "And pour me one of those." He placed his drinking vessel on the table next to the wine.

The sudden appearance of the mercenary shocked Denis so much that he felt like if he had been close to a window, he would have jumped out of it.

"We arrived here, three weeks ago, in the middle of a storm. Had you told me then that a half month later I would be standing here, ready to get married – even for pretend – I would have laughed." Denis massaged his temples. "I have no idea if we have managed to keep the news secret from Betsy's mother and the rest of our friends in Grantville. I'm certain that Grandmama wrote to Mirari with the particulars."

He tilted his head as he regarded the captain. "By the way, where have you been? I haven't seen you since we confronted de Rhizoy in the street."

"Laying low," Captain Pohl said. "We spooked de Rhizoy just enough that if he didn't know he was being watched, he would have run like frightened doe during a stag hunt. My men tell me that he has been borrowing money about town. I would not be surprised if some of the ladies in your family find that their personal jewelry has suddenly gone missing."

"Perhaps we should apprehend him now?" Denis asked hopefully.

"Not yet," Pohl shook his head. I would like to give de Rhizoy just a bit more rope to hang himself with. Besides," here the corner of the captain's mouth turned up. "I would not be the one to make Betsy to miss out on her grand performance."

Just then the prelude music started, signaling to Denis that it was time.

"You don't know Betsy like I do," Denis shook his head as he turned. "Every day for her is a grand performance."

* * *

Betsy looked radiant.

Denis had always thought she was pretty, from their first meeting when she burst into the offices of the *Grantville Times,* screaming at Mr. Kindred, angry because he had changed her copy.

But standing next to her in the chapel with his kin looking on, Denis realized just how pretty Betsy was. He really couldn't understand why he had never *really* noticed it before.

In spite of the fact that he knew that the ceremony was not real, he nevertheless found himself wiping sweaty palms on his trousers.

Although he'd never entertained thoughts of being married, he was certain that if he had, it wouldn't have been with a redhead in pink standing next to him like one of Mirari's fluffy dessert confections.

Nor would his Great-Aunt Serina be standing there as a matron of honor in her own version of the pink monstrosity, wailing as if at a funeral, to say nothing of his Grandmama Julianna standing off to one side, her face unemotional and stoic. To distract himself, Denis side-eyed Betsy again. Which was when he realized that she was wearing her diamond earrings, the same ones she had used in France to pass herself off as an art buyer when they busted the art forgery ring.

"I thought you never got those back, he whispered to her out of the corner of his mouth.

"Captain Pohl just returned them." Betsy muttered back. "As a 'wedding gift."

"Shhhh!" Great-Aunt Serina hushed them, which caused the faux pastor to bestow a glare on the entire wedding party. The pastor was a wide man; even in his vestments Denis could almost envision him swinging a sword on the Russian steppes. Denis wondered if this particular bit of deception fooled anyone.

"Have you the rings?"

Denis glanced over at his cousin, who with a swooping gesture brought forth the two rings. Denis took one, looked at Betsy, and then slipped it onto her ring finger. She followed suit, placing an identical one on his hand.

"It fits," she sounded shocked.

"Madamoselle," The pastor paused the ceremony to direct a stern glare at Betsy. "You have the rest of your life to speak with your intended. Would you mind not jabbering on at this moment so that I can finish the ceremony and make him your husband?"

Behind him, Denis could hear his cousins titter and Grandmama shush them all.

"Sorry," Betsy whispered.

"I'm sorry," Denis added.

"You'll both be sorry if you don't let him finish," Grandmama Juliana chided.

The pastor glared at them, completed the liturgy, and snapped his bible closed. "Très bien ! You're married! You may kiss the bride, sir."

Betsy and Denis looked at each other in surprise. "I didn't think about kissing," Betsy whispered to him. Denis tentatively reached for Betsy, wrapping his arms about her as he drew her closer. Their faces were only an inch apart when a boom echoed through the chapel. The two of them jumped apart as if caught misbehaving.

Denis's grandmother and Great-Aunt Serina let out identical huffs of exasperation. "What now?"

Captain Pohl entered the back of the chapel, along with one of his soldiers. The captain carried a staff in one hand. The dragoon was pulling Jean LaRue de Rhizoy along by the scruff of the neck.

"I'm sorry to have to stop the ceremony, but I've caught a thief!" Pohl cried, then slammed the staff down against the stone floor, producing another attention-catching boom.

Both Denis and Betsy visibly relaxed.

"What is going on? How dare you insult this family by interrupting my great nephew's wedding!" Great-Aunt Serina threw her hands in the air in an overwrought manner.

Betsy watched in fascination. "I could take lessons in stealing the show from her," she whispered to Denis.

Pohl tilted his head and stared down at Great-Aunt Serina. "I dare because it is necessary, madam. I caught him trying to ride away through your compound gates with his saddlebags filled with silver candlesticks and jewels."

As if on cue, Sergeant Dimitri entered the room with a set of saddlebags. He reached into one and produced a silver goblet.

Great-Aunt Serina ran to Dimitri. She pulled the bag away from him forcibly and began pulling contents out "That silver candlestick belonged to Cousin Yoshia! And these are Sheila's earrings! How did he manage to get all of these things? My emerald ring! No wonder I couldn't find it this morning!" As she cataloged the contents of the bags at the top of her lungs, a few more women in the chapel cried out in anger over finding prized possessions among the missing items.

Grandmama strode over to Jean LaRue de Rhizoy. Under her imposing glare, the faux poet cringed as if expecting her to slap him. Instead she turned to Captain Pohl. "I assume you have something suitably grim in mind for this man's punishment, Marcus?"

"I can think of a few things," Captain Pohl said.

"Good! I'll leave him to you." With a final glare at de Rhizoy, she strode from the chapel.

Betsy watched Grandmama go with wide eyes. "That is a classy lady. I would have spit on him, or something. But where is she going?"

"She's got to see to the festivities," Great-Aunt Serina said as she gathered up the treasures into the saddlebags in order to distribute the stolen items back to their owners. "Who has time to dwell on feeling foolish when our Denis is finally married?"

Still clucking over the saddlebags, Great-Aunt Serina left the chapel, trailed by various family members intent on retrieving their lost possessions. At last only Betsy, Denis, Captain Pohl, and Dimitri were left.

"Wait just a minute!" Denis narrowed his eyes suspiciously at Captain Pohl. "How does she know your first name?"

"Oh, that," said Captain Pohl. "It happens that my mother was her god-daughter. I didn't realize that you were related to this Sesma family the first time we met."

Betsy traded astonished looks with Denis. "Small world." She said.

"Indeed," Captain Pohl said. "At any rate, your Grandmama knew about Jean LaRue de Rhizoy, and when the little scum showed up here she wrote to me. You know the rest."

"Then Grandmama Juliana was never besotted with the poet?"

Betsy began to laugh, then ran her finger along the side of her nose. "It was all a con game, straight out of *The Sting*. She lured us here, and the two of you used us to set up de Rhizoy."

"Indeed," said Captain Pohl. "I wish I could have told you, but then your performances in front of him might not have been so convincing."

"I'll have you know sir," proclaimed Betsy, "My performance would have been worthy of an Academy Award!"

Betsy stared longingly down at the third finger of her left hand for a moment, running her finger across the ring that Denis had so gently slid on there.

"It looks good there," Denis said softly.

She pulled off the ring and handed it back to Denis. "Maybe you should save this for the girl who you really do decide to marry."

"By the way," asked Dmitri. "Where did you find such a convincing pastor at the last minute?"

Denis, Betsy, and Captain Pohl all froze in place.

"What do you mean, Dimitri?" Captain Pohl asked slowly. "I didn't get a look at the pastor; wasn't it Illya?"

"No, I just spotted him through the window; something must have held him up. When I came in earlier and he wasn't at the front of the chapel, I figured you got someone else to do the job."

Denis and Betsy looked at each other with wide eyes.

"You don't suppose." Betsy trailed off with a gulp.

"Betsy . . ." Denis said slowly. "I think that might have been a real man of God."

"Then," she said slowly. "That means that you…. and I…. are…."

"Really married!" laughed Captain Pohl. "Looks like your Grandmama had one more trick to play on us all. And it is about time!"

"By the authority vested in me by Kaiser William II, I pronounce you man and wife. Proceed with the execution," Betsy said.

"HONEYMOON IN GENOA"

By: Tracy S. Morris

Curses! Foiled again! thought Denis Sesma as he plucked at his beard in agitation while Grandmama Juliana pressed a bag of coins in his hand.

"Your lovely new wife has told me all about this thing called a "honey moon." I think you should take one. It will be good for your future as a husband and wife."

Translation:, he thought as he stewed inside. *I tricked you into marrying; now I'm going to meddle further.*

"Actually Grandmama –" Here he tried to push the bag of coins back into the old woman's hands. "I hoped to just go back to Grantville. Betsy and I should really check in at the *Times* and get back to work."

A cough over his shoulder alerted him to the fact that Betsy had just entered the room. "Hold your horses there, Denis," the red-haired girl said as she reached out and grasped the coin pouch, "a honeymoon sounds wonderful! I always wanted to go to Myrtle Beach as a child."

"Where is this Myrtle Beach?" Grandmama Juliana inquired.

"Someplace in my past and your future. I'm sure the actual beach is still on the coast of North America, but there probably isn't a Hilton or a Ripley's Aquarium there, so maybe we should choose another location."

"Then might I suggest Genoa?" Grandmama nodded her head as if the matter was already settled. "And while you are there, the two of you can pay my regards to an old friend."

Denis felt a prickling sensation at the base of his skull. It was similar to the one he felt when Grandmama Juliana was arranging the wedding plans: Like a noose tightening around his neck.

"That old friend wouldn't happen to be Castiglione, would it?" He asked.

In response, Grandmama looked away.

"I knew it!" Denis pointed an accusing finger at the older woman. "You're trying to get me back into painting!"

"They do good landscapes in Genoa. But not as good as yours." Grandmama lifted her head in defiance. "I don't see why you won't – to use one of Betsy's phrases - at least give it a try." Her voice turned cajoling. "I'll even provide you with a letter of introduction to my banker there. You should live quite comfortably."

"The least we can do is look around," Betsy stepped on Denis's foot.

With a sigh, Denis rolled his eyes and said "Yes, dear." He was becoming proficient in those words.

* * *

Several weeks after that fateful conversation with Grandmama Juliana, Denis found himself standing atop one of the Genoese city walls, sketching as workmen mixed mortar in the ongoing effort to modernize the ancient structures.

They'd done as Grandmama asked and visited with several artists in the Genoese school. And while Denis still felt no particular pull to rejoin the world of the landscape artist, Betsy had come up with a project that sounded more promising.

"We'll publish a travelogue." She said. "As Kim Basinger said in *Batman*: 'My words, your pictures. Pulitzer Prize material.'"

Whatever a Pulitzer Prize was.

Which was how he ended up making sketches of everything that caught Betsy's fancy: from the Piazza de Ferrari, which had nothing to do with a sports car, much to Betsy's disappointment; to the Doge's Palace, not to be confused with the one in Venice; and to the Holy Grail, or one of them, as there seemed to be a grail in every monastery between here and Paris, though this one was carved from an emerald. Betsy had said, "Indiana Jones had it right. What was a carpenter doing with an emerald cup?"

As if the very thought summoned her, Betsy stepped up next to him. She beamed in satisfaction at his work. "That'll look great in the book!" She said, and clapped her hands in enthusiasm.

Denis put the final touches on the sketch before folding away his book. "Where are you dragging us off to today?"

His question prompted a wicked smile to hug Betsy's lips. "How would you like to investigate a real live sea monster?"

Denis raised his eyebrow. "Sea monster? Where?"

"That's the best part." Betsy said. "Upstream from here, in the Bisagno River. There is a ferryman who swears that he saw the beast. I want to get an interview."

Denis sighed at that. He doubted that a sea monster swam right up to the city, and then up the river just to torment some rural ferryman. But Betsy wouldn't rest until she'd ferreted out this monster. Which meant that he got to spend the day tramping around the Bisagno River, probably with some kind of butterfly net.

At least we'll have another story for the Inquisitor *when we get back to Grantville.* Denis thought. Some days he wondered if the only reason that Mirari's tabloid stayed in business was because Betsy kept supplying it with stories.

* * *

"Look out, Denis!" Betsy leapt from rock to rock, pants rolled up and red hair flying as she threw her head back in laughter. Here the Bisango River spread wide, and was shallow enough to let Betsy wade across. "We must be careful while we cross this mighty river!"

"I've read that the Rio Grande River in your uptime United States could be just as shallow, Betsy." Denis scratched his head. "The word Rio is Spanish for River. Why do you uptimers call it the Grand River River?"

"Do we? I never noticed. Probably because it was just the Grand River in Spanish, and then the English thought that *Rio Grande* needed an English clarification. 'This is the Rio Grande River. As opposed to Rio Grande City or the Rio Grande Valley." Betsy climbed back up the riverbank and put her shoes back on. "We'd better get going. We won't find a river monster here. Maybe a river minnow."

The river deepened as they traveled farther inland. After what seemed like hours walking, they came to the ferry crossing. A thick rope that spanned the river had been tied to a tree on either side. Beneath the rope on their side of the crossing a rough plank raft large enough for a horse and cart had been pulled partially out of the water.

Denis looked around, but the ferryman was nowhere in sight. Had he been here, he could have pulled them across the river using the rope.

Betsy walked up to the ferry and cocked her head sideways. "Someone chalked a message onto the boards here, Denis. It's too long to just be an "Out to Lunch" sign. Can you read it?"

Denis scanned the lines. "It says that there is a monster in the river and that the ferryman will not risk his skin trying to help travelers across the river." He scoffed. "But that we are free to head downriver and cross in the shallows."

"Very helpful." Betsy strode upriver, one hand shading her eyes as she peered into the brackish water.

Denis stepped onto the raft and put a hand to the rope. The craft bobbed under his weight.

"Where are you going?" Betsy asked.

Denis waved to the boards under his feet. Where he was going should be fairly obvious. "Out onto the river."

"Where the sea monster is? Because I've seen *Jaws* enough times to know that never ends well."

Denis squinted. "Another movie?"

"*The* movie." Betsy said. "Before *Jaws*, there was no summer blockbuster event."

"What's it about?" Denis asked.

"A great white shark eats tourists," Betsy said. "I saw it when I was a kid. Then I wouldn't take a bath for months. I really thought that a great white shark was going to swim up the bathtub drain and have me for dinner."

Denis bowed his head to hide a smile at Betsy's antics. Something long and gray flashed by in the water. "What was that?" He asked.

Suddenly, the raft bucked beneath him, as if something was trying to surface underneath the craft.

"Denis!" Betsy yelled as she backed up the riverbank, face twisted in horror. She tripped over a rock and crab-crawled the rest of the way up the embankment.

Denis leaped off the raft and sprinted to Betsy. When he reached her, he flopped down and watched the raft drift downstream.

"Denis?"

"Yes dear?"

"We're going to need a bigger boat."

"Or a boat at all," Denis said.

"That couldn't have been a shark." Betsy shook her head, whipping her long red hair into her eyes.

Denis's jaw dropped. "You're skeptical? *You*–a believer in werewolves and government conspiracies and aliens?"

"What can I say?" Betsy shrugged. "After time travel, anything is possible. But there is a difference between possible and probable. Possible – in uptime 1916 a shark swam into a creek in New Jersey and ate two people. In 1937 two fishermen caught a shark on a trot line in the Mississippi river north of St. Louis."

She held her index finger in the air. "Not probable – that a shark swam up that stretch of river that I just waded across."

"It couldn't have swum here when the river was up?" Denis argued.

Betsy stood and turned back toward Genoa. "I have my doubts, but there is one way to know for sure. We have to catch the river monster. And to do that, we'll need a net and a gun. Maybe a scuba tank and a rifle? That worked in the movie."

"Yes dear," Denis fell in step next to her.

* * *

A crowd had gathered in the square before the San Lorenzo Cathedral when Denis and Betsy returned to the city.

Denis grabbed the arm of a passing city watchman. "What's going on?" He asked.

"Someone has taken the Holy Grail." The guard shook off Denis's hand and turned to march on. But Betsy stepped into his path.

"Betsy Springer. I'm a reporter for the *Grantville Inquisitor*," She flashed her library card at the watchman. "When was the holy relic stolen?"

The guard stepped back half a pace, looking impressed at Betsy's credentials. Denis thought it was more to do with the word "Grantville" than with the *Inquisitor*.

"You're an uptimer, then?" The guard looked her up and down.

"About as uptime as one gets," Denis said. "She cut her teeth on Rick Springfield."

"Bruce Springsteen," Betsy corrected.

"And Grantville is interested in the grail? Is ours the true grail?" The guard's eyes grew large.

"I can neither confirm nor deny," Betsy said. "But we are interested in seeing justice served. When did you say that the grail was stolen?"

"Sometime last night," the guard said.

Once the guard had moved away Betsy whirled on Denis, rubbing her hands together. "Pinky, are you pondering what I'm pondering?"

"Is this another movie quote?"

"Narf!"

"Why did you mention being with the *Inquisitor* and not the *Times*?"

"I figure that old man Kindred would appreciate it if we didn't throw the *Times's* name around too freely."

"When it comes to you, I think he expects that sort of thing," Denis said.

* * *

"Over there!" Betsy pointed into the river. The ferryman's raft lay wedged between two rocks in the shallowest section. She slid down the dirt embankment, and then turned back to him. "Keep a lookout for the river monster."

She splashed her way across the river, soaking her boots and her denim trousers up to the knees. When she reached the raft, she hooked her fingers under one corner and yanked with all her might. "It's heavy! Find a pry pole?"

Denis followed at a slower pace, picking his way over slick rocks and managing to keep his feet dry. He scanned the riverbed and spotted a long branch piled amongst some fallen leaves that had been swept through the current.

"This will serve as a good pole." He picked up the improvised tool, grimacing as his foot slipped off a rock and into the water up to his ankle. He slid the branch over a large rock and under the corner of the raft. Then he bore down with all his weight on the raised end of the pole. The corner of the raft lifted out of the stream, dripping water as it rose.

Betsy wriggled like a snake under the raised corner of the raft. "Ah ha!" she drew back, soaked from the neck down and clutching a canvas bag in her arms. "I'll bet the missing grail is in this sack!" She sat on a rock and worked the knotted mouth of the bag open with her teeth.

"It could just be the ferryman's earnings." Denis leaned against the pole and mopped his brow.

"Seems like a big coincidence that the stories about the river monster started up right before the grail disappeared," Betsy said. "I bet the ferryman started the stories to keep people away while he hid the loot."

"Brilliant deduction, if you're right," Denis said. He wondered how they would get the grail back to San Lorenzo Cathedral without the authorities arresting them. He wished they knew the Genoese equivalent of their friend, the dragoon Captain Pohl.

Suddenly, something large and gray erupted from the river next to them.

"Shark!" Betsy flailed about, and then flopped backward into the water.

Denis whipped the tree branch up between himself and the monster. It stumbled back and he caught a good look at it for the first time.

It looked more like a man in a diving costume than a shark.

Denis swung the pole, but the man in the costume ducked under it and punched Denis's face, then pushed him down into the water. With a jolt of panic, he realized that whoever this man was, he was stronger: strong enough to hold him under indefinitely.

I'm going to drown! he thought in panic.

Just then, Betsy popped up behind the man and clubbed him with the canvas bag. Denis heard a sound like breaking glass, and the mystery man slumped over.

He put a hand to his chest and sighed in relief. Then he pulled the monster suit open to reveal an ordinary man. Probably the ferryman.

"He chose . . . poorly." Betsy smirked. Then she pulled her knife from her belt and cut the bag open. She looked inside, lips twisting in a moue of displeasure. "I don't think this grail is made from an emerald the way that they said it was. After a hit like that, it shouldn't have shattered."

"Shattered? Betsy!" Denis spluttered, raking his fingers through his hair. The good citizens of Genoa wouldn't take kindly to the two people who broke the grail. Especially if they thought those same two had also stolen it in the first place. "This is terrible! Now what are we going to do?"

Betsy stood, tying the sack closed again. "Now we dump Mr. Monster on the steps of the magistrate's home when no one is looking, tie the bag round his neck and get out of town."

Denis slumped in defeat. "So much for the honeymoon."

"Hey! No one died. So . . . there is that?" Betsy grimaced. "As far as traveling goes, I'd say this trip worked out better than our usual."

Denis grumbled while hoisting the man-monster over his shoulder. Maybe that's what they should call their book: *At Least No One Died.*

A CLINICAL LESSON AT MT. VESUVIUS

By: Tracy S. Morris

Denis Sesma finished his sketch with a flourish. The red-haired woman on the blanket before him leaned on one arm, the other held under her chin as if contemplating Mt. Vesuvius, the volcano beyond her in the distance. She would have appeared peaceful if not for the stiff grin plastered across her face.

"All right, Mr. DeMille, I'm finished with my closeup," she said through gritted teeth.

"Yes, we're finished." Denis put away his pencils and drawing paper.

With a groan of relief, Betsy threw herself backward onto the blanket, bouncing her denim-clad legs in the air dramatically. "What a relief! Remind me never to pose for you again! I thought I was going to sit there forever!" She pressed the back of her right hand to her forehead. "I swear I have the vapors!" She exaggerated her accent into what she had once told Denis was a Scarlett O'Hara impersonation.

Denis chuckled. "So tell me, Mrs. Springer-Sesma, what masterpiece of the cinema made you want to visit the Campania region?"

"Why do you think it's a movie that made me want to visit?" Betsy lifted her head, nose wrinkled in puzzlement.

Denis paused from latching the picnic basket to give her an incredulous look. "With you, it's always either a movie or a conspiracy. Since you haven't mentioned anything about the Pope or the Illuminati, I assumed a movie was involved."

"That's because there's always a conspiracy! It's the Pentavirate! They meet tri-annually at a secret country mansion in Colorado: The Queen, The Vatican, The Gettys, The Rothschilds and Colonel Sanders. He puts an addictive chemical in his chicken that makes ya' crave it fortnightly!" Judging by Betsy's affected Scottish accent, this was yet another of her innumerable movie quotes.

"I rest my case." Denis rolled his eyes.

She sat up, crossed her arms and stuck her nose in the air. "Well, the joke's on you, Mr. Smarty! This little side trip has nothing to do with movies or conspiracies! I just wanted to see Mt. Vesuvius."

"The volcano?" Denis looked past her at the jagged peak which locals told him had changed shape considerably after the recent eruption.

"Don't look so surprised! I have a geology degree, after all."

"Yeah, but you told me that was your father's idea. 'West Virginia was coal mining country,' you said. 'You could always find work when you had a geology degree,' you said."

"It was! But some of the classes were actually pretty interesting. One my professors even grew up in Naples! Professor DiGulio loved to talk about Vesuvius. How could I pass up the chance to put the only active volcano on the European mainland into our travel book? It would be practically dishonoring his memory!"

"He's probably still alive back in the future you left, you know."

"Yeah, probably. But that's hardly relevant." Betsy said.

Denis carried their picnic basket and his supplies back to their horses. Betsy followed with the blanket. "I assume you want to go up to the caldera?" He asked.

"You assume correctly."

"And it's not going to erupt while we're up there?"

"It just erupted. So, no. It's not scheduled to erupt again for another thirty years, butterfly effect willing and the creek don't rise."

"Then we can probably just make it up the slopes and then back to Portici before sunset."

Betsy threw him a cheeky grin over her shoulder as she climbed into her saddle. "OK, Denis! Let's get dangerous!"

"I hope not!" Denis rolled his eyes.

* * *

"That's a whole lotta' hole!" Betsy whistled as she lay on her belly in the dirt and looked down into the crater. "I bet this caldera is nearly a mile across!"

"If you say so," Denis said as he stood well away from the chasm edge, shielding his eyes from the evening sun and staring into the volcano's crater.

Oblivious to Denis's trepidation, Betsy pointed to the center of the smoking, sulfurous caldera.

"That last eruption blew the volcano's plug, see! You can look right into the throat! The Ancient Greeks and Romans believed that the bones of a giant who fought Hercules were buried under this volcano."

"Interesting." Denis deadpanned as he eyed the loose soil around the edge of the gaping hole. "Could you back away from the edge of the volcano, dear? I'd rather not sacrifice you to a volcano god the way they do in those b-movies you love to tell me about."

Betsy rolled her eyes at Denis as she inched back from the edge. "Happy?"

"Ecstatic." Denis said.

"Good. Where was I?"

"Hercules." Denis said.

"That's right. Around here the Romans kind of loved Hercules more than Disney does-did." Betsy corrected herself. "That may be why one of the buried cities was named Herculaneum."

"Is that one of the lost cities?" Denis asked.

"According to Professor DiGulio, the *lost cities* were never really all that lost." She held up two fingers on each hand and twiddled them to make air quotes. "More misplaced, like a set of car keys. The Neapolitans have a vague-ish idea of where they are. There just won't be any interest in digging them up until antiquarians come along in the next century or so and realize that there is all kinds of intact ancient stuff under the ground. Or at least that's the way it played out in my old past."

The sound of a clearing throat behind them caught Denis's attention. He turned to see a portly, balding man standing a respectful distance away.

"Pardon me, but are you . . . Americans?" The man asked.

"We are from the USE. Why do you ask?" Denis asked cautiously. Most people who they met in their travels thought that Americans from the future were a myth: like unicorns, or Betsy's little green men. And the people who did believe in uptimers thought that they were all like that MacGyver fellow from Betsy's television: able to make magic from duct tape and a bent paperclip.

The stranger smiled. "Allow me to introduce myself. My name is Lucas Holstenius. And I think it may be divine providence that I met you today, of all days!" He bowed to Denis and Betsy. As he did so, a cheaply-made copy of a magazine with a familiar gold border fell from the man's jacket.

"That looks like a *National Geographic*," Betsy observed as she stood, brushing dirt from her clothes.

"Well spotted Mrs . . .?"

"Springer-Sesma." Betsy said. "But you can call me Betsy. And this is my husband, Denis." She held out her hand in a silent request for the magazine.

Lucas handed it to her.

Over Betsy's shoulder, Denis could see the image of a half-buried skeleton that appeared to be clutching a set of gold rings. "*Herculaneum, May 1984*. This was copied from the Grantville Public Library," she said.

In his time in Grantville, Denis had observed how ubiquitous the *National Geographic* was. Something about looking at full-color photographic covers depicting half-naked people, polar bears, mountain climbers, and Egyptian mummies must have made the average West Virginian feel worldlier.

The magazines collected in attics, basements, and garages across the city, where they seemed to multiply in the dark until they filled multiple cardboard Bankers Boxes. Betsy told him that in the future that was, issues moved from home to home via garage sale, where they were sold for ten cents a copy.

Last time he'd checked, an authentic uptime copy of *National Geographic* cost as much as one of his Grandmama's fine coaches.

"How do you know that the artist sourced this from the library?" Denis asked.

"Because whoever hand-drew this copy also drew the library's *property of* stamp." Betsy pointed to the illustration. She looked at Lucas archly as she returned his magazine copy to him. "If you're looking for Pompeii, you won't find it up here."

"I am aware of that, Mrs.— Betsy" Lucas smiled wryly. "I couldn't help overhearing your conversation, and I hoped you could tell me what you know about the lost cities."

Denis and Betsy traded wary looks. It seemed that Lucas was the other type of person who believed in uptimers: The type who thought that every single person from the future somehow knew nebulous Important! Future! Secrets!

Lucas would probably be disappointed to find out that the only thing that Betsy could share from her past was the name of nearly every Oscar winner for best picture since 1929.

Seeing their wary expression, Lucas held out a reassuring hand. "Perhaps I should explain. You see, I'm the personal librarian to Cardinal Francesco Barberini. I've recently come to Naples looking for new tomes for his library. While I'm here, I thought to tour La Civita. I've long thought that community was the site where Pompeii had been buried. But until recently I'm the only one in academic circles to make that argument. And then . . ." He waved meaningfully at Betsy. As if the whole of the Ring of Fire were her doing.

"And then a whole city from the future appeared in Thuringia, with lots of *National Geographic* magazines that showed what exactly was buried under the ground." Betsy said.

"Just so," Lucas sighed. "And now the whole of the hillside surrounding La Civita looks like it is infested with particularly giant moles."

Betsy winced in commiseration. "That happened in my past as well. It looks like here in this time, it all just started a little sooner."

"I have an appointment with Viceroy Zúñiga tomorrow to discuss the matter," Lucas said as he followed Denis and Betsy down the steep mountainside trail. "Hopefully, he'll see the prudence in regulating the excavations. Especially since the canal that supplies Torre Annunziata with water runs beneath that hillside. The last thing he would want is for the water supplying his munitions factory there to be disrupted. But if I told him that I'd spoken with an uptimer, and shared what Pompeii meant to Naples back in your past . . ." He trailed off with a hopeful look.

Betsy shrugged helplessly. "I'd like to help you, Lucas. But at this point you probably know more than I do about Pompeii." She pointed at his copied *National Geographic.* "In third grade history, all I learned was that a Roman city was preserved by an erupting volcano. I saw a mosaic with "Cave Canem" on it, and a bunch of plaster bodies that made me sad to look at. That's pretty much it."

"Are you sure?" Lucas looked hopeful.

Betsy nodded. Then shook her head. "Well,in college I learned a little more from one of my geology professors, that there was actually more than one city destroyed. But Pompeii gets all the attention because it's easier to dig up. Professor DiGulio said that it's buried by maybe 25 feet of loose soil and ash. Herculanum would be harder to excavate because it was buried 65 feet deep by a mudslide, which hardened into solid rock."

"Then you heard nothing about the private library in Herculaneum." Lucas sounded disappointed.

"Sorry," Betsy said with a wince. "I don't know anything about a library. How did paper books survive a volcano?"

"Not books, scrolls!" here Lucas sounded frustrated. "Workmen in your time thought that they were carbonized logs. Many were thrown away before anyone knew what they were."

"I'm sorry," Denis said placatingly. "As a librarian, I know that must frustrate you."

"I wish we could help," Betsy said. Then her eyes lit up. "Hey! We work for the *Grantville Times.* I'm sure the people in the USE would like to know what's happening to Pompeii."

Lucas grunted. "I doubt the people of the USE could do much to help us here when they are all the way up in Thuringia. Interest from my own patron will be more useful, since the Viceroy is of the Catholic faith."

A slightly desperate look crossed Betsy's face. Denis recognized it as the look of a reporter about to lose out on a good story.

"Still, it couldn't hurt for us to report on what's happening," Betsy wheedled.

The librarian nodded his assent. "I will be sure to find you after my meeting with the Viceroy. With any luck, you will have good news to report."

* * *

By the time Denis rose for breakfast the next morning, Betsy had already claimed the end of a trestle table outside. A crowd of admirers gathered around her as she spun a tale of intrigue, danger, and shooting Nazis. Denis hung back to admire the way she talked, hands waving in front of her as if weaving the tale from pure imagination on an invisible loom.

"So Rick said: "Louie, I think this is the beginning of a beautiful friendship."

The entire table cheered.

"What happened after that?" Denis asked, once the applause died away and Betsy's table-mates started to get up.

"What do you mean, what happened after that?" Betsy put her hands on her hips. "That's the end of the story!"

"But it's not, really." Denis signaled for his breakfast porridge and settled next to her at a newly vacated spot. "It's just a good stopping point. Stories never really end, do they? Even this —" He pointed in the general direction of the volcano. "Pompeii. Centuries ago ash buried the town. Now here people are digging it up and squabbling over the remains. What looks like a new drama is just a sub-plot of the same story."

She hummed thoughtfully as she took a drink from a mug. "That was poetic, Denis. Why haven't you tried writing for the *Times*?"

"Because I would rather paint with brushes and leave the words to my beautiful wife."

Betsy put her head on his shoulder. "Flattery will get you — Oh hey!" She sat up suddenly. "There's Lucas Holstenius. Hey Lucas! We're over here!"

Denis patted his suddenly cold shoulder. A line from one of Betsy's cliffhanger serials came to mind: "Curses! Foiled again!" he muttered.

Lucas waved to indicate that he would be over in a moment. Then he retrieved a mug of beer and drank deeply before crossing to their table.

"How did your meeting with the Viceroy go?" She asked as soon as he sat across from them.

"Not well," he said, slamming down his half-full mug for emphasis. "A so-called archaeologist from France has already struck a bargain with the Viceroy to plunder the hillside for whatever treasures he can strip from the earth."

Betsy looked at Denis and raised her eyebrows. Which meant that she wanted him to come up with something tactful to say. Denis shrugged helplessly. *Sorry your priceless treasures are getting ground under the wheels of politics.* didn't quite seem empathetic enough to cover it.

"It's a tragedy, is what it is!" Lucas said. "All that knowledge! Perfectly preserved and just waiting there!"

"Don't we already know most of it?" Betsy asked in a soothing tone. "That's the kind of thing they talk about in your copies of the *National Geographic* and *Encyclopedia Britannica*, isn't it?"

Lucas scoffed. "Broad strokes! I know that the Romans had what you uptimers call takeout restaurants, but I can't tell you what they served at them! They had gardens, but what did they grow? What did they make? The scholarship didn't come back in time with your town. All that detail is in danger!"

He set his jaw, as if coming to a decision. "I'm going to have a word with this treasure hunter! He must see the wisdom in using scientific archaeological techniques." He repeatedly slammed the beer mug onto the table as he said the last three words for emphasis.

Denis darted a concerned look to Betsy. She made a frantic chopping motion with her hand to indicate that he should cut the idea off at the knees, before Lucas got *himself* cut off at the knees — and ruined her story in the process.

Privately, Denis agreed with her. They'd already had to run out of Genoa ahead of the law because they'd broken the town's fake holy grail. If Cardinal Barbarini's personal librarian got himself killed after talking to them, they would probably be blamed for *that* as well. How much further would they have to run to escape that kind of trouble?

He seized Lucas's sleeve. "Are you sure you should do that?" He asked.

Lucas looked down at Denis's hand on his wrist in confusion. "Why not?"

"Because treasure hunters aren't generally happy to be interrupted," Betsy said. "I've seen enough Indiana Jones movies to know that shouting '*it belongs in a museum*!' leads to getting shot at."

"No one would shoot at a churchman!" Lucas laughed as if the very thought was ludicrous.

"Tell that to half of Europe," Denis muttered.

"Maybe we should go with you, just in case." Betsy added.

Lucas stared off into space, drumming his fingers on the table as he considered this. At last, he nodded. "If you think it's best."

"We do!" Betsy said as she wiped her chin with her napkin and reached for her sun hat.

Denis sighed. He should have realized by now that when he traveled with Betsy, it was best to order his breakfast to go.

* * *

The two reporters had to rush to keep up with Lucas. The librarian muttered to himself while marching double-time up the road leading to the hillside settlement of La Civita. Betsy watched him from the corner of her eye with a sinking feeling. If they confronted any diggers while Lucas was in such high dudgeon, the confrontation would not go well.

As they approached the hillside, Betsy could see a large pit carved into the earth. Walking along the edge, she spotted the skeletal brick and stone walls of a long-forgotten building rising from the soil like the derelict ribs of a shipwreck upon an ocean reef. Paint and plaster clung to some of the walls, making them look like they'd contracted a case of the pox.

Workmen clustered along the base of those walls with shovels, throwing dirt haphazardly into baskets. More men hauled the baskets up wooden ladders, then carried them to a pair of mule-drawn carts, which were each half-filled with the soil. Betsy noted that the workmen hadn't even bothered with the pretense of looking like they were conducting a scientific archaeological study. There were no perfect grid lines, no crawling around on hands and knees with trowel and toothbrush, no meter sticks for measuring.

Lucas drew up as if he'd been slapped. "Travesty!" He hissed.

Denis put a restraining hand on the other man's shoulder. "Whatever you're thinking of doing: Don't."

"I only wanted a word with them!" Lucas said in protest.

"You look like you wanted to have more than one word. And none of them would befit a holy man," Denis replied.

Betsy dismissed the argument between Denis and Lucas as she moved closer to the carts in order to pet the nearest mule on its velvety nose. The animals stood ground-tied, patiently waiting for the command to move. The one she was petting lipped at her hands. She wondered where they were taking the soil. Probably dumping it not far away, she surmised.

Just then, a man wearing a better quality of clothing than the average workman rounded the back end of the carts, moving toward Betsy. He held a shovel loosely tucked into the crook of his arm and resting on one shoulder. A map, stretched between two hands, obscured his face.

He must be the *head archaeologist*, she decided. If so, this was the dude that Lucas would want to talk to. Or the one Lucas would be punching in the nose, if Denis hadn't talked sense into the librarian yet.

"Um? Excuse me? Are you in charge here?" She asked.

He stopped, slowly lowering his map. Betsy recognized him as Justin Quinniaro, the art forger who was *supposed* to be in jail somewhere in France.

Guess he gave Captain Pohl the slip, she thought.

Quinniaro's eyes narrowed as his face turned purple. "You!" He hissed.

"Yipe!" Betsy squeaked.

Dropping his map, Quinniaro seized his shovel with both hands and raised it over his head. With a gulp of fear, Betsy whirled and darted between the two mules.

Quinniaro followed, attempting to swing his shovel. But the blade of the implement got caught in a mule's harness.

Betsy ducked under the other mule's belly and between its front and back hooves. She popped up on the other side. Over the back of the nearest beast, she could see Quinniaro struggling to free his shovel from the other mule's harness. The startled beast began to rear and kick.

I'd better hide while he's distracted. Betsy thought. Glancing around desperately, she spied a loose tarp over the dirt in the nearest cart. Betsy flung herself into the back, covering herself with the tarp. Then she peered at Quinniaro through a gap between the boards along the side of the cart's bed.

Quinniaro had been tugging fruitlessly at his shovel all this time. When he gave a mighty heave, the implement came free, smacking him in the face. The con man fell backward in the dirt and lay still. Meanwhile, the mule darted away, pulling the other half-filled cart with him.

Holy cow! Is he dead? she thought, slipping from her hiding place.

When she rolled Quinniaro on his back, she was relieved to find him still breathing.

At the sound of pounding feet, she glanced up to see Denis round the cart. He clutched at his chest as he looked down at her. "Are you alright?"

"I am, but he is going to have a massive headache when he wakes up."

Denis threw a panicked look back the way he came. "We're lucky the other diggers are still down in that pit! But Lucas is standing at the edge of the pit and shouting insults down at them. I think they're going to pound him into paste once they do climb up if we don't get him out of here."

"We can't just leave Quinniaro! If someone spots him lying on the ground, they'll think we killed him!"

"Why does this kind of thing always happen to us?" Denis moaned as he looked back at whatever trouble Lucas was stirring up.

Betsy drummed her fingers on Quinniaro's sternum as if it was a table and she were deep in thought. What to do? What to do? Then she remembered a movie she once saw. "I have an idea!"

Denis shut his eyes and shook his head. "I'm going to regret this, but what's your idea?"

"Have I ever told you about *Weekend at Bernie's*?"

* * *

Quinniaro's dead weight hung between them as they marched him, three-legged-race style away from the wagon.

"Yoo-Hoo! Lucas!" Betsy called out to the librarian where he stood arguing at the top of his lungs with a rapidly growing mob of angry diggers that was fast forming a circle around him.

Everyone stopped shouting long enough to turn and stare at them.

Denis held Quinniaro's head up from behind while Betsy pulled their tied-together wrists up. She waved her hand. Quinniaro's own hand flopped along with the motion like a dead fish.

"Don't oversell it," Denis hissed out of the corner of his mouth. "They're already not buying this."

"Yes they are," Betsy hissed back. "Think positive! Just — Don't get too close to them." Lucas and the diggers were all looking at Denis, Betsy, and Quinniaro with various expressions of confusion.

"It turns out that the boss here is our old friend Justin Quinniaro from Gévaudan! He wanted to catch up with us, since it's been so long!" Betsy's smile was starting to hurt her face. She felt like it might meet in the back of her head and the top of her head would fall off. Just like Alice imagined Humpty Dumpty's head doing in *Alice in Wonderland*. "Why don't you come along, and you can discuss your concerns with Justin, here?" To emphasize her point, she waved Quinniaro's hand again.

"Annnnd we're walking away now," Betsy hissed to Denis.

Denis sighed. "Yes, dear."

Once they'd frog-marched Quinniaro's body far enough away, Betsy felt safe to speak in a normal tone of voice. "This guy probably escaped Captain Pohl's custody and left France," She hit the unconscious man across his chest with his own hand.

Denis nodded in agreement. "He already has a sketchy history of selling copies of uptime art. He probably read about Pompeii and decided to get the Viceroy to sponsor his dubious archaeology project."

"I wouldn't be surprised if he kept the best treasures to sell himself and sent the Viceroy the leftovers." Betsy grunted. "How much further are we going to walk? He's getting heavy!"

Denis glanced at the side of the road, where the brush looked broken back. "That looks like a good spot to dump Quinniaro. I bet the mule and cart went that way."

Just as Denis surmised, the mule stood grazing placidly just beyond the stand of mauled bushes, still hitched to his cart. He cut Quinniaro free and dropped him like a sack of flour into the dirt in the back of the cart just as Lucas stomped into the bushes. The holy man drew up short at the sight of them.

"What is going on?" Lucas asked incredulously.

"We figured out how to stop your looters," Betsy said as she rubbed her sore wrist. "All you need to do is let the Viceroy know that his master archaeologist is wanted for art forgery in France. In fact, send a message for the dragoon Captain Pohl. He can confirm it for you. He'd probably like to know where one of his prisoners went."

Lucas looked delighted. "I knew that meeting the two of you was providence!"

"Never had anyone say that about us before." Denis grunted as he took up the mule's reins and turned the cart toward Naples. "Usually they're too busy looking for their tar and feathers."

* * *

Lucas was frowning again the next morning when he sat down to breakfast with Denis and Betsy for her follow-up interview.

"I take it things didn't go well with the Viceroy?" Denis asked tentatively.

"What?" Lucas blinked. "Oh, no. Quinniaro is in prison. The looting has stopped, for now at least."

"Then what's the problem?" Betsy asked as she opened her notebook and took out her pencil.

"The Viceroy wanted me to recommend the best places for him to send his workmen next." Lucas said glumly. "He's not interested in preserving the knowledge. He's looking for Roman statues and frescoes for his palace."

"What are you going to do?" Betsy asked, pencil poised to write.

Lucas shrugged. "I'm going to tell him what I know."

"Exqueeze me?! Baking powder?" She pretended to clean her ear with her eraser. "What we have here is a failure to communicate."

"This is not what you uptimers call a rescue operation. It's what you call triage." Lucas held his hands out in a Gallic shrug. "According to your *National Geographic*, Pompeii is so large that by *your* time a full third of the city was not yet uncovered. Meanwhile, Herculaneum lies undiscovered with its library and buildings that survived in better condition after the eruption. Not to mention the other ruins, like Stabiae, that might be missed altogether until your uptime archaeologists can train up the next generation to properly study them."

Denis realized that his jaw was hanging open. He hastily closed it. Then reached over and lifted Betsy's chin out of her lap as well.

Lucas sighed. "This is the way of things. The only reason we have extant works by Plato or Pliny the younger is because a librarian like myself saw fit to save those writings. If I must choose to sacrifice Pompeii to save Herculaneum for the future, I think Pompeii can survive."

"I suppose that makes sense when you put it that way," Betsy said dubiously.

"It's ironic," Lucas said. "I was barely a footnote in your histories of Pompeii: Simply an antiquarian who made a good guess about the provenance of a rock with a bit of paint on it. I'm afraid that this time around, future generations will curse my name."

"Maybe," Denis said. "Or perhaps they'll remember you as the man who saved Herculaneum?"

"It's a nice thought, though I doubt I'll be alive to see it." Lucas stood, nodding goodbye to them. "At any rate, I won't cling to that hope." With that he turned and slipped out the door.

Betsy threw down her pencil, crossed her arms, and stuck out her lip. "I hate it when there is no happy ending."

Denis rubbed comforting circles on her back "Who knows? Maybe your story can spur someone to action? It's like I told you: there are no endings," he said. "Just a new chapter."

"Maybe," Betsy groused. Then she brightened. "Well, if we're going to be the ones to turn the page on this chapter, then we'd better get this story back to old man Kindred." She stood and settled her notebook back into her pocket. "Let's get back to Grantville, Denis! Time's a wastin'!"

IF IT AIN'T BAROQUE, DON'T FIX IT

By: Bradley H. Sinor and Tracy S. Morris

Betsy Springer-Sesma sat at a corner table in the chocolate shop which belonged to her cousin-by-marriage, Mirari. She drummed a teeth-mauled pencil on a battered notebook as she stared off into space.

Mirari filled her cup from a steaming carafe of cocoa as she passed by and gave her a sympathetic smile. "Still stuck?"

"Yes!" Betsy threw the pencil down in a fit of pique. "I don't get it. I'm not one of those people who believes in writer's block. But I'm absolutely stuck on this manuscript."

"What are you writing?" Mirari asked.

"It's the text for the travel book that Denis and I are putting together: *We Came, We Saw, We Got Out of Town Before the Authorities Could Arrest Us.*

Mirari made a face. "Was the title your idea?"

"It was that, or How to See the World on Your Grandmama's Dime. Needs work?"

"Needs work," Mirari agreed. "You're writing about how you broke the Holy Grail and fought a shark, right?"

"Yeah, but old man Kindred told me to tone it down. He said:." Here she cleared her throat, puffed out her chest and made air quotes with her fingers. "It sounds like a pulp era Indiana Jones pastiche. Not a factual account of your travels." Betsy said in a deep voice.

"It doesn't help that he knows of your obsession with movies." Mirari swept the crumbs off the table. "Or your love of conspiracies."

"I lost him at Holy Grail." Betsy muttered. She picked up the pencil again. "I need to just . . .wax lyrical about the pretty scenery, or some crap like that."

Mirari looked up as the bell over her door rang, heralding a new customer. "I know something that might break your writer's block." She pointed.

Betsy turned to see her husband Denis Sesma walk into the shop, leading Cyrano de Bergerac with him. "Look who I found outside!" Denis announced.

"Cyrano!" Betsy clapped her hands. She slid out of the booth and ran to the two men, sweeping them both into a bear hug.

"Miss Springer. Or is it Mrs. Sesma now?" He raised an eyebrow. "I understand congratulations are in order."

Betsy scuffed her toe in the carpet. Denis put his arm around her shoulders, grinning.

"We sort of fell into marriage. Apparently, everyone but us saw it," Betsy said.

"And when Grandmama commands, one must obey," Denis added.

"You must admit, he's certainly better than Albert." Cyrano said.

"Much!" Betsy shuddered at the mention of her former suitor. "So what brings you back to Grantville? Last we saw, you left town just ahead of your chaperone."

Cyrano scratched the back of his neck. "My tutor and I have an agreement. He leaves me alone and sends glowing letters back to my family. In return, I don't mention to them that he spends more time with his mistress than minding me."

"Oh, . . . how . . . nice for you?" Betsy looked askance at Denis. He shrugged in response.

"I actually need your advice," Cyrano said.

Betsy raised an eyebrow. "Really? What kind of advice could a well-known seventeenth century French writer need from a time-displaced twenty-something with a degree in geology and a spotty career in yellow journalism?"

"It's about my latest creation. I believe I spoke of it when last I was here." Cyrano said.

"You were going to call it "I Love Betsy," Denis said.

"Oui," Cyrano said. "The play is complete. I have put together a theatre company. Now I must promote my play in order for it to be successful."

"I don't see where I can help," Betsy scratched her head. "I was in high school drama. But other than playing Wilbur the Pig in the senior production of Charlotte's Web, my drama days are behind me."

"But you know about movies!" Cyrano spread his hands. He waved them around as if he were standing at center stage, delivering oration into the middle distance before an audience. "Breakfast at Tiffany's, The Maltese Falcon, The African King and I!"

"I think you mean The African Queen, and the King and I," Denis said. Betsy took his hand in hers.

"Do I?" Cyrano said. "Seems like a long, complicated title for a movie."

Betsy opened her mouth, but Denis shook his head. "Never mind," he mouthed to her. She shrugged.

"The point is, you know how those famous movies were promoted. You can share their secrets with me!"

Betsy chewed her bottom lip. "A play is a different thing than a movie, Cyrano. There are plenty of uptimers here who are already revolutionizing performance arts. Look at the ballet."

"Yes, but if I want to stand out I need to be different!"

Denis's eyes narrowed. He jerked his head toward the corner of the room. Betsy nodded in understanding.

"Cyrano, would you mind if I talk this over with Denis for a moment."

"Certainement," he bowed. "I shall go order a beverage."

Betsy turned to Denis once Cyrano was out of earshot. "He's not telling us the whole story, is he?"

Denis put his hands in his pockets. "I think," he said slowly, "that it would probably help his play if the original Betsy happened to be supporting it."

Betsy made a wry face. "I don't get it. We're all friends. Why wouldn't he just ask us?"

"If the play is a success he would make money off of it, "Denis reasoned. "Maybe he is worried that we would want a stake in it."

"It sounds like he's basing it more on Lucile Ball's character than on me. He just changed the name "Lucy" to mine. I don't get into that many misadventures."

Denis gave her a sideways look. "Right," he said slowly. "At any rate, we should ask Cyrano what is really going on."

They turned to find the Frenchman sitting at Betsy's table, stirring a cup of coffee. Denis and Betsy sat down as well.

"Which theater in Paris are you staging your play in?"

Cyrano winced. "I've got a slight problem there," he said to his coffee.

"Do you have a theater?" Denis asked.

"Not as of yet." Cyrano said slowly. "Just recently, The Cardinal formalized the Académie Française. A couple of years ahead of schedule, too." He clasped his hands, fingers threaded between one another like rungs on a ladder.

Denis looked to Betsy for an explanation. "What is the Académie Française?"

Betsy shut her eyes, tilting her head sideways. "I know this. I know this." Her eyes popped open. "Oh! Oh! It's the French Academy!"

"Helpful." Denis said in a deadpan tone.

"The French Academy is kind of a ruling council of writer muckety-mucks." Betsy said. "In my future-past. Or past-future. Whatever. They protected the French language by standardizing it. Mostly by publishing the dictionary."

"How do you know this?" Denis asked.

"I once took a research detour while studying Marie Curie for history class," Betsy said. "When I found out there was an Academy of Sciences in France, I wanted to find out what other academies there were. Turns out there were a lot of them."

Cyrano nodded. "Here and now the King and the Cardinal have invested the French Academy with the power to judge whether a play is worthy of being disseminated in France. If they don't like it, they can keep it from being staged. And there are a lot of things that they don't like."

Betsy grimaced. "I'm sorry to hear that. But what can we do to help?"

"If I can stage the show outside France and get everyone who is anyone talking about it, perhaps I can sway enough members of the Academy that they'll let me put the show on in France." Cyrano said.

Betsy's eyes lit up. "It sounds like what you need is a good old-fashioned press junket."

"What's that?" Denis asked.

"It's where producers of a movie will put on a special screening for critics and members of the press," Betsy said. She held her hands out, bracketing Cyrano between them. "Say you're the producer."

"He actually is the producer." Denis told her.

Betsy snapped her fingers and pointed at him. "Right. So you find a swanky place to put on your play. Hopefully some place isolated, with few distractions."

"You mean so they can't get away from you." Denis said.

"Then you spend the weekend plying them with booze. Get them predisposed to like what they see." Betsy continued as if Denis hadn't spoken.

"Not that we think your play is so bad that you'd have to be drunk to like it." Denis put in.

Betsy rolled her hands at the wrists. "Then you show them the work. They go home and write good reviews in all the papers. Or the Sixteenth century equivalent."

"Seventeenth Century, Betsy," Denis corrected mildly.

She scratched her head. "I can never keep that straight. It's the 1630's, but the seventeenth century." With a shake of her head, Betsy continued. "My point is: if you generate good buzz then everyone will want to see the play. When everyone wants to see the play, the muckety-muck judges at the academy will have to let you put it on."

"They're called the Immortals," Cyrano said. "The members of the academy."

"There can be only one!" Betsy giggled.

"No." Cyrano looked confused. "There are actually forty of them. But if I invite them to see the play outside of France, they'll only send one or two representatives."

"Can you get some influential movers and shakers to leave Paris to see the play?" Betsy asked.

"I'm certain I could." Cyrano rubbed his hands together. "Some of the actors in my company have influential friends. If I pull the right strings, they will come. Of course, the two of you must also be there."

Denis made a triumphant noise.

Betsy looked down at the blank page of her manuscript-in-process. Maybe what she needed was a break to get the creative juices flowing on her own work. "We wouldn't miss it," she said.

CHAPTER TWO

Betsy stared distastefully at the bright yellow, horse-drawn sledge that came surging out of the mud flats and up to the dock where they stood.

Cyrano hopped out, patting the horse. He waved his arms at the vehicle with a dramatic flourish. "Sir and Madam, your chariot awaits. Or Wattwagen, in this case."

"Watt is right. As in what is this?" She put her hands on her hips.

"It's obvious; he's going to take us out to sea and drown us," Denis muttered under his breath.

Betsy continued her rant as if Denis hadn't spoken. "Cyrano, when I said to stage the play somewhere the critics couldn't get away, I was thinking in the Basque territories. Not the middle of the North Sea!"

"No, it's perfect!" Cyrano explained. "In the play, Betsy and her friends are marooned on an island. So I'm staging a play on that very island."

"What island?" Denis asked.

The driver of the sled, a ruddy-faced, jovial-looking man turned to them. "It's called Neuwerk."

"Denis, Betsy, this is Soren Bruit. Soren's family is one of the farming families that live on Neuwerk Island. Soren drives the wagons back and forth from the mainland each day. They'll be hosting us while we're on Neuwerk."

"You can get there by this contraption? Is it safe?" Betsy asked.

"Perfectly safe, although the sea water does get up to the horse's chest sometimes." Soren said cheerfully. He strode over to a pile of packages waiting on the dock and began tossing them into the back of the sledge. "Neuwerk is a tidal island. We make the crossing whenever the tide is out."

Betsy looked at Denis with an uncertain expression. He shrugged, and tossed their baggage into the sledge with the packages. "He does it every day. Must be safe."

"So we're cut off from the mainland for however long the tide is out every day?" Betsy said. "Perfect to get critics rip-roaring drunk and make sure they're in a good mood to see the play."

"Or make them blackout drunk and forget the play if they don't like it," Denis added.

They climbed into the sledge, and Soren started them on their way with a jingle of the horse's reins.

"Technically we're part of Hamburg, although the council leaves us be. There are five families on the island. Two fishing families, and three farms," Soren said.

As he steered them across the mud flats, Betsy could see a series of poles set into the mud with what looked like giant bird cages attached to their tops. "What are those?"

"They're a safe place to go for anyone who gets caught out here when the tide comes in."

"Have you ever had to use one?" Betsy asked.

"No," Soren laughed. "I learned how to drive the team from my grand-uncle. I've done this often enough that I can time myself by the sun."

While they slid across the sodden ground, Denis pulled out his sketchbook and began drawing the desolate landscape.

The wind tugged at Betsy's red hair until it flew about her head like a kite. She twisted it into a rope and tucked it under her shirt. Then she looked over Denis's shoulder. "Mud. More mud. Tide pool. Look! More mud!"

"It has its own unique beauty," Denis said mildly. "Very austere."

"I'd question your sense of beauty, but you find me attractive, so you must have some good taste." She turned to Soren. "Why is the island called Neuwerk?"

Soren gave her a half-smile. "It's named after the island's watch tower. The new work," he said. "The island used to be a summer pasture for livestock. Then they built the tower to defend against pirates gone a-Viking. About the time of my great-granddad, they build the dikes. Then my great-granddad's family moved to the island. We've been there ever since."

"Doesn't sound much like a place where French muckety-mucks would be comfortable," Betsy whispered to Cyrano.

"It has its own mystique," Cyrano said. "Like Mont Saint-Michel."

"So why didn't you set your play there?" Betsy hissed back.

Cyrano pretended not to hear.

As they traveled Soren waxed lyrical about the types of fish found in the North Sea, the sea life found in the tide pools, and the bird life in the marshes in the outland area beyond the dikes. He described the livestock on the island, and their rotation through various pastures.

After a time, Soren pointed to a square structure rising out of the glistening mud like a mirage. "The watchtower."

The tower seemed to grow larger as they approached. Betsy could see that it was a red brick building with a pyramid-shaped roof. "It looks very solid."

"It's withstood every bad storm Mother Nature has thrown our way," Soren said.

The mud flats gave way to a marshy swampland. Startled birds took to wing as Soren pulled the sled along the marked path. "You're from Grantville, correct?" Soren said. "We had a Grantville citizen visit last year to see the birds."

"Really?" Betsy had the feeling that Soren could make enthusiastic conversation with a wall. After being trapped in the wagon with him for two hours she had sympathy for every animal that ever chewed its own limb off to in order to escape a live trap.

Soren pulled the sled past a dike and into a barn.

"I'm afraid you must carry your bags," Cyrano said. "I hired a couple of the farmers to carry the belongings for tomorrow's guests. But . . ." He spread his hands.

"We're not muckety enough to keep from walking in the muck," Betsy surmised with a shrug.

"Fortunately, nothing on the island is too far away. We'll take you to see the tower and the pavilion outside where we've set the stage up. After that, I'll show you to your tent."

"Tents?" Betsy scratched her head.

"The man at the army surplus store where I rented them said they were made of army duck canvas," Cyrano said. "Guaranteed not to leak. Plus cots and oil-fired camping heaters."

"The novelty of staying in uptime tents would probably even entice the King of France," Denis said. "I'll bet King Louis has one stashed somewhere at Fontainebleau."

"This will be just like attending Woodstock," Betsy said. "I just hope it doesn't go as poorly as the last one of those."

Once Denis hoisted the bags, the three of them set out. Cyrano pointed out that they could navigate anywhere on the island by the stone tower on the man-made hill. He led them to a ring of tents and let them put down their bags before taking them to the tower and the large tent set up at its base. Inside was a crude stage made of planks set across a bunch of barrels. In front of the stage, someone had set up a half-dozen wooden chairs for their audience in a semi-circle.

As Denis and Betsy looked over the performance area, a red-haired lady put her head into the pavilion. "Oh, there you are," she said with little enthusiasm. She withdrew her head. "He's back!" Betsy heard the red-haired lady call out.

Immediately, five people entered the tent.

"Wonderful! You're all here!" Cyrano said. "Come, let me introduce you all to the inspiration behind the play!"

The new people formed a half circle around Cyrano.

"Denis Sesma, Betsy Springer-Sesma, this is my acting company." He swept his arms wide to present the players to them. Then waved to the red-haired actress. "Angelique Paulet plays the part of Betsy Ricardo when she can be pulled away from her prayers." Cyrano muttered the second half under his breath to Betsy. If Angelique heard him she pretended not to, instead nodding her head in greeting.

"Madeleine Bejart is Vivian Mertz." Here a much younger, blonde girl simpered at them. It seemed odd to Betsy that someone who looked to be half Angelique's age would be playing Ethel Mertz to Angelique's Lucy Ricardo. In real life, Lucile Ball wanted Vivian Vance to look a lot older and more frumpy than her.

Cyrano moved on to a statuesque woman with a dancer's figure. "Beatrice Crossno does her best to understudy both parts." Beatrice cocked an eyebrow at him. Betsy wondered if Cyrano meant that comment in such a backhanded way.

A well-dressed man stepped up to them, sweeping off his fancy plumed hat in a bow. Cyrano rolled his eyes. "This peacock is my investor, Francois de Thou. Francois is playing the part of William Mertz." Francois took Betsy's hand and kissed it before stepping back.

"Of course, I am playing Denis Ricardo while Oliver Bourdon is our understudy." Cyrano waved to Bourdon, who seemed absorbed in reading a copy of the play. He looked up and nodded to them before turning back to his reading.

Cyrano clapped his hands together. "Please take a seat. We've time to run through the play before supper tonight."

"Why don't you let me help you get settled?" Angelique dragged a chair up to the front for Betsy.

Betsy blinked in confusion. "Sure?" She settled in the chair, brushing her long hair back over her shoulder, then finger combing the wind-blown tangles out of it.

Once Denis dragged over his own chair and sat down, Betsy leaned on his shoulder to whisper in his ear. "Cyrano seemed rather dismissive of his acting troupe, didn't he?"

“Cyrano is still very young,” Denis said. “At some point he’ll either pick up the finer points of interacting with others, or he’ll have it knocked into him.”

Betsy rolled her eyes. “He’s old enough to be staging his own play, Denis.”

“You mean he’s wealthy enough. No one much cares about his age so long as his coin is good.” Denis chuckled darkly.

“Still.” Betsy shook her head. “Maybe we should be the ones to knock some sense into him. I feel a little like he’s the annoying younger brother I never had. Especially after he helped me out with the whole Albert fiasco.”

"Perhaps. But they are actors. Big egos and drama are part of the territory. Look at Angelique."

Betsy turned to see Angelique brushing her own red hair back and combing through it with her fingers just as Betsy had been doing moments ago. "So?"

"Never mind," Denis sighed.

"My point is that if Cyrano is tossing out backhanded insults right and left, then he's going to create pointless drama in his company. That's going to come out on stage where everyone is supposed to look as if they like each other. It'll go just like it did in another play that they made a movie about: *Noises Off*."

"It's called acting for a reason, Betsy." Denis said. "Don't write the play off before we even see it staged."

Betsy made a face.

"Yes dear?" Denis smiled at her.

"Better." She hugged him.

CHAPTER THREE

Denis found Betsy in the pavilion the next morning, nursing her coffee, and blinking sleepily at the players on the stage.

Cyrano and Angelique stood on the platform, rehearsing one of the early scenes.

"Betsy! You have some 'splainin' to do!" Cyrano proclaimed to the tent's awning while waving a frayed rope in Angelique's face.

Angelique pressed the back of one dainty hand to her forehead and wailed dramatically. "Wahhhhhh!"

"You know," Betsy said to Denis. "*I Love Lucy* really does translate into a neoclassical comedy better than I thought it would."

"How so?" Denis asked, scratching his bearded chin absently.

"It fits all the rules of a neoclassic play: You don't mix comedy and drama. Comedy only has commoners as characters. The whole thing has to take place in a 24 hour period and the whole shebang has to take place in one setting."

Denis blinked at her. He hadn't yet had enough coffee to process a doctoral dissertation this early in the morning. "This is what you learned in high school English?"

"I'm a font of useless trivia, conspiracy theories, and movie quotes, aren't I?" Betsy gave him a winsome smile.

Denis kissed her cheek. "That you are." Over her head, he watched as the two characters stumbled around, pretending to be fighting gravity on a storm-tossed ship's deck. "What have I missed?"

"Lucy -- sorry, Betsy lost the anchor and a big storm just came up. The four of them are about to be marooned on the island."

"How well do these particular actors work together?" Denis asked.

"They seem fine on stage," Betsy said. "But once the ladies think no one is watching, they all look like they want to murder Cyrano in his sleep. I wonder what the story is there."

"No doubt something suitably theatrical," Denis said. "They haven't gotten to the scene where Betsy loses the boat's paddles?"

"That's next."

"Then they've got enough time to run through the whole play once before Soren returns with the dignitaries," Denis noted. "I take it Cyrano wants us to interact with all the guests."

Betsy grunted affirmatively. "He said that he's sure they'll have questions about Grantville, and what life was like back in the good ole' U S of A. So we're supposed to hobnob. How'd you guess?"

"Didn't you tell Cyrano that movie stars would attend the press junkets to scrub elbows and impress the critics?"

"Rub elbows. But yeah," she chuckled.

Denis pointed from Angelique on stage to Betsy. "Well my dear, you are "*The* Betsy." In this case you are Cyrano's elbow rubber."

Betsy made a horrified expression. "That sounds dirty, Denis!"

Just then François de Thou and Oliver Bourdon entered the tent. Spotting Denis and Betsy, de Thou's eyes lit up.

"Good morning to our inspiration!" His booming voice carried across the enclosed space. On stage Cyrano stumbled and then recovered. He shot de Thou a dirty look before continuing with the play.

Betsy waved awkwardly. "You're more awake than I am this morning."

"Is this coffee?" De Thou turned his nose up at Betsy's drink. "I've heard that you uptimers can't live without it. How do you drink such vile, bitter sludge?"

"With an i.v. drip, preferably," Denis said.

Betsy took a sip of her beverage. "In a few hundred years Parisians will still wonder the same thing. But only because they've perfected the art of drinking teeny tiny cups of it in sidewalk cafes." She held her thumb and forefinger an inch apart.

"How do you find our play thus far?" De Thou asked.

She set the mug down and clapped her hands together in enthusiasm. "It's just delightful! I know that it's going to wow the critics."

Bourdon grimaced. "I fear our critics might have less progressive tastes than you do."

"Hush, Oliver!" De Thou held his finger in front of his lips. "I won't hear doubts."

Bourdon shrugged and turned his attention to Cyrano and Angelique on stage.

"Is . . . everything ok?" Betsy asked hesitantly, her eyes darting from de Thou to Bourdon.

De Thou gave her a blank stare. "Shouldn't it be?"

Betsy held her cupped hand up toward Angelique and Cyrano. "There seems to be some tension between our young star and the leading lady. Not to mention the best supporting actress and their understudy."

"Bof," de Thou puffed out his cheeks then let the air out explosively. "That? Nothing."

Bourdon rolled his eyes.

"I must go pretend to be on a sinking ship." De Thou stood, patting his pocket. "Oliver, please mind my lucky dice. I'd rather not lose them while I flail about."

Bourdon scoffed, yet held out his hand. De Thou kissed his dice then handed them over. He stood, set his hat on his head, and walked to the stage.

"Lucky dice," Bourdon spat.

Betsy and Denis traded concerned looks.

"Everyone seems tense. Did someone mention that Scottish play that no one is supposed to name because it invokes the thespian curse?" Betsy asked.

Bourdon looked to Denis in confusion. Denis shrugged. "Since none of us know which Scottish play you're talking about, Betsy, I'm sure we haven't invoked a curse."

"I'm talking about Macbeth -- oops!" Betsy clapped her hands over her mouth, eyes going comically wide. "I jinxed us!"

Bourdon's smile didn't reach his eyes. "I wouldn't worry about your play or Macbeth, my friends."

Betsy groaned.

"Young Cyrano is simply reaping the rewards of his youthful indiscretions."

"Youthful . . . ?" Betsy's forehead puckered.

Bourdon sighed. "Vous êtes obtus."

Betsy had no idea what he just said, but she didn't think it was complimentary.

Betsy held her hand over her stomach in hopes that it would settle the churning within. Any moment the muckety-mucks would be here. Those sledges would pull into the barn and the dignitaries would disembark, fully expecting to meet *The* Betsy.

Bringing up the Scottish play didn't help matters! They'd all be lucky to get through this play without anyone *actually* breaking a leg now.

She directed a sour look at Denis. Why did he have to point out that she was, for all intents and purposes, a less-skinny Kate Moss at this shindig? She'd been fine before. But now she had stage fright. And she wasn't even expected to be onstage!

Out of the corner of her eye she watched Angelique hold her own stomach. At least someone else here had stage fright as well! The other actors seemed fine. Bourdon even looked amused, judging by the way he smiled and poked de Thou in the gut before pointing at Angelique's nauseous expression when the actress wasn't looking.

With a snort, Betsy re-focused on her own problems. Imagine being a star to a bunch of Haute French Dignitaries!

She didn't know how to cope with that.

As a writer her name was out there for people to see every day. But that wasn't celebrity. If she did her job right, people talked about the story, not the writer. Or if they did, she could sit next to a reader in Mirari's shop while they told her all about a Betsy Springer-Sesma story, all the while never knowing that she herself was Betsy.

Celebrities were not her. They were Audrey Hepburn, swanning through life wearing sunglasses and a Givenchy dress while smoking a cigarette from one of those long holder things.

She was more like Lucile Ball: stumbling around with good intentions only to wind up with chocolate stuffed down her shirt.

Except, wasn't that the point? *I Love Betsy* was about a crazy redhead who managed to "help" her friends and family into a shipwreck.

Betsy could do that sort of Manic Monday personality without even trying. With a nod to herself she squared her shoulders. She was going to "Betsy" the heck out of this.

Out of the corner of her eye, Betsy watched as Angelique went from holding her own stomach to squaring her shoulders. Betsy wondered what *that* was all about.

Just then, two more people walked into the barn and up to Cyrano. One was a craggy older man, the other a careworn girl about Betsy's age. Judging by their hook-like noses and blue eyes, the duo was related. And probably related to Soren, as well.

"Everyone, this is Magnus and his daughter Astrid Bruit." Cyrano said. "Magnus is the closest thing the island has to a mayor. He's offered to give us a tour of the island when our guests get here. Astrid will be serving as our all-around chef and camp-keeper while the guests are here. Please remember that she's here to serve our guests first."

In other words, Betsy thought, *she's not your maid. Don't make more work for her.*

Soren's sled pulled into the barn with six passengers, three men and three women. Two of the men were dressed in what Betsy thought of as the 'musketeer' style, after the fashions she remembered from the Leo DiCaprio movie in which he played both the King of France (the next one), and The Man in The Iron Mask. The third man wore priestly vestments, though he also had his beard and mustache trimmed in the musketeer style and his hair in long ringlets.

The ladies were all dressed in riding habits with coats and hats similar to the men's. If not for the long skirts and the padded hips, Betsy would have taken them for men. She felt a surge of disappointment at not seeing any fancy French clothing. After all, these were court ladies.

Then again, they were traveling. Maybe she'd get to see them all dressed up to view the play later.

One of the ladies, an older woman who reminded Betsy of Susan Sarandon in –*Dead Man Walking,* only without the nun's habit, strode to Angelique with her face alight. "Darling!" She kissed the red-haired actress. Angelique smiled demurely back, bowing slightly to the woman.

"That is Catherine de Vivonne, Marquise de Rambouillet," Cyrano whispered to Denis and Betsy. "And her husband, Charles d' Angennes, the Marquis de Rambouillet." He nodded to the man following closely on his wife's heels. "They run the most influential salon in Paris, the Hôtel de Rambouillet. The group that became The Cardinal's academy first met one another at the Hôtel de Rambouillet. Even if I'm not allowed to produce my play publicly in France, a good word from them would make the nobility seek my play out wherever I choose to go."

"Who is the priest?" Denis asked.

"François le Métel de Boisrobert. He is a particular friend of Richelieu, and one of the Immortals we must win over," Cyrano said.

"*He's* a man of the cloth?" Betsy wondered. "Shouldn't he be off preparing a sermon somewhere?"

Cyrano patted Betsy on the shoulder. "He'd laugh to hear you say that. His verse is legendary. Some say the Pope elevated him to his august position in appreciation for his poetry, despite his proclivities."

Betsy cocked her head at Cyrano, shooting him a blank look.

"How shall I put this delicately? Your husband's charms would impress him more than yours, dear lady." Cyrano cleared his throat.

"Oh!" Betsy looked started. "Ah."

"The other Immortal here to evaluate the play is standing next to him."

Betsy turned her attention to the man with a nose that could slice butter and a chin that could launch a thousand ships.

"Valentin Conrart." Cyrano said. "The group that formed the Academy held their meetings in his house before the Cardinal formalized them with his blessing. I . . . think he might have thought himself a poet at some point. Now he's one of the King's counselor-secretaries. He changes the work of others if the spelling displeases him."

"A know-it-all editor," Betsy frowned. "Charming."

"I confess, I'm ignorant to the identity of the last couple." Cyrano scratched his head.

"The siblings Madeleine and Georges de Scudéry," A voice behind them caused them to turn. De Boisrobert stood there with an amused expression on his face. Betsy ducked her head against the flush she felt creeping up her neck. She hated that her pale complexion and red hair made her look like a tomato when she blushed.

"Forgive me, I couldn't help overhearing," de Boisrobert said. "My favorite topic of conversation - in addition to myself- is other people. And God, of course. I'm obligated to work him in."

Betsy and Denis traded looks. "Hm." Denis said neutrally.

"You were asking about our enchanting companions, the de Scudéry siblings. They are here as guests of the de Rambouillets since none of their own seven children cared to make the journey to this charming backwater."

Cyrano frowned at the description of the island. Betsy wasn't quite certain why Cyrano would take offense. He'd chosen Neuwerk for the junket for that very reason.

"Georges is a writer himself, though half his work is probably his sister's." De Boisrobert made a careless gesture. "If you listen to him long he will have you believe that he single-handedly saved France when he was in the army.

"Now Madeleine," de Boisrobert put the back of his hand beside his mouth as if disclosing a great secret. "You uptimers have an expression that nicely sums up her personality: 'If you don't have anything nice to say about anyone, come sit next to me.' If there is a disagreement anywhere in the salon, she has probably started it. If she is not the source, you will find her in the background watching as if she is at the ballet. Then she publishes her opinion on the whole matter as if it were a work of fiction with the names changed."

Denis and Betsy gaped at him.

He smiled thinly at their discomfort. "Forgive me. I heard that Americans were more forward than we are in France."

"We are," Betsy stammered. "But we usually introduce ourselves before dishing dirt on someone." She stuck her hand out. "Betsy Springer-Sesma. This is my husband, Denis Sesma."

"Enchanté," de Boisrobert shook her hand, his smile turned enigmatic. "Though I have not yet met young Monsieur de Bergerac, his reputation precedes him. Perhaps more so than his famous nose."

"On that note," Cyrano cut in. "Why don't I show you all to your quarters? I'm sure everyone would like to freshen up before we tour the island."

A second sled driven by another Bruit cousin pulled in. The poor horse pulling the sled foamed with sweat from pulling the heavy load of trunks.

"Dear boy," Catherine said. "We'd like to do more than simply freshen up. My gowns need a good airing before I promenade." She waved carelessly to the baggage-laden sled.

Cyrano bowed. "Of course! Astrid will show you all to your lodgings. We'll all be staying in tents in the uptime style." He eyed the bags. "The tents are all rather spacious. I'm sure your wardrobe will fit."

Betsy thought that the downtime definition of spacious was very different from the uptime version.

When the party assembled in the pavilion, Betsy's hope to see fancy French court dress was fulfilled. The ladies all wore off-the-shoulder gowns bedecked in ribbons and lace, with corsets and artificially widened hips. They'd put white powder on their faces, applied little black patches made of velvet as a sort of beauty mark, and painted their lips and cheeks bright red. The men all wore wide-brimmed hats trimmed in feathers, long coats, short pants, stockings, and heels.

And wigs. So many wigs!

The actors were all similarly garbed. Betsy might have felt self-conscious about her lack of finery, but since she was more-or-less playing herself she decided to treat it like a trip to Colonial Williamsburg and assume that she wouldn't be out of place in her patched jeans and grubby canvas sneakers.

Besides, uptime clothing, no matter how grubby, had its own cachet.

The group set out on foot across the island. The cold wind buffeted their cheeks. Soon the nobles were holding their hats on their heads and trying desperately to keep their wigs from flying away.

"If you wish to see the wildlife," Cyrano shouted over the wind, "We can cross the dikes into the marshes. But it is rather muddy."

The less than enthusiastic sounds the group made told Betsy that they would not be seeing the birds.

"In the play, our characters are marooned on this very island." Cyrano waved his arms like an albatross trying to take off. "We can circle the land inside the dikes in under an hour. It gives you a sense of the atmosphere I portray in the play's setting."

As they walked, Denis took Betsy's hand. Betsy smiled at him. This was turning out to be kind of fun.

They weren't the only ones with this idea. The de Rambouillets were also holding hands. With the heated looks the two exchanged, Betsy had an idea just how they'd ended up with seven kids.

Her smile turned into a frown of confusion when Denis tugged her sleeve to get her attention. Her eyes followed his to Angelique. The actress seemed to be copying Betsy's manner of walking.

"What?" Betsy mouthed. Denis shrugged in reply. While they looked on, Madeleine Bejart and Beatrice Crossno walked up alongside Angelique. The three actresses put their heads together and began to giggle. Occasionally they cast a sly look at Cyrano. If the young playwright was aware of their scrutiny, he ignored it.

Madeleine de Scudéry looked at the three actresses with an interested expression. When she noticed Betsy also watching, she shared a conspiratorial wink.

"What do you think of the French?" Betsy asked.

"In general?" Denis teased. Betsy elbowed him in the ribs.

"We have two Madeleines: Mademoiselle Bejart and Mademoiselle de Scudéry, as well as two Francoises: de Thou and the priest de Boisrobert."

"The chatty priest, bless his heart." Betsy said. "I suppose we can differentiate by using their last names."

Denis scratched his head. "Why do you do that?"

"Do what?" Betsy wrinkled her nose.

"I've noticed that you say 'bless his heart,' when you mean the opposite. All you uptimers seem to do it."

Betsy smiled. "There's an old Southern saying: if you don't have anything nice to say, don't say anything at all. I guess saying 'bless his heart' is better than saying nothing."

"Perhaps someone should teach that saying to de Boisrobert." Denis said.

Betsy quipped, "His motto seems to be: Let me tell you something you'll like about someone you don't."

Denis wrinkled his brow. "Charming."

Betsy laughed.

As they neared the island's dock, they saw a couple men loading a boat in preparation to put to sea.

"This is Henrik Erikson," Cyrano said. "He captains the fishing boat here on the island."

Cyrano seemed to have met everyone in the community. Betsy's eyes widened at the thought. The young playwright really must have wanted this play to work out if he was invested enough to learn the names of all the locals. She hoped that his play was a success beyond his wildest imagining.

"How long will the fishermen be gone?" Denis asked.

"Several days," Henrik said. "We catch what we can, then sell it on the mainland before returning."

"What kinds of fish are in the North Sea?" Betsy asked.

"We catch mainly sturgeon, shad, rays, skates, and salmon," Henrik said. "But there are lots of sharks: dogfish, Greenland shark, kitefin, basking, nurse."

Betsy made a face. Soren hadn't mentioned sharks in his long diatribe about the types of fish found in the sea. "Now I'm not sure I want to go back by wagon if the water gets up to the horse's chest."

"Are you afraid of sharks?" Bejart asked.

"I'm fine with sharks so long as they stay where they belong." Betsy said. "It's when they go where they're not supposed to be that we have issues."

Bejart looked confused at that.

Cyrano clapped his hands. "Let's all return to the encampment! Astrid has put out a picnic of uptime sandwiches just like the kind described in the play."

The group walked back to the pavilion. Along the way the three actresses continued to giggle. At Cyrano's expense, Betsy presumed.

"A fine day for a promenade!" De Thou proclaimed as he and Bourdon fell in step beside Denis and Betsy. Betsy thought that his booming voice could be heard all the way across the island.

They watched as Georges de Scudéry chased his fine hat across a field, stumbling in his beribboned heeled shoes. "It's diverting at least," she said. "Do you know our guests well?"

"Cyrano knows them better than I," de Thou admitted. "I've provided the funds for this venture, but he is the one with the connections. Though if he is optimistic about our play, I am as well."

"He should be! It's a good story." Betsy said.

Bourdon harrumphed.

"Do you not like the play?" Denis looked surprised.

De Thou looked amused. "Ignore Oliver; he fancies himself a misanthrope. I invited him to partake in this production. Despite his doubts, he has indulged me with the favor of his company."

"What doubts?" Betsy asked. "It's a well-written work! In my time, it could have been a classic."

"Perhaps the piece is too much a product of your time, dear lady," Bourdon said. "The Immortals are committed to producing work in the Baroque mode."

Betsy supposed that made sense. In the original timeline, the Catholic Church encouraged the Baroque movement with all its grandeur to counter the simplicity of the Protestant movement. Since the Cardinal supported the Immortals, self-interest would dictate that they adhere to the company line. Cyrano's simple, neoclassical comedy was at least 100 years ahead of its time. Perhaps more.

"I fear that our little play is too uptime for the Immortals to embrace." Bourdon echoed her thought.

Betsy crossed her arms. "So what? If the Parisians don't like it, I'm sure the USE would love it! It's like the little clock in *Beauty and the Beast* always says: If it ain't Baroque, don't fix it."

Bourdon and de Thou both looked at her in confusion.

"Best not to ask," Denis told them.

CHAPTER FOUR

"You're staring at the Marquise again," Denis noted. "Why?"

Betsy flopped onto her back and took a bite of her salmon salad sandwich.

They'd been left with the muckety-mucks to have a picnic lunch under a borrowed canvas awning while the actors rehearsed the play. Betsy thought that the borrowed tent might have come from a funeral home, judging by the scalloped edging and the white "Coffee Brothers" lettering stitched into the side.

But she didn't plan on sharing that bit of speculation.

"Her beauty mark is distracting," she said.

Denis squinted in Mme. Rambouillet's direction. "It's just a teardrop. Madeleine de Scudéry is wearing one in the shape of a schooner in the center of her forehead. How is that not more interesting?"

"It just reminds me of a prison tattoo." Betsy shrugged.

He scoffed. "When have you seen prison tattoos?"

"Television." Betsy sang while spread her palms outward like a dancer in a Bob Fosse musical.

Denis rolled his eyes. He lay back on the picnic blanket pulling his flat cap low over his face. "Of course! Do continue." He rolled his hand lazily.

"On TV, a teardrop under the eye meant that you'd killed someone." Betsy sat up and propped her chin on her knee. "Or maybe it was just that you planned to kill someone."

"I doubt Mme. Rambouillet has been in prison," Denis smiled. "Though if looks could kill, the ones she's been directing at Cyrano would surely end him."

Betsy finished her sandwich and washed it down with water. "Is there any female on this island who isn't mad at Cyrano?" she asked once she'd swallowed.

"Other than you? Astrid didn't seem to mind him."

"As long as Cyrano's money is good, I get the feeling she'll tolerate a lot. " Betsy said. "Unless she plans to poison us with bacteria-laden sandwiches."

"Cyrano told us that the fish was fresh caught and the mayonnaise made this morning. They do have a little too much mayonnaise on them, but I doubt the sandwiches are worse than anything you've *tried* to make. And before you argue with me, remember that Mirari banned you from her kitchen."

Betsy considered her sandwich with a shrug. "Fair enough." She crammed the rest of the food into her mouth and brushed the crumbs off of her hands.

Denis stood and helped Betsy to her feet. The two of them nodded politely to de Boisrobert and Conrart as they passed.

"Those two are odd companions," Betsy commented.

"How so?" Denis asked.

Betsy nodded to a cross Conrart was just tucking into the folds of his cloak. "Huguenot cross. And de Boisrobert is a member of the clergy."

"I gather that de Boisrobert is less committed to the faith than other men of the cloth," Denis said.

"Yeah, he seems amused that somehow he wound up in service of God."

"I wonder who is more amused by that, him or God?"

Their conversation was cut short as a gunshot echoed across the grounds from the stage area.

"That sounded like a flintlock," Betsy said. "Cyrano didn't say that they were using a gun in the play."

A woman's scream chased the gunshot. It sounded too hysterical to be faked. Denis and Betsy exchanged a look, and then broke into a run.

They raced full-tilt across the open ground to the stage. As they neared, Denis put his hand out to block Betsy from thundering right into the center of things like an elephant in a tearoom.

Francois de Thou lay on his back in the middle of the stage in a spreading pool of his own blood. Across the proscenium, Cyrano held his hands in the air. A pistol lay at his feet where he had obviously just dropped it. The other actors clustered at the front of the stage, clutching at one another with expressions of terror. Madeleine Bejart wrung her hands, teeth clenching her bottom lip. Angelique had fainted into Bourdon's arms.

"I knew I shouldn't have said Macbeth!" Betsy said.

"What does Macbeth have to do with it?"

Betsy stabbed the air between them with her finger. "There! You said it this time! We've got to stop using that word!"

Denis shoved her hand down as the two of them approached Cyrano.

"There wasn't supposed to be a bullet in the barrel!" Cyrano said so quietly that Betsy barely heard him.

"Didn't you check before you fired the gun?" Betsy asked, then immediately felt stupid. Of course he hadn't checked. If he'd checked, then this wouldn't have happened.

Denis climbed onto the stage and held his fingers over de Thou's pulse point. But Betsy could tell by the gray-pallor of de Thou's skin that the man was already gone. When her husband shook his head, it only confirmed it.

The others from the picnic ran into the tent behind Betsy. There was another chorus of gasps as they spotted de Thou. The Marquise de Rambouillet immediately moved to check Angelique. Her husband trailed uselessly behind her.

"What happened?" Valentin asked.

"Someone put a bullet in my prop pistol." Cyrano spoke woodenly, his eyes still locked on de Thou.

Madeleine de Scudéry turned to de Boisrobert. "You're a man of the cloth. You should do . . . something?"

De Boisrobert rolled his eyes. "I suppose I could administer last rites." He walked to the stage with a huff.

“Aren’t you supposed to do that before he dies?” Denis asked.

“Am I?” De Boisrobert quirked an eyebrow. “Well then.” He brushed imaginary dirt from his hands and shrugged in the Gallic fashion.

Georges de Scudéry scoffed. "What was the name of that man in charge of the island?" When Cyrano didn't immediately respond, Conrart snapped his fingers under the younger man's nose.

Cyrano shook himself as if physically dislodging his lethargy like a blanket. "Magnus Bruit,” he said.

"Sister, run fetch this man," Georges instructed. "Tell him what has happened."

Madeleine de Scudéry gathered up her skirts and took off surprisingly fast for a woman wearing enough finery to resemble a parade float.

"Why?” Bourdon asked. "What can he do?"

"He can get us all off this island." Georges cut a sidelong glance at Cyrano. "This may have been an accident, but it seems suspicious. I would prefer to be far away from Mondemoiseau de Bergerac as soon as possible."

Denis squeezed Betsy's hand. Things suddenly looked grim for their young friend.

Madeleine de Scudéry returned with Magnus and Soren Bruit. Soren carried a large canvas tarp. The two men wrapped de Thou in it and Soren carried the body away.

"Unfortunately, the tide is in and Henrik left with the fishing boats an hour ago. We won't be able to reach the mainland for another 12 hours." Magnus shook his head. "Until then we can keep the body in my root cellar."

"What about locking this scoundrel up?" Beatrice pointed at Cyrano.

Denis winced internally. Even before this, his young friend had made enemies among the guests and actors. Now when he could least afford to have enemies, it had come back to bite him.

"Just a minute! Whatever happened to innocent until proven guilty?" Betsy spluttered.

Denis leaned over to whisper in her ear. "I don't think that's a concept they're familiar with."

"Mondemoiseau de Bergerac says that it was an accident. As he is a gentleman of standing, I see no reason to hold him until the magistrate from Hamburg determines otherwise," Magnus said. "It's in his own interests to cooperate. Else he risks his family's reputation."

"Very well," Georges nodded. "I suggest the rest of us pack. And for our own safety, none of us should be alone. Particularly with Mondemoiseau de Bergerac."

The various dignitaries and actors drifted away, leaving Denis and Betsy alone next to the bloodstained stage.

"We can't let Cyrano get arrested over this!" Betsy said.

Denis spread his hands. "What do you suggest?"

Betsy looked around as if searching for something. Then her face brightened. "Cyrano said that the pistol wasn't supposed to have a bullet in it. So someone must have put the bullet into the gun! Maybe we can prove that Cyrano wasn't the one who did it!"

Denis wasn't sure how Betsy planned to do that. "I know we've caught murderers in the past, Betsy. But we're not exactly the police. What do you suggest we do?"

"We can dust the weapon for fingerprints!" Betsy said. "I've seen how they do it on TV. All we need is some powder, a brush and something sticky to capture the print. I bet the actress's makeup will have everything we need. We might even be able to get a print off of the bullet!"

Denis thought of trying to dig a bullet out of de Thou's corpse with a shudder. "I am not touching a dead body, Betsy!"

Betsy sighed. "The bullet probably wouldn't have a print left on it anyway. Not if it's inside poor Mr. de Thou." She turned in the direction that the de Rambouillets had taken Angelique. "I'll be back in just a second."

Denis frowned thoughtfully at the pistol, still laying on the stage. What possible reason would anyone have to kill de Thou? Surely it had to have been an accident. But who loads a pistol and just leaves it lying around? Uptimer weapons could be loaded and left with a bullet in the chamber. Denis had heard uptimers talking about a loaded weapon discharging accidentally and killing someone.

But a flintlock was too cantankerous and complicated a weapon to simply leave loaded. You only loaded it with shot and powder before firing it, and then you cleaned it to keep it working.

Denis shook his head. They needed to speak with Cyrano.

"I have it!" Betsy called out as she entered the tent with a lady's valise. She put the case down on the edge of the stage, pulling out a brush and a container of fine white powder. She brandished them with an arch look. "Lady Catherine will never miss this in all her other makeup baggage. Let's look at the gun a little closer, shall we?"

Denis pulled his sketching pencil out of his pocket and inserted it into the flintlock's barrel. He then lifted the weapon using the pencil. Then he carried it out into the sunlight so that they could see it better.

Gunpowder-smudged fingerprints covered the weapon.

"First we add the face powder to enhance the print's visibility," Betsy said as she opened a jar of white powder and pinched a bit with her thumb and forefinger. She sprinkled the powder over the pistol the same way she sprinkled salt over her dinner. Then she blew over the butt of the weapon.

"Lastly we brush away the loose powder with a brush." She pulled a sable powder applicator from the valise and used it to gently brush away the powder. "And voila! Visible fingerprints!"

"You seem a little too familiar with the process to have merely seen it on TV." Denis observed.

Betsy grinned impishly. "Almost every kid I knew learned how to do fingerprints when we were in grade school. They used to sell kits at book fairs. We'd all walk around with black powder on everything for weeks after. Our teacher finally banned it at school after one too many of us turned in homework assignments covered in fingerprint powder."

"What about the something sticky you mentioned earlier?" Denis asked. "That powder looks like it would smudge."

Betsy trailed off as she rummaged through the valise. She pulled out another of those arcane-looking vials of lady's cosmetics and a square of black cloth. "We have a bit of adhesive and some of that velvet the ladies were using to make those fake moles all over their faces."

She brushed the adhesive over the cloth, and then waved the fabric around and occasionally touched the edge until she seemed satisfied with something. Then she draped the fabric over the pistol. When she pulled the cloth away, the white fingerprints came with it.

"We'd better put that pistol somewhere safe and then speak with Cyrano," Denis said. It wouldn't do to accuse everyone on the island of murder before they determined that the fingerprints belonged to someone other than Cyrano.

Even if someone else handled the weapon, Cyrano might have obliterated his or her fingerprints when he picked up the gun himself.

"We could give it to Magnus," Betsy suggested. "If anyone is in charge here, it would be him."

Denis nodded his agreement.

They found Magnus Bruit in the tower with Cyrano. The younger man was packing his things under the watchful eye of the elder. The older man seemed stoic as ever, while Cyrano looked miserable.

"Are you okay?" Betsy asked Cyrano.

Denis turned away so that the other gentlemen wouldn't see him roll his eyes at his wife. Whether he was innocent or not, Cyrano had just shot a business partner. Of course he wasn't all right.

"Bad business with de Thou," Cyrano sighed in a melancholy way. "I swear to you, I loaded the pistol with powder earlier this morning. But I didn't put a ball into it." He held his hands out in an imploring manner. "Now my father is going to wonder why I was not with my guardian. And once he settles this matter, I shall doubtless be kept on a shorter leash.

"Perhaps it's for the best," the young man continued. "I have inadvertently shot dear Francois. Perhaps I should be sent to prison despite whatever influence my father curries."

"Cyrano," Betsy put her hand on his shoulder. “Is it possible that someone wanted de Thou dead?”

Cyrano's eyes widened. Magnus leaned forward in interest.

"You think perhaps he was murdered?"

"Betsy and I have a theory that somebody might have loaded the flintlock knowing that you would be pointing it and dry firing at de Thou," Denis said.

"Did he have any enemies?" Betsy asked.

Cyrano tilted his head from side to side as he thought. "Francois was a jovial sort. He made friends easily. Although..." He chewed his lip. "He did owe a lot of money."

"To whom?" Denis asked.

"Everyone." Cyrano rolled his eyes. "Except you. But only because he hadn't had the opportunity to talk you into a game of dice yet."

"This is true," Magnus confirmed. "He lost money to me last night."

"That's less than helpful." Denis scowled. "Perhaps we'll have more luck with the fingerprint angle."

Off Cyrano's curious look Betsy held up the pistol and her scrap of cloth. "We were able to take prints from the weapon. I'd like to see if any of them are not yours. If they don't match, it's possible they belong to the one who loaded the flintlock."

Cyrano held out his own hands. Betsy smeared them with rouge. Then she pressed them onto a piece of blotting paper.

While Cyrano washed his hands, Denis, Betsy and Magnus compared the white blotting paper with red prints to the black cloth with the white prints.

"That one!" Magnus pointed to a fingerprint near the corner of the black cloth. "That print is different."

"I think I lifted it from the barrel," Betsy said. "Someone might hold the pistol by the barrel to ram the slug down inside. But if Cyrano thought he was only dry firing it, he wouldn't have touched the barrel. He would just pick it up by the butt and pull the trigger."

"We need to collect fingerprints from the rest of the people on the island," Denis said. "Starting with the most likely suspects." He turned to Magnus. "I don't mean to offend, but would you mind terribly if we took your prints to be certain. Then once we eliminate you as a suspect, could you hold all the evidence for us?"

"Not at all," Magnus said. "We have a strongbox here in the tower."

"I would speak with de Boisrobert if I were you," Cyrano said. "He takes an interest in everyone. If de Thou had any particular enemies, de Boisrobert would know."

"We've noticed," Betsy muttered. "He seems to have sat next to quite a few people."

Cyrano wrinkled his brow. "What?"

"Don't ask . . . Wait! I actually understood that reference," Denis said.

CHAPTER FIVE

They found de Boisrobert near the marshland feeding bits of bread from his lunch to the seabirds.

"Admiring God's wonders?" Betsy asked.

He threw the rest of the sandwich on the ground and cleaned his hands with his pocket-handkerchief. "Feeding some stinking birds that don't have the sense not to eat this strange soggy bread."

"It did have a little too much mayo," Betsy agreed.

"I knew this trip would be a waste of my time but I didn't expect . . . this!" De Boisrobert's wave took in the entire island. "If I had my way I'd never travel far from Paris."

"Is that where you serve as priest?" Denis asked.

"I'm a canon of Rouen. I was able to visit on my way here, in fact. That took care of the better part of my obligation for the next six months."

Betsy rolled her eyes. "Then not such a waste of your time, after all."

"I suppose not." De Boisrobert gave her a knife-thin smile. "God and I have an understanding. I stay out of his business and he stays out of mine. We're all happier that way."

"How did you become a churchman?" Denis asked.

"Cardinal Richelieu appointed me," de Boisrobert said. His smile tilted in a sardonic slant. "I rather think he took a liking to me."

"What do you think of The Cardinal?" Betsy asked.

De Boisrobert pursed his lips. "You're an uptime reporter, yes? Is this an interview? Or are my words, as you say, off the record?"

"I doubt anything you say about Richelieu would be surprising," Betsy said. "By the Twentieth century we know everything there is to know about Richelieu."

"I think the Cardinal may yet surprise you, dear lady," de Boisrobert said.

Betsy changed the subject. "What about the people you traveled here with? You were quick to tell us about the de Scudéry siblings, but what about the others?"

"Monsieur Conrart is, of course, one of my fellow Immortals," de Boisrobert said. "I hold him in the highest esteem. He has fine tastes in literature. I do feel that he lets his honor get in the way of his own greatness."

"How so?" Denis asked.

"He is His Majesty King Louis's secretary over publication of books. He could publish anything he wants, including his own work. Yet he chooses to abstain from publishing. He feels that to do so would be a breach of his own morals." de Boisrobert shuddered. "A bit too subservient to God, if you ask me."

"What about the de Rambouillets?" Betsy asked.

"Aren't they just sickening?" de Boisrobert asked. "It's unhealthy to be that much in love with your spouse. That kind of thing leads to having too many children."

"One would presume," Denis said dryly.

"The Marquis is under no illusions about his place in the world: His wife is the shining star of the two of them. I think he's content to bask in her glow, and even more content to make sure that we all bask in her glow as well. As for the Marquise, she only agreed to come out to this godforsaken island in support of Angelique."

"They seemed to take an instant dislike to Cyrano," Betsy said. "Is that because of Angelique?"

"The Mondemoiseau de Bergerac has that effect on people, when he's not shooting them. Then again, don't you uptimers have a saying: hell hath no fury like a woman scorned?" de Boisrobert spread his hands. "Bof! To be young and foolhardy again."

"Is that one of ours?" Betsy asked. "I thought it was older than that."

"Sadly, no," de Boisrobert said. "But it is accurate."

* * *

"Is that a parade float?" Betsy squinted, shading her eyes. Denis followed her gaze, to see Madeleine de Scudéry walking toward them. "No, it's just Madeleine de Scudéry. Wearing her court dress."

Denis squeezed her hand in warning. "Behave, Betsy."

"Sorry." Betsy said unrepentantly. "I think talking to de Boisrobert puts me off my dinner."

"The Sesmas! Just the duo I wished to see!" Mademoiselle de Scudéry said.

"You found us." Betsy said with a forced smile. "What can we do for you?"

"I wanted to hear about your Grantville!" Madeleine clapped her hands to her chest. "I considered it as a setting for my next story. It sounds like a perfectly exotic location!"

Betsy traded a knowing look with Denis. In the time since the Ring of Fire, there had been a whole wave of fictional stories set in their hometown. *Grantville* was practically synonymous with *exotic and wondrous location* to the average down-timer in the same nebulous way as *the orient* or *the West Indies.*

"What would you like to hear?" Betsy asked. She and Denis had a set of rote answers for most questions asked of them whenever they were outside the USE. No, Elvis Presley wasn't one of the uptime saints. Nor was Michael Jackson. Yes, The Beatles were the best band to come out of the 60s. But *Spice World* was exactly the same movie as *A Hard Day's Night.*

"Where would one be taken in Grantville were one being kidnapped?" de Scudéry leaned in closer to Betsy.

Betsy raised an eyebrow. "To the police station, once the cops caught the kidnapper. We don't truck with that kind of thing back where I'm from."

"She means it's not tolerated," Denis said.

De Scudéry waved dismissively. "Yes, yes. But assume that you have an innocent highborn lady, kidnapped for the purpose of marriage so that the dastardly villain can gain her lands and titles. Where would they go to hide in Grantville?"

"This no-account kidnapper better stay away from the USE." Betsy crossed her arms. "We disagree with that sort of behavior. Sometimes violently!"

"How is my heroine supposed to find the freedom to wander about unchaperoned unless she escapes the clutches of her vile kidnappers?" de Scudéry stuck her lower lip out in a pout.

"If you can't think of a few ways, maybe you ain't trying hard enough." Betsy muttered.

Denis put out a placating hand. "Maybe your villain takes your heroine into the USE by mistake? Then once she's freed by the local authorities she has the liberty to explore Grantville on her own? If you like, we can give you the address of the Grantville tourism bureau. They'd be able to answer most of your questions."

De Scudéry looked off into the distance, brows knitted.

"Does Grantville have a tourism bureau?" Betsy whispered to Denis.

"I have no idea," Denis whispered back. "I was going to give her Paul Kindred's address and let him figure it out."

"Good thinking," Betsy nodded in approval.

De Scudéry seemed to reach some kind of decision. "That would be acceptable." She smiled at them. "I'm sorry to have bothered you. I had hoped to speak with you at leisure over the weekend. With this business over Monsieur de Thou's death, I was afraid that we'd part ways before I could ask you about Grantville."

"We understand," Denis said. He pulled his art book and a drawing pencil from his satchel and presented both to de Scudéry. "If you would like, I'll be happy to take a note to the tourism bureau."

"Oui!" Madeleine beamed gratefully. She scrawled out a letter in haste and signed it with a flourish. "Thank you both. This has been most productive! I hope I shall see you again once I've packed my things."

Once de Scudéry was gone, Denis handed the book and pencil to Betsy. "Let's dust that for prints too. We can at least eliminate one suspect from our list."

"Two!" Betsy held up a penknife.

"Where did you get that?" Denis frowned at Betsy.

"It was laying next to de Boisrobert's lunch bag. So I helped myself."

Denis looked at her in horror. "You stole from a priest!"

"God stays out of his business, remember?"

"Still."

Betsy huffed. "Fine! We'll put it back after we dust it for prints. Besides, it's not like he's much of a priest, anyway."

Denis sighed. "Yes, dear."

* * *

Unlike the muckety-mucks, who seemed bent on repacking everything they'd brought over including the kitchen sink, the actors gathered in the dining tent. Perhaps, Betsy thought, they were drawing comfort from one another's presence. After all, it was one of them that had died. Possibly shot by another of their number.

When Denis and Betsy joined them in the tent, Bourdon was placing de Thou's dice onto a table for all to see.

"Shouldn't we put them into the pocket of his coat?" Angelique asked. "It seems like something he would've wanted. That way when he goes to heaven, he can challenge St. Peter to a game of dice."

"Or Old Scratch if he went to the other place," Bourdon said.

Angelique put her hands on her hips. "Don't speak ill of the dead, Monsieur Bourdon!"

Bourdon shrugged.

Betsy rested her hands on the table and her chin on her hands scrutinizing the dice. Across the table Angelique copied her movements.

"Why are you doing that?" Betsy asked.

Angelique blinked, then looked self-conscious. "Cyrano told me to study you, since my character is based on . . . well, you."

"I figured that out," Betsy said. "I mean, why are you still doing it?"

"It's part of my process. I wouldn't expect you to understand, “Angelique said haughtily.

Beatrice scoffed at Angelique. "You may as well give up. After this, no one will ever touch this little play again."

The redheaded actress sniffed at Beatrice. "I want the satisfaction of knowing that I could have played Betsy to perfection whether the play goes on or not."

"I wouldn't count it out just yet," Madeleine Bejart said. "I'm sure there will be a scandal, but that is all to the good in my mind. Infamy is almost as good as popularity, and anyone who is anyone will want to say that they have seen the play."

"Assuming Mondemoiseau de Bergerac can talk, or at least write his way out of prison," Angelique said scornfully.

"Do you think he murdered de Thou?" Beatrice asked.

Angelique shrugged her shoulders. "He says it was an accident."

"How did shot *accidentally* find its way into his weapon?" Bejart scoffed.

"You three don't seem to like Cyrano very much, considering he's your director," Betsy said.

"He has very few qualities to recommend himself," Angelique said.

"Least of all his pen," Bejart added.

Betsy tilted her head to the side, inquiringly, causing Madam Bejart to huff.

"He wrote a few nasty verses about myself and Angelique." She waved between herself and the other woman.

"I'm sure we've all written things that we regret later," Betsy hedged. Out of the corner of her eye she could see Denis shake his head in disbelief as he stared at her. She kicked him under the table, while pretending to ignore him. Her work for the *Inquisitor* was serious journalism, thank you very much, husband! She would never regret a word of it.

"It didn't help that he published it." Angelique said. "I had patrons laughing into their sleeves wherever I performed. I couldn't even show my face at the Hôtel de Rambouillet."

Bejart shrugged. "Eh. They'll find some new diversion next week."

"Couldn't you just move to a different hotel?" Betsy asked.

"Hôtel, not hotel, Betsy," Denis said. He pronounced the French word carefully, omitting the H sound. The others nodded in approval at his pronouncement.

"What's the difference?" Betsy scratched her head.

"A hôtel is a fancy mansion. A hotel is a guest lodging."

"How Avant Garde." Betsy said, glaring at Denis as if to reprimand him for derailing their investigation. "Getting back to our previous topic: why would Cyrano shoot de Thou? Did they dislike one another?"

"Hardly," Angelique said. "De Thou was Cyrano's financier for the play. He even asked Bourdon to understudy."

"Promised to pay his debt to me once the play succeeded." Bourdon winced as if physically pained. "Not that it matters now."

"Cyrano needed de Thou." Angelique said with a sage nod. "I'm sure the magistrates in Hamburg will all agree that this was just a tragic accident."

Just then Madame de Rambouillet appeared at the entrance to the tent. "There you are, Angelique! If you would be a dear and assist me in packing my things, I should be happy to return the favor to you!"

"La! Perhaps we should also pack," Angelique brushed her hands as if wiping them clean of the matter.

Bourdon put the dice back into his pocket. "I'll do as you ask, Angelique, and place these dice with Francois."

Once the actors had cleared the tent, Betsy turned to Denis. "I bet we can get everyone's prints and match them at the same time if we just collect them from the luggage."

"Good idea," Denis said. He held his thumb and finger an inch apart. "Small problem: how do we do that without being seen?"

"We need a diversion." Betsy crossed her arms, drumming her fingers along her biceps in thought. Just then an idea hit her. "I know!" She stood, holding her index finger in the air.

"What?" Denis asked.

"We need Cyrano!"

CHAPTER SIX

Cyrano looked doubtful when Betsy explained her plan. Denis couldn't blame him.

"Are you certain, Betsy?" Cyrano asked. "I'm not sure anyone trusts me right now. What makes you think they would agree to stage the play?"

"Because they're bored?" Betsy put a hand on her hip. "It's several hours until the tide goes out and we can leave. Considering that de Thou was a gambler, passing the time with cards or dice might be a little gauche even for someone who wears a powdered wig and a mole shaped like King Louis's head."

"Some would say that staging a play when de Thou's body isn't even cold is a bit gauche as well," Cyrano said.

"Some would." Betsy waggled her eyebrows. "I doubt those people are among our guests. If you can keep their attention for a few hours, Denis and I can probably clear your name."

Cyrano plucked at his chin, looking thoughtful. "We can, as you say, give it a try. What do we have to lose?"

Denis could think of several things. Their lives, if there was a killer among them. Their sanity, for another. Though considering he was married to a redhead his sanity might already be shaky.

He glanced at his wife. 'But, oh, what a way to go,' he thought.

Cyrano led the two of them back to the avenue of tents where the guests and actors were dragging their suitcases out.

"Ahem, ahem!" He cleared his voice several times loudly. The others stopped and looked, some curiously, others with hostile expressions. "My friends!"

"Don't push it," Denis whispered.

"It seems a shame that the play de Thou worked so hard on will never see the light of day."

"Should have thought of that before you murdered him," Georges murmured with a dark look at Cyrano.

Cyrano continued as if he hadn't heard Georges. "Since it appears we're at loose ends for a few hours, perhaps we could stage the play just once as a diversion. We can do it in the style of the uptime "poor theatre" without props, set or costumes. Very avant-garde! It can be our final tribute to Francois de Thou."

The others looked at each other incredulously. Finally, Angelique shrugged. "I don't see as it would hurt anything provided we stick together and watch out for one another. Honestly, I want the chance to act the part just once."

"Splendid!" Cyrano clapped his hands together. " Bourdon, you can stand in for William."

Now that the group had decided to go through with the play, the actors seemed to vibrate with energy. They drifted toward the viewing pavilion.

"Are we really going to watch this?" Mademoiselle de Rambouillet furrowed her brow.

Her husband offered her his arm. "It appears so. At least we will have a story to tell when we return to Paris."

De Boisrobert said nothing. But when he passed them, he gave Betsy a bemused smile.

Once the guests and actors had departed, Betsy turned to Denis. "Let's hurry before they miss us."

The two of them strolled to the barn where the wagons had been loaded with baggage for the return trip. Betsy broke into a run once they'd moved into the shelter of the barn. She tore boxes from their resting place, dusting the handles of each valise and trunk with face powder. Denis came behind her, comparing the prints to the one they'd taken from the weapon.

"This is the last bag," Betsy said, kicking the side of a robin's-egg blue box.

Denis squinted at the handle of the valise. "None of the prints on any of the bags match."

"None?" Betsy sat down in defeat. "Great! That was a waste of time!"

"It's just a dead end." Denis put his arm around her. She rested her head against his shoulder and sighed.

"Maybe the person who left the print didn't handle their own baggage? Or they don't have bags?"

"Or the fingerprint on the pistol wasn't made by the person who put the shot into the weapon? Perhaps it's a random fingerprint."

"Back to the drawing board," Betsy sighed.

Suddenly, the sound of women's screams cut through the air.

Betsy and Denis exchanged a look. "That came from the stage," Denis said.

Betsy turned on her heel, and ran for the pavilion. "Knew I never should have mentioned Macbeth!"

"Then stop mentioning it now!" Denis said as he ran alongside her.

The two of them entered the large pavilion to find it empty. The guests and actors were nowhere to be seen.

"Where is everyone?" Betsy called out.

"Out here!" Conrart yelled from the other side of the canvas wall beyond the stage.

Denis and Betsy rounded the structure -- to find a tablecloth-shrouded body on the ground. Denis's blood ran cold to see a shock of red hair spilling from beneath the covering. The person under the cloth must be Angelique.

Madam de Rambouillet's wailing drew his attention. The woman stood in the circle of her husband's arms, her shoulders shaking with silent grief. Madeleine de Scudéry hovered next to them, wringing her hands, a troubled look on her face. On the ground behind them, Madeleine Bejart, Oliver Bourdon and Beatrice Crossno sat in a quiet huddle. Beatrice held a compress to Bourdon's head.

"What happened?" Denis asked.

Georges rounded on them as if he suspected that they'd been responsible for the murder. "Where the devil did the two of you go?"

"We snuck off so that I could have a moment with my husband!" Betsy grasped Denis's hand. "We're married. We can do that kind of thing."

The former soldier rolled his eyes. "While you two were having fun, someone snuck up on Angelique, Oliver and Madeleine Bejart." He waved his hand at the three of them as if it proved something.

"Angelique and I were going over our lines," Madeleine Bejart said in a shaky voice. "Someone must have been hiding around the corner of the tent. They threw that over me." She pointed to the tablecloth that now covered Angelique's body. "I heard a scuffle. Then Angelique screamed." She put a hand to her throat as she swallowed convulsively. "By the time I fought my way free, she was . . ." She broke off, biting her closed fist. "She'd been stabbed. You can see the knife still in her back."

"I heard the scream," Bourdon said. "By the time I got here, it was too late. Angelique was dead. I never saw who did it, but they struck me from behind." He pointed to the lump forming on the side of his head.

George looked at the collected group. "I think the question we should ask ourselves is: where is Cyrano de Bergerac?"

Almost on cue, Cyrano rounded the corner of the tent. When he caught sight of the grim assembly, he stopped short. "What happened?" He asked, his face turning pale.

"You murderer!" Madame de Rambouillet shouted. Her husband pulled her away, making comforting, shushing sounds.

"Mondemoiseau de Bergerac, I must ask as to your whereabouts just now," Conrart asked.

The young playwright blushed red. "I . . . was at my toilette."

"A convenient place to clean away blood. Can anyone vouch for you?" Georges asked.

Cyrano looked helplessly at Denis. "N . . . No."

"Just as I suspected!" Georges waved his hands at Cyrano with a triumphant flourish before bringing them to cross at his chest. "We should lock him away for our safety until we can deliver him to the magistrate in Hamburg. In chains, if I have my way!"

"For going to powder his nose?" Betsy squawked.

"I would not speak presently, young Madame Sesma," de Boisrobert muttered to her. "Lest in his zealousness, Georges tries to have you locked away as well."

"He's got a point, Betsy." Denis whispered to her.

Madame de Rambouillet wailed inarticulately, beating at her breast. Her husband put his hands over her shoulders as if to lead her away. But the formidable woman shook off his grip. She glared at her husband in denial of his subtle command. Then choked off her cries with a shaking breath. "Someone go find that brute of a man!"

"I think you mean Monsieur Bruit." Madeleine de Scudéry sighed. "I suppose I'll go."

Georges scowled in a forbidding way. "Don't go alone!" He said while reaching for his sister as if to bodily stop her.

The female de Scudéry evaded her brother with a humorless smile. "What have I to fear? You've already caught the murderer."

* * *

Madeleine de Scudéry returned with Magnus and Soren Bruit. The two men tisked at one another and shook their heads in a vague sort of way while bundling Angelique in the tablecloth. As Soren carried her body away to the cold room where Francois's body also lay, Magnus took Cyrano to the lighthouse to lock him into a room.

Denis drew Betsy's gaze and jerked his head in the direction that Soren went to indicate that they should follow him. Betsy nodded her agreement.

The two of them ambled after Soren. They caught up to him as he was exiting the cold room.

Soren narrowed suspicious eyes at them. "Yes?"

"We wanted to see the murder weapon," Betsy said. "in case the killer left his fingerprints on them the way he did with the gun."

Soren looked from Betsy to Denis, then sighed. He stepped out of the doorway of the cold room and waved them through.

The temperatures in the cold room raised gooseflesh on Denis's arms. Betsy clutched at her own arms and shivered. Soren pushed past her and pulled the sheet away, exposing the knife that stuck out of Angelique's back.

Denis once again found himself staring at the actress's red hair, so like Betsy's.

"Well fudgsicles!" Betsy said. "There are prints, but they're too smeared."

"Then we're done here?" Soren said.

“Yeah,” Denis looked away, glad when the younger Bruit covered the body again.

“Soren wasn’t very talkative, for once,” Betsy noted once they had left the cold room.

“Can you blame him?” Denis said. “There have been two murders since lunchtime.”

"I get the feeling that Magnus will be glad when we're all off his island." Betsy said wryly.

"I'll be glad, too." Denis clasped his wife’s hand.

She squinted at him. "What is it?"

"I can't help but think that Angelique was killed by mistake."

"Mistake?” She wrinkled her nose. “The killer thought she was a steak and accidentally stabbed her? Oops! She fell on my knife?"

Denis pulled Betsy into his arms and stroked her hair. "She was imitating you, Betsy. From the back the two of you looked indistinguishable."

Betsy leaned back, her face pale beneath her numerous freckles. "Are you saying the killer wants me dead?"

"I'm saying that maybe the killer knows we're investigating him, and he or she doesn't like it." He looked over to the ground stained with Angelique's blood. "Not one bit."

Betsy pulled one of Denis’s grease pencils from her pocket, strode into the pavilion and crawled up onto the stage. "We need to make a murder board like they do in crime scene shows. Think spatially. Draw our findings up,” she said as she got down on her hands and knees. In sticky red she wrote:

Murder of Francois de Thou and Angelique Paulet.

Below that, she wrote:

Motive.

"Separate the two incidents," Denis said. "I'm pretty sure Angelique was murdered by accident."

"Thanks for that reminder," Betsy grumbled. "I like to dwell on the fact that someone wants to kill me."

Denis drummed his fingers on the edge of the stage as he chewed over a thought. "It just means that we're on to something, and someone did kill Francois. It also means that it wasn't Cyrano because we're actively trying to clear his name."

"So . . . motive?" Betsy wrote the word on the flooring:

Frame Cyrano?

He nibbled his lower lip. "That feels wrong. Framing Cyrano would have been convenient. But this feels personal. Remember how Cyrano said that Francois had gambling debts?"

Betsy crossed out her scribbling and wrote:

Who benefits: Indebted Gambler.

At the sound of footsteps, both of them looked up.

Astrid stood at the entrance to the tent, hands on her hips, scowling at them. "What are you doing?" She lifted an eyebrow.

Betsy looked from the smudged flooring to the grease pencil in her hand. "Thinking. You weren't planning on using this stage after we left, were you?"

"It's going back on the side of the barn where it belongs."

"Oh!" Betsy swiped at the grease with her sleeve, smearing it. "I'll . . . just . . . clean it up when we're done. Yeah?"

"See that you do," Astrid said tartly.

Betsy sighed. She'd forgotten in her excitement that life would go on for the people who lived here once they left. She blinked, sitting up at that thought. If she'd forgotten about Astrid; the others would have, too. After all, they were haute société. Betsy would wager that people like the de Rambouillets wouldn't think twice about a servant being in the room.

"Astrid!" she called out just as the other was about to leave the tent.

Astrid halted with a put-upon sigh. "What is it now?"

"You've been here the whole time. Did you see anything that struck you as odd?"

The girl raised both eyebrows at this.

"Specifically about Monsieur de Thou, the murdered man." Denis added.

Astrid's eyes took on a faraway cast as she nodded slowly. "I did hear Monsieur de Thou in an argument outside his tent before the promenade."

"Who was he arguing with?" Betsy asked.

"I couldn't see or hear the other person." Astrid's mouth slanted in an apologetic line.

Denis and Betsy exchanged a weary glance. It seemed that every new lead they chased led to a dead end. "Thanks anyway, Astrid." Denis said.

They returned to the tower to find Magnus Bruit sitting outside Cyrano's room.

"Can we talk to Cyrano?" Betsy asked.

The patriarch of the Bruit clan shrugged his shoulders. "I don't see why not. I've just been asked to keep him from leaving."

They opened the door to find the young man sprawled like a pile of laundry across his bed, an arm thrown over his face.

"What is it?" He asked without looking up.

"It's just us," Betsy gave an awkward wave as if he could see her through his arm.

Cyrano looked up, rising from his reclining position. "My friends!" He tried to sound upbeat, though Betsy detected a quaver in his tone. "I trust you've been working on my defense?"

"We've been talking about it," Betsy said. "We spoke with Astrid Bruit. She said de Thou was arguing with someone in his tent. I know he had gambling debts, but was anyone leaning on him to repay them? Is there anyone on the island that he might have been arguing with?"

Cyrano rubbed his chin. "His creditors were hounding him, that much I know," he said. "De Thou really needed our play to succeed. He needed the steady income so that he could pay back his debts. Mayhap he was arguing with one of the critics."

"How did he end up funding your play if he was in so much debt?" Denis squinted at Cyrano, tilting his head to the side.

"I caught him at the right moment during a windfall." Cyrano rubbed the back of his neck. "I couldn't ask my father, or any of his friends. De Thou was my only option."

Betsy scratched her head. "I know Oliver Bourdon thought the play was not Baroque enough to please Conrart and de Boisrobert."

"Just so!" Cyrano said. "Perhaps it was one of them de Thou was arguing with, trying to get a fair airing of our work."

"I suppose we should go talk to Conrart. De Boisrobert said he had high moral standards," Denis said.

"I get the feeling that de Boisrobert wouldn't know a high moral standard if it bit him on the tush. High on the tush."

"Yes, dear," Cyrano said.

Denis laughed. "That's my line."

* * *

Valentin Conrart sat on the sandy shoreline with a book in one hand and a ballpoint pen in the other. He seemed to be contemplating the grey line of clouds in the distance, the marsh grasses, and the gently lapping waves. He smiled when he saw Denis and Betsy approach from along the shoreline. When they were near enough, he held up the writing implement.

"Marvelous invention," he said. "I'd like to visit your Grantville someday and see what other wonders the future-that-will-never-be held."

Betsy shrugged. "I took them for granted, to tell you the truth. And now that I'm down the rabbit hole, everything is curiouser and curiouser."

"I've read that book, you know." Conrart said. "The word play was a bit too English for my tastes. But I enjoyed the math jokes."

"I was thinking of the Disney movie." Betsy tucked her hands behind her back and rocked on her toes. "But the meaning is the same. It's kind of shocking to see lords and ladies sleeping in old Army tents. When I was twelve, my dad saved up for a month to take my mother to a fancy lobster dinner. Here, no one wants to eat lobster. It's a cheap food that poor people pull off the seashore.

I suppose if you wanted to feel the way I do, imagine if you met an Ancient Sumerian who used clay tablets. Think how amazed he'd be at the paper in your hands." She pointed to the writing journal in Conrart's lap.

"That was very poetic. You write for a newspaper, correct?"

"Not in a literary sense." Betsy said. "We're investigative journalists. Which means we try to ferret out the truth. Right now we're figuring out if Cyrano murdered two people."

"You think him innocent?" Conrart surmised.

Betsy tugged her ear. "I think he doesn't have a reason for killing de Thou. Not if it meant that his play would fall apart."

"To be honest, Mademoiselle, this play didn't have much hope anyway." Conrart sighed. "Myself and de Boisrobert were both of the mind that it was too much a product of the uptime."

"A play is too uptime, but a pen is not?" Betsy asked.

"The pen is useful," Conrart said. "Ideas are like a contagion. They spread whether you want them to or not."

She bared her teeth, leaning away from Conrart. "Are you calling *I Love Betsy* a disease?"

"I mean no personal insult," Conrart said blandly. The corners of his lips quirked in the barest hint of a smile. As if he thought Betsy's personal anger was entertaining. "I'm sure it's fine, for what it is. But it's too uptime for Parisian tastes."

"What makes you the authority on what the Parisians want?" She put her hands on her hips.

"That's what it means to be an Immortal, Mademoiselle." Conrart said. "We tell them what they like."

"You probably ought to read *Les Misérables*. It's very instructive about what happens when people get tired of being told what to think." Betsy's glare slid off of his mild expression like water off a duck's back.

"You make my point for me, Madam. Contagions are dangerous."

"We didn't come here to discuss the merits of *I Love Betsy*." Denis cleared his throat to break the tension. "We're trying to retrace Monsieur de Thou's last hours. He was heard arguing with someone just before we all took the island tour. Cyrano thought he might have been trying to change your mind about the play. Were the two of you talking at that time?"

"No," Conrart said. "We did talk briefly, but not in his tent. And it never became heated. He did try to change my opinion. But, as you and your wife see, that is quite impossible."

"Clearly." Betsy snapped.

Denis put his hand on her shoulder. When she looked his way, he shook his head. This was not the time for another "spirited discussion."

"Thank you for your time, Monsieur Conrart." Betsy said. She drew her lips into a tight line. With her head held high, she marched back toward the pavilion.

Once they walked far enough that Monsieur Conrart could no longer see or hear them, Betsy whirled on Denis. "Why did you do that?"

"To borrow one of your sayings: Never try to teach a pig to sing."

Betsy's angry expression cracked. She giggled. Then held her sides as she bent over laughing. "Because it wastes your time and annoys the pig. Oh Lord, Denis! Imagine Conrart's face if he knew you just compared him to a pig!"

"Seemed apt." Denis said. "Besides, while you distracted him with your argument, I grabbed this." He held up Conrart's pen. "It should give us a nice set of prints to check, don't you think?"

Betsy's smile was feral as she put her hand on his elbow and the two of them continued on their way.

CHAPTER SEVEN

"Why do you want to search the suitcases a second time?" Denis asked as Betsy steered him back to the barn.

"All we did was dust for prints before," Betsy said. "Maybe if we search the bags, we'll find something incriminating. Besides, it'll give us a chance to put those little things we stole back where they belong. I can't believe that none of them had useful prints on them."

Denis sighed. "Betsy, maybe you're just not good at taking fingerprints." He said gently.

Betsy sniffed at him. "I did just fine with the gun."

And found nothing on my art book, the luggage, the knife or the pen. Perhaps we should stop chasing that avenue of investigation."

"Fine!" Betsy crossed her arms.

"We better make this fast," Denis said. "I don't want to get caught."

"We can just say that we're searching for something in one of our own suitcases."

"They're not going to believe that if our suitcases are back in our tent."

Betsy tapped her fingers against the side of her leg. "This hypothetical person who catches us doesn't know that."

The barn seemed too quiet to Denis. As Betsy crawled into one of the wagons, he moved to search a second one. Before he could reach it, he saw a pair of boots sticking out from beneath the vehicle.

He drew back. The scene reminded him of the dead witch with the red shoes under the house in the movie about the wizard that Betsy liked.

Denis's heart sank. *Please, just be someone taking a nap,* he thought as he kneeled next to the feet and looked under the wagon. There lay Astrid Bruit.

She was not taking a nap.

"Betsy?" Denis called weakly.

"Yeah, hon?"

"Could you go get Magnus? And try to be sneaky about it?"

"Huh?" Betsy looked over the top of an open trunk, one of Mademoiselle de Rambouillet's wigs in her hands. She gasped as her eyes fell on the pair of feet sticking out from beneath the conveyance. Her face paled. "Oh!"

"Yeah, oh."

Betsy put the wig back, closing the trunk with a click. "I'll just go do that." She hopped out of the wagon and took off running.

While Betsy was gone, Denis searched the barn for clues. He found nothing. Which meant that Astrid was possibly murdered elsewhere and then carried here so as not to be found immediately.

Denis shook his head. Astrid was probably a target because she talked to the two of them. Which meant the killer was getting desperate and sloppy.

Betsy returned to the barn with Magnus and Soren. Both men looked grim. Soren's eyes were red-rimmed.

Magnus looked under the wagon, letting out a dark curse.

Soren shut his eyes and shook his head. A single sob escaped him before he clenched his fist over his mouth.

"You have my condolences," Denis said.

Magnus turned to him, a stormy expression on his face. "You're trying to find the murderer, yes?" He choked out. "Save your condolences and find them!"

"Cyrano was confined in his room, correct?" Denis asked.

"The whole time," Magnus said through gritted teeth.

Denis nodded. "Can you conceal this from the other guests?"

“We’ll try.” Soren’s voice was thick with emotion.

"Why do you want to keep it secret?" Betsy whispered.

Denis plucked at his chin. "Right now we four and the murderer are the only ones who know. That may make them slip up."

"Then we'd better hurry to question the others,” Betsy said.

* * *

A lively, staccato sound from the pavilion caused Betsy to pause as she and Denis crossed the avenue where the Bruit family had pitched the army tents. She furrowed her brow. Denis shrugged, pointing toward the open pavilion flap to suggest that they see what the sound was.

Betsy peeked through the flap to find Beatrice Crossno leading Madeleine de Scudéry in the steps of a spirited dance. The two women broke apart when they saw Betsy.

"I was teaching Mademoiselle de Scudéry the Gavotte," Beatrice said as she waved the two reporters into the tent. "It's very popular at court."

"Georges has no time for newer forms of dance," de Scudéry added. "Beatrice has danced for the Marquis and Marquise de Rambouillet before. Who better to learn from?"

"Do you Gavotte?" Beatrice asked Betsy.

"Only when I think the song is about me." Betsy winked at Beatrice and elbowed Denis in the side.

Beatrice tilted her head sideways in confusion, while de Scudéry blinked.

"It's an uptime song," Denis explained.

“Ah,” They said in unison, nodding as if they understood. Betsy doubted they did. No one ever seemed to get her sense of humor.

"I look forward to corresponding with your contact in Grantville," de Scudéry said. “Perhaps when I tire of Paris, I'll convince Georges to visit there.”

"Some days I hardly recognize it. Last week some tourist stopped me on the street and asked me what the town was like before the Ring of Fire." Betsy stared into the middle distance, her mind transported into a past that existed somewhere off in the future. She shook off the thought, focusing on de Scudéry and Beatrice. "Then again, some days I hardly recognize myself."

"Tragedy is like a refining fire." de Scudéry nodded sage-like. "One never moves through the fire without becoming stronger."

Betsy groped for a change in topic. "Have you lived in Paris long?"

"Not overly. My brother invited me to stay with him when our uncle passed away. We've made the tour of literary salons. When the Marquise de Rambouillet asked us to accompany them, I thought it would make a nice change of scenery."

Beatrice laughed at that. "Well, it's certainly not Paris."

"Then again, what is?" de Scudéry yawned.

"Did either of you know Angelique very well before the play?" Betsy asked.

"Poor Angelique," Beatrice sighed. "She was, of course, a favorite at the Hôtel de Rambouillet."

"Owing to her friendship with the Marquise," de Scudéry said. "We'll all feel her absence at the salon. Particularly in Madame de Rambouillet's melancholy."

"I'm just fortunate I wasn't murdered as well. Mondemoiseau de Bergerac and I also didn't get along." Beatrice clapped the back of her hand to her forehead.

Behind Beatrice's back, de Scudéry rolled her eyes. "He seems like a perfectly callow youth," she said. "Did he get along with anyone?"

Betsy tucked her hands in her pockets. "We like him. He helped me get rid of an unwanted suitor, once."

"Did he write something about you as well?" Denis asked Beatrice.

"Fortunately not," Beatrice said. "But it would be improper to gossip." She turned to de Scudéry. "I must finish packing before we depart. When we reach Paris, you should meet me at the Hôtel de Rambouillet. I'd love to continue teaching you to dance!"

De Scudéry clasped Beatrice's hand warmly. "That would be magnifique!" she said with a placid smile. Once Beatrice's footsteps faded into the distance, de Scudéry's beatific expression melted into annoyance.

"What a perfectly odious woman!" She shuddered, drawing her hands in to her sides and twisting her face in revulsion. "I'd sooner be dropped into a pit with a bear than spend another minute alone in that grasping social-climber's company!"

Remembering de Boisrobert's description of de Scudéry as an unrepentant gossip, Betsy sat on the stage, swinging her legs and patting the space next to her for the other woman to come sit next to her. "What did she have against Cyrano?"

"Less than she would like." De Scudéry sat down next to Betsy. "Beatrice always seems to make herself the center of attention. If she can't be part of the spectacle, she'll invent new pageantry and recast herself in the starring role."

De Scudéry spread her hands to indicate their encampment. "Take now, for instance. People have been murdered. Yet she's complaining that young Monsieur de Bergerac slighted her in some minor way." De Scudéry leaned closer. "Do you know what I think really happened?" She whispered behind her hand.

"What?" Betsy whispered back.

"She thought she could ensnare his affections, owing to his age. And once she had them she planned to lead him around by the nose. Perhaps then he would give her Angelique's part in the play?"

Betsy rubbed at her chin and nodded.

"But this is all just speculation, you understand." de Scudéry rubbed away imaginary dust from her puffy sleeve. "A humble writer's passing fancy. Who knows, perhaps I shall turn this weekend into another one of my clever little stories? I believe you uptimers called them roman à clef?"

"I just call it real person fanfiction," Betsy said. "But my degree is in geology, so what do I know?"

De Scudéry slipped off the stage, brushing her hands over the backs of her skirts. "At any rate, I should make sure that the Marquise is ready to depart." She wiped her hands together as she left the tent.

"Real person fanfiction?" Denis asked.

"I used to exchange stories about my favorite TV shows with college classmates on Usenet, and one or two university-sponsored e-mail groups. Back when there were enough computers to have an Internet." Betsy said. "Where do you think I learned to write?"

"So much about your work with the *Inquisitor* is clearer now," Denis put his hands on his hips.

* * *

Cyrano once again lay across his bed with his elbow over his face when Denis and Betsy returned.

"Anything?" he asked them, barely lifting his arm.

Betsy winced.

"Thought not." Cyrano said. He dropped his head back onto his bed. "The tide is going out. There's no choice but to face whatever messy legal snarl awaits us in Hamburg."

"They can't hold you!" Betsy said. "You were here in your room when Astrid Bruit was murdered!"

"Astrid Bruit was murdered as well?" Cyrano yelped.

"Oops," Betsy muttered. "Forgot to mention that."

Cyrano put his face in his hands. "No matter. Even if my good name isn't tarnished beyond all repair, this has been a disaster from start to finish!"

Betsy sat next to Cyrano, squeezing his bicep in a sisterly fashion. "I'm sorry all this is happening," she commiserated. "If only your play had been anticipated in Paris! Maybe de Thou could've made the money to pay back you and Bourdon and everyone else. Then no one would have been upset."

Cyrano looked at her in confusion. "Oliver? Oliver was the one who owed money to myself and de Thou."

"What?" Denis asked flatly.

Cyrano nodded. "He settled the debt by understudying for us. Once the play succeeded we would have all been quite wealthy."

"And you made it clear that the debt was forgiven, even if the play wasn't a success, correct?" Betsy asked.

Cyrano blinked at that. "Maybe?"

Denis rolled his eyes. "We need to detain Oliver. Now!"

They opened the door, only to find Magnus Bruit blocking the way, intent on preventing Cyrano from leaving.

"We know who killed all three people, and it wasn't Cyrano," Denis said. "It was Oliver Bourdon!"

Magnus set his jaw in a grim line. "Lead me." He picked up a walking stick, brandishing it like a club.

The party ran down the stairs, out the door of the Neuwerk, and through the camp, weaving around various Bruit relatives in the process of taking down the tents.

They ran past the barns and up to the departure wagons. Ahead, they could see the guests milling about like hens in a chicken yard, and looking just as disorganized.

In the distance, the tide had nearly gone out.

"Are we leaving?" Beatrice asked. "Only, Monsieur Bourdon just rode past on a horse."

Magnus blistered the air with the most inventive foul language that Denis had ever heard this side of the army. A look of fascination crossed Betsy's face. Denis winced, knowing that he'd probably be hearing some of those choice phrases again the next time Betsy stubbed her toe.

"Bourdon is the one who did it," Magnus said to Soren. The younger Bruit man swore in a couple languages Denis hadn't even heard of as he jumped from his wagon and set to work unharnessing the horses.

"Did what?" Valenin Conrart asked.

"Everything! At least we think so." Betsy said. "He killed de Thou and framed Cyrano because he owed them money. Then he killed Angelique thinking she was me, and Astrid when he thought she saw something and was going to tell us."

"Who is Astrid?" Madeleine de Scudéry piped in.

Beatrice looked from Betsy to Madeleine de Scudéry in confusion. "Eh? One of the servants?" She wrinkled her nose.

"My sister!" Soren shouted as he jumped onto the back of one of the horses. "I'll run him down!" The broad, stocky young man rode his horse out into the surf.

"Come on, Denis!" Betsy vaulted from a wagon to a second horse. She landed across the horse's back like one of the bags of flour that he unloaded for Mirari in her shop. "We have to make sure that Soren doesn't kill Oliver Bourdon!" With that, she kicked the horse's flanks and chased Soren into the ocean.

Denis huffed in exasperation at Betsy. It was just like her to go charging blindly into the tidal flats on a horse she'd never even ridden before. But as Betsy went, so went his nation. And at the moment, he had to make sure his nation didn't fall into the ocean and drown. With a shout, he jumped onto another horse and kicked it into action.

They rode through water that was up to the horse's flanks in some places. Denis glanced into the murky depths, but couldn't even see the bottom. He reminded himself that the horses made the trip across the tidal flats daily, they were within sight of those elevated birdcages, and Soren knew the way.

"There!" Betsy pointed into the distance.

A rider who could only be Oliver Bourdon sped away. He seemed to be struggling with his mount, fighting to turn it in a direction that it did not want to go and whipping it mercilessly.

Betsy clicked her tongue to urge her horse into a gallop. Water sloshed off of the animal's flanks. Soren blinked as she sped past him, then he urged his own horse to follow.

Denis sighed, twitching the reins to get his horse to keep up.

Little by little, Betsy drew even with Oliver Bourdon. He threw a dark look over his shoulder as he whipped the horse's flanks with a horsewhip that he'd probably snatched out of Soren's hands. When she drew into his range, he took a swing at her with the whip. Betsy ducked the swing and then football-tackled him from the back of his steed into the receding waters.

Denis clung to the horse's mane as he scanned the tide for his wife. Betsy's red hair stood out in stark contrast to the brown muddy water. He grasped the back of her shirt and fished her, dripping and spluttering, onto the horse before him.

Betsy coughed, wringing her hair out. Then she let out an ear splitting shriek.

"Get it off me!" She shouted. "Get it off! Get it off! Get it off!" She flung some kind of long, glistening pink, tube-like thing from her hair. "Ugh! What was that thing?"

"Hagfish," Soren Bruit grunted. He hauled an unconscious Oliver Bourdon from the water and threw him unceremoniously across the horse's withers in front of him. Bourdon looked like he'd swallowed half the ocean, but he was still breathing.

"Hagfish huh?" Denis rubbed comforting circles across Betsy's shoulder blades. "At least it's not a shark."

CHAPTER EIGHT

Denis and Betsy stood on the pier, waving at Henrik Erikson on the departing fishing boat. Once they'd captured Bourdon, Soren had insisted that they go on to Hamburg rather than delay justice by taking Bourdon back to Neuwerk and then having to wait another day to bring him back once the tide went out again.

Erikson's fishing boat brought over Magnus Bruit, Cyrano, the French dignitaries, the actors, and everyone's luggage that night, along with the bodies. The Frenchmen and women left immediately. But the Bruits and Cyrano lingered to see justice done.

Now Cyrano drifted up to them, hands tucked behind his back. "Magnus said that he and Soren would be staying to give testimony against Bourdon," he said. "I suppose they'll take their horses and ride back to the island when they've gotten justice."

"Are they alright?" Betsy asked.

"They told me that they wish I'd never come to Neuwerk." Cyrano raked his hands through his long, messy hair. "I told them that I wish the same thing."

"I'm so sorry." Betsy rubbed his shoulder, twisting her lip into a sympathetic grimace. "I know a thing or two about life not working out how you planned it." She put her free hand in Denis's. "But sometimes it works out for the best anyway."

The young playwright nodded "Look for the silver lining, eh?" He sighed. "Monsieur Conrart told me that *I Love Betsy* is officially banned in France."

Denis frowned. "That's horrible."

Cyrano shrugged. "That's the silver lining, I suppose. Thanks to all that has happened, I've been asked to stage the play here in Hamburg. Who knows? If audiences here are ready for the neoclassical movement, perhaps we can take the production on a tour?"

"That's good." Betsy said tentatively.

"I need to re-cast my Betsy and William characters." Cyrano eyed the two reporters with a hungry expression. "Would the two of you be interested?"

Denis and Betsy exchanged a wary glance.

"Sorry, Cyrano," Denis said. "I think we've had enough of show business."

"I'm just happy to go home," Betsy said. "But this'll be a wonderful story to write up for the *Inquisitor*. Once it's out there, you'll sure have lots of theater patrons coming out to watch the play."

"What will you call your story?" Cyrano asked.

Betsy held her hands up as if picturing a headline. "I'm thinking: *If It Ain't Baroque, Don't Fix It!*'